LIZARD RADIO

PAT SCHMATZ

WITHDRAWN

CANDLEWICK PRESS

For the lizards

Copyright © 2015 by Pat Schmatz

First edition 2015

Library of Congress Catalog Card Number 2014960012
ISBN 978-0-7636-7635-3

15 16 17 18 19 20 BVG 10 9 8 7 6 5 4 3 2 1

Printed in Berryville, VA, U.S.A.

This book was typeset in Adobe Devanagari.

Candlewick Press
99 Dover Street
Somerville, Massachusetts 02144

visit us at www.candlewick.com

In a world similar to ours

with some genetic twists

and decisional turns . . .

Chapter One

I DO NOT BELIEVE. Not in any corner of my heart or scrap of my soul do I think that Sheila will carry it through. Not when she makes me pack a duffel. Not when she hustles me into the gov skizzer, not when we pedal through the grit-gray morning, and not when she takes me for the first time beyond city limits, into the afternoon countryside. Still, I will not believe.

Not until we turn onto a gravel drive and pass under the wooden CROPCAMP sign do the first fear-flavored tendrils of belief creep in between my ribs. Sheila steers across the wide lot, takes her feet off the pedals, and parks. She steps out, reaches in the back for my duffel, and drops it on the gravel. It lands with a puff of dust. A woman strides across the lot to greet us. I get out of the skizzer.

"Hello." She is tall with light brown skin. "I'm Ms. Mischetti, the CropCamp director."

"Hello, Ms. Mischetti." Sheila pronounces each syllable carefully. "This is Kivali Kerwin."

"Hello, Kivali." The director moves closer to me, and I hitch a step back, against the skizzer. "Welcome."

I cut a look at Sheila. She won't meet my eyes. The director watches me. Nobody's eyes connect.

"I'll be going now," says Sheila.

Her voice is as tight as her face. For the past two weeks, she's been all about the opportunity: an opening at a CropCamp close to home, how I'll like living outdoors, how SayFree Gov is pressuring for early camp entrance for me, how it might be better than either of us can imagine. Now I see that she doesn't believe it any more than I believed she'd bring me here.

The director still looks only at me. Our triangle-gazed standoff lasts another beat, and then another, and then Sheila breaks it by stepping in the middle, turning her back on the director. She takes me by the shoulders and pulls me in — not quite a hug, but close — and whispers in my ear.

"Be brave, my sweet gecko."

Then she leaves me.

I don't watch her go. The CropCamp director stands on the head of my shadow on the gravel. I refuse to look up and see her seeing me. I concentrate on standing still, not letting my inner shiver show.

"Lacey!" Her feet shift, releasing my shadow-head as she turns to someone across the lot. "This is Kivali Kerwin — Pie Five, Slice Nineteen. Show her down, would you? She'll just have time to drop off her things before orientation."

Ms. Mischetti walks away. I lift my head and look over my

shoulder to see if Sheila is skizzing back under the CropCamp sign to get me: joke over, let's go home.

She's not.

I look up at the sky, searching for the saurians. Are they just on the other side of that puffy cloud, watching me? Can they see through clouds? Do they breathe human air? I've never been good at the science part.

"Hey, you! Come on, get moving."

A girl in light green coveralls stands at the edge of the parking lot with her hands on her hips. I sling my bag over my shoulder. She starts walking, and I trudge along behind her. Her streak-blond ponytail bounces as we pass the L-shaped wooden office building and cross a large five-sided green lawn.

"This is the Quint," she says. "We have social time here every evening."

The straps of the duffel dig into my shoulder. Why did Sheila do it? Pressure or no, she didn't have to. She could have put them off for at least two years. I just turned fifteen last week.

"Over there is the Pavilion; that's where orientation is." Lacey points to a round-roofed structure with some people clustered outside. "The gong will ring in about ten ticks, and you need to be there. We have Cleezies there, too, every day and twice on Sundays. Over there, that's the Mealio. We eat there."

I can't imagine eating there. Not for one meal. Certainly not for three months of meals. As we cross the Quint, another long, L-shaped building with a low roof comes into view, and Lacey points.

"That's the Study Center. That's where you'll have class. The ayvee pod is there, too."

She leads me on a dirt path between spreading fields. Girls in pairs and threes and a few solos meet us along the path. I play the you-can't-see-me-if-I-don't-look-at-you game.

"Greenhouse over there. Boys' Pieville on the east side. Toolshed just past the greenhouse. Our Pieville's down here."

At the edge of the field the path drops off, down a steep slope into a deep shade with a sharp, tangy smell. It's a real forest. Trees, tall ones with green pine needles. The westering sun reaches through the gaps and spaces to create long streams of golden light through the shadows. The smell comes in not just through my nose — it seeps into my pores, gentling my shivery stomach.

"The pies are in numerical order." She points at a round, fabric-covered structure that comes to a point at the top. Others are smattered irregularly through the woods. "The privo and spigot are over there. Shower house is behind. No showers tonight; you'll get your first chit from your crew guide tomorrow, and after that you have to earn them in the power room. That's your pie, the far one back there. Slice numbers are stamped beneath the doors. You're nineteen. Drop your duffel, and then get yourself back to the Pavilion for orientation. Everything happens strictly on time here."

She turns away and leaves me.

I follow the path back to the last pie. Light gray synthie fabric stretches over wooden rods that converge at the top. Four doors.

I locate the number nineteen stamped beneath the back door, the one facing a tangly copse of leaves and grasses and branches and brush. Kaleidoscope green.

There's a zipper tag at the bottom corner. I zip the door open and step into my slice of the pie. Cot along one wall, desk on the other. Three sets of beige coveralls stacked on the shelf unit in between. I drop my duffel and pull the komodo dragon out of my pocket. Tiny and fierce in constant frozen motion, it steps forward with its right front clawed foot. I set it on my palm and bring it up to my face.

"Lizard time." I speak aloud in the silence.

Something rustles in the far side of the pie. We are not alone. I curl my fingers over the toy dragon and hide it away in my pocket, still holding tight.

"Lizard time?"

I close my eyes. Yes. Time for the saurians to get me out of here. Right now. Hurry up. A door unzips, and footsteps round the pie. I clutch the komodo. Its sharp metal edges dig into my palm. A gong rings in the distance.

"That gong is for us. You coming?"

I release the komodo, wipe my sweaty palms on my pants, zip my door open, and step out. My new comrade has a rampage of dark curls around her face, backlit by the angled sun. She looks me up, down, and up again.

"Lizard time?"

"Just kidding," I say, and she breaks open a big grin.

"Kidding, huh? Not everyone pulls a lizard out of their kidding bag. I'm Sully. I think you should be my new best friend. We can terrorize the camp."

Her eyes are warm, and her smile and stance confident. Social power rolls off her, the kind that everyone wants to get close to. The kind that is dangerous when it turns on you. She walks, and I follow a half step behind. We pass the other pies and scrabble up the steep path. Roots crisscross the dark earth beneath our feet. That dank tangy smell fills my whole head.

We pop up next to the fields. There's no longer a crowd near the Pavilion. They're all inside. We sprint past the fields and scramble up to the door at the same time as a couple of breathless latecomers from the boys' side. They open the door, letting us in first. Rocks rattle underfoot as we slink into the back row. We sit on a rough-hewn bench, breathing hard.

Low wooden walls form the round structure. From waist-level up, it's all screen until the high wooden-domed ceiling. Sparks and smoke dance from a fire up through the hole in the center of the roof.

Ms. Mischetti stands. The murmurs and fidgets hush immediately.

"Welcome to CropCamp," she says. "Welcome to the beginning of the end of childhood. Welcome to community, to comradeship, to finding your place in the world. Welcome to work and learning, to responsibility, to growth and connection."

Her voice is a smooth-humming motor.

"This is a safe place, putting you on the road to safety in

life. I've never had a vape from this camp. Expuls are rare. There are thirty-nine of you here today, and I expect thirty-nine of you to receive your camp certifications at the end of August. With a cert from this camp, your chances of ever landing in Blight are less than three percent. You'll enter the adult world ready for further education or a fulfilling career in agriculture.

"The regs are strict here. I suggest that you comply and let us make this a good experience for you. If you leave here certless, you'll face consequences that your MaDa cannot fix. If you are of age, you'll go directly to Blight. If not, you will be relocated to fosters who can prepare you for a RepeaterCamp. So consider your actions carefully. Your choices here will follow you for the rest of your life."

She then launches a flow of suggestions and advice, weaving a steely web of restrictive assurance with promises to care for us and help us and teach us. She waves her hand, and Lacey and the other guides in their pale green coveralls stand. Then the teachers, and the counselors.

More words, words like citizenry and safety, responsibility and open air and honest labor. Same words I saw in the infodocs that Sheila made me read last week.

"I'm not seventeen," I said. "You always said no camp before I'm seventeen, not over your dead body. Are you planning to die?"

Sheila looked like I'd slapped her, and I was a little bit sorry. Only a little, because I still didn't believe. But now I wonder: what if she really *is* planning to die? Maybe she has a horrible disease and is on her way to a medcenter right now. Or maybe she regrets picking me up off the sidewalk fifteen years ago, and this is her chance to finally be free of me.

Ms. Mischetti is still talking, but her words fuzz and morph and slide on by without meaning. My comrades are all nearly grown, like Sully. Some lean forward, listening hard. Some gaze into middle space in front of them. One pair of eyes looks up across the fire, grabs mine, and holds.

He's a midrange bender. He has pale skin with a shadow of shave on his cheeks and chin. Straight dark hair sweeps across one eye. His features are chiseled and delicate, his nose long and sharp. He sits with one leg draped over the other. He smiles and dips his head ever so slightly, a nod of recognition.

I check my own posture. I uncross my ankle from my knee and bring my legs closer together. He sees me do it and tilts up one corner of his mouth. He leans forward, face propped on his hand. Not on a fist beneath his chin, but with his fingers spread open on his cheek, and I realize that my own hands are clenched into fists. My every natural movement reveals bender, just like his. At least I try to keep mine under control. Especially here, among strangers.

Sully elbows me and nods down at her right hand. It's stretched out, palm up. Everyone else is lifting their hands to the same palm-up position. Two of the guides, Lacey and a tall guy with a scruff of blond whiskers, walk the circle in opposite directions from Ms. Mischetti. They carry baskets and lay something on each upturned palm.

"Wait until everyone has one," Ms. Mischetti says. "We do this together — it is your official entrance to summer CropCamp."

The guide sets something on my palm. It's the size of a grape, light brown with an irregular surface.

"Close your eyes," Ms. Mischetti orders.

Everyone does it, all the way around the circle. Everyone but me and the bender guy.

"Close your eyes."

She looks directly at me. I cast my eyes down, still open.

"On the count of three." She lets me slide. "Put it in your mouth. Together, we'll savor the sweet taste of community. One. Two."

My stomach is hollow, empty, caving in on itself. I didn't eat anything when Sheila and I stopped just an hour outside of CropCamp. Too busy not-believing and refusing to participate.

"Three."

I glance at the bender. He drops the thing to the rocks and puts his foot over it.

"Now," the director says. "All join hands."

The director's eyes have me pinned, and hands reach for me on either side. I put the thing in my mouth. Saliva springs so fast and hard that I almost drool.

Sully's hand finds mine, interlacing fingers. *Hmm*ing passes around the circle, from taste to taste and palm to palm, and the sweet crunchy texture and softness inside spreads all through me. Sully moans, and the vibration tingles up my arm and the back of my neck, across my scalp.

9

"Open your eyes now."

Ms. Mischetti speaks softly, no longer looking at me. I run my tongue around my mouth to be sure I haven't missed anything. This sensation, it's good, way beyond the taste. It sparks a big happy inside, bigger than the fear or dread or worry about Sheila.

"Again I say: Welcome to CropCamp. Welcome to the world of discipline, diligence, cooperation, and camaraderie. Welcome to the gateway to your adult life."

She lights a long match, and I realize the sun has set. The guides step forward to light candles off the match. They enclose the candles in glass wind-covers.

"The guides will escort you back to your Pievilles. Do not turn on any leddies until you're in your own slice, and then only for what you absolutely need. Do not speak when you leave here. Just feel. Listen to the trees, to the wind and stars. Settle into your new home in silence. The gong will ring at six tomorrow. You will put on the camp coveralls and prepare for the day. We meet at CounCircle — that's on the east side of the Mealio — promptly at the seven o'clock gong. Breakfast will follow."

She ends with the customary farewell, the one used in public gatherings throughout the country.

"Come from One."

"Live in the light," we reply.

"Return to One."

We all say the last line together. I rise with the others, a unified mass in motion. Sully unlaces her hand from mine, running a fingertip across my palm as she lets go. She smiles as if she sees the tiny shiver dance up and down my spine. Her pupils are dark enough to fall into. She puts hands to my shoulders and turns me to follow the flickering lights at the doorway.

We split as we exit, boys to the east and girls to the west. No one speaks, but the air is full of the sound and taste and sensation of the moment. The guides lead us down into the woods. Other comrades drop off as we pass their pies. At the privo, Lacey lights a candle in the torch-holder. Only Sully and I and one other girl follow Lacey to the last pie. The other girl is tall, with hair gathered in a poof at the back of her head.

Lacey points the candle toward our pie, and then continues along the path beyond. The three of us watch her candle dip and flicker. It angles to the left, flicks between trees, and finally disappears.

"You must be number eighteen." Sully turns to the third girl. A fullish moon is on the rise, just beginning to stream through the pines. "Or are you twenty? I'm Sully."

The tall girl turns her back and zips into slice eighteen between mine and Sully's without a word.

"Oh, right," says Sully. "No speaking."

She lightly punches me in the arm and enters her slice. I round the pie and stand in front of my own door. I tuck my hands up under my armpits and face the darkness of the woods. The odd happy feeling continues to spin in my chest. It's all so strange. The strangest part of all is that in this moment, I almost like it here.

11

Chapter Two

BRIGHT MOONLIGHT PRIES MY eyes open. My toy komodo glows in the beam, and I jolt up. The komodo hovers on the very edge of the shelf as if it's about to leap onto my head. That's not where I left it. Is it?

I check my door. Yes, closed. No one has been in here — I would've heard the zipper. Slowly, I reach out to the dragon, half afraid it'll leap at my finger and chomp it. But no, it doesn't move as I touch the sharp tip of its cool metal nose. I turn it around so it faces the door the way I thought I'd left it. On guard.

The night lies still around us. A slightly wheezy breath rises and falls, the sound leaking through the synthie wall that I share with number eighteen. Everything else is quiet except for the blood thudding in my ears. I sink back onto the pillow and put a hand on my jumpy heart.

Deep breath in, two, three. I follow the air in and out. Shift my attention away from the here and now, shut it out the way I shut out the walk-a-day noise of machinery and humanity at home. I sink into the chitter and murmur, the moving shapes on the backs of my eyelids, the removal from the world and the day, and I tune in. Lizard Radio is the best place I know, the quietest and calmest, the furthest from anything bad or scary or —

Go to the fields.

I bolt straight up. Lizard Radio never speaks human words.

The breathing in the next slice continues. The komodo remains frozen where I put it. The moonlight shines steady. The words pulse, not out loud but strong and clear. *Gotothefields.* *Gotothefields.* Like someone whispering in my ear from the inside.

I pick up the komodo again and run my fingers back to the end of the tail. I touch the space between the eye socket bumps, feel the curve of the claws. I bring it to my mouth and kiss it. My clothes are on the floor where I dropped them. I pull them on and tuck the komodo in my pocket, strap on my frods, and kneel at the doorway. I slow-tick the zipper up, quiet, no-wakey.

A light breeze moves through the rustling woods, and the night air shivers across the back of my neck. The moon casts shadows of spooklight. A small flame still dances inside a glass shield by the privo, and I head that way. I pass it by and continue into the dappled darkness, slinking past the sleeping pies. I climb the steep slope, placing my frods carefully on the unfamiliar terrain. My breath dances in and out. Now is the time. The saurians are here. They'll take me to the Lizard Radio world.

At the top of the rise I sense motion and immediately drop, belly-flat, heart hitting the earth. Head down. The treetops whisper and hiss. The wind's light fingers touch my hair. Slowly, I lift my head. A solitary silhouette stands awash in the moonlight to my right. Not a lizard. A human.

The moon has begun to drop to the west, and the shadow of the treetops falls several paces in front of me, drawing a clear line between more-dark and less-dark. I belly-crawl forward for a closer view, right up to the edge of the shadow line.

The figure in the field shrugs out of his coveralls. They fall to the ground, and he steps clear, completely unclothed. Moonlight splashes the long plane of bare hip and the curve of back. He stretches arms to the sky, fingers reaching. His hair flows as he tips his head back and the moon shines on his face.

It's that bender boy I saw in the Pavilion.

"Please."

His solitary word carries on the night air and punches my heart. It's soft but clear, and reverberates through my skull with all of the longing in the world.

"Please."

His voice quavers. Silvery liquid light shines between his out-stretched fingers. My whole body leans in his direction, listening, feeling. He collapses to the ground, hugging his legs into his chest. His hair falls over his face.

I want to help him. Whatever he wants, I want to give it to him.

A light comes on in the far side of the office building, the short leg of the L-shape. He can't see it, not with his head down like that. He'll be caught. Maybe expulled. Ms. Mischetti was very clear about curfew, and about culpas and expuls.

14

"Hey!" I huff out a whisper-yell. "Ssst!"

His head comes up. He turns and looks directly at me as if he can see me. Another light comes on, an outdoor one. A door slams. I flatten again. I cannot risk an expul. I'm too young to go to Blight, but an unknown foster and RepeaterCamp? Away from Sheila and Korm, maybe forever? No.

A figure moves through the circle of yard light, toward the fields. Tall and broad-shouldered. Ms. Mischetti, on her way to collar him. She stops mid-stride with a strangled cry, as if she's run into a wall. I look to see what the boy has done.

He's gone. I arch up, propped on my hands, searching. The dark crumple of his clothes is still there in the field, but the boy is not. Ms. Mischetti sinks to the ground with her arms over her head. "No." She mirrors the posture of the boy who was there only seconds ago. "No."

Suddenly, I understand. In those few seconds when I watched Ms. Mischetti approach the field, the boy vaped. But nobody has ever vaped from this camp. Ever. Maybe that's why Ms. Mischetti is — well, it looks like she's crying.

I ease back into the deeper shadows and crawl until I find the path. Soft-frod back down to Pieville and slip into my slice. Get in bed and stare into the moony night with a pounding heart. That boy vaped. Korm says that vaping is good, a privilege, a treat. It's supposed to be a terrible thing, but Korm says that you only get to do it if you're worthy. She says she'll vape any day now.

Of course, she's been saying that the whole time I've known her, and that's more than seven years. Sometimes when I was younger and she didn't show up for our sessions, I was sure that she'd vaped. But she always came back.

Benders and samers, defectives and defiants and violents, that's who vapes. People just like Korm. It's the ultimate threat, vaping. Scarier than Blight because no one knows for sure what it is. But that bender boy wanted it. Begged for it.

Sheila says if and when Korm does vape, it'll mean the gov finally caught up with her. She also says that Korm has a tenuous grip on reality. Korm says that Sheila's too attached to the reality of this world, and that's why she's so unhappy. I kind of think they're both right.

Before they started the camp system, lots of teens vaped. Almost 5 percent. SayFree Gov called it a growing epidemic and set out to cure it, first with the strict bender regs and then with the camps. Vapes are rare now. Almost unheard of.

But I just saw one with my own eyes. Well, almost.

Chapter Three

THE GONG RINGS, AND I open my eyes to daylight leaking through the fabric walls. I look quickly to the shelf. The komodo is not there. I bolt up in the cold shiver of dawn and grab my pants from the floor, rifling in a panic through the pockets.

My fingertips hit the reassuring shape.

"Lizard! Are you over there?"

Sully calls me Lizard. As if she's speaking code to my heart, which answers with a speedy thud-thud.

"I'm here," I manage to say.

"How about Number Eighteen?" she yells. "Are you there, too? Did we all survive the night?"

I take the top coveralls from the stack of three on the shelf, shake them, and pull them on over boxers and T-shirt. The coveralls are lightweight, roomy, and comfortable. I drop the komodo in my pocket, strap on my frods, and step out into the ray of sunshine slanting through the pine needles.

I rub my eyes, shake my head. The bright sunshine makes the night and the moon shadows seem distant, unreal. The tall girl steps out of the slice next to mine. She looks to be nineteen or twenty, but that can't be — eighteenth birthday is the upper limit for camps. She has a thin, olive-skinned face, and her fuzz-poof of hair is dark brown. Her dark eyes are fierce, daring me to speak and daring me not to.

"Hi," I say.

"I'm Nona Raglisch."

"Nona Raglisch," Sully repeats, coming up behind her. "I'm Sully, and this is our Lizard. Let's hug and be alla-One."

Sully steps in close, her arms out. Nona stares at her without moving, expressionless. Sully stops, her arms in an arc.

"No? No love for your new piemates?"

Nona doesn't move.

"No." Sully answers herself and drops her arms.

Nona's eyes slide over me as she turns away. Feeling released, I walk with Sully toward the privo.

"That was the icy-coldest dose of shut-up I ever got," Sully says. "What did you do to make her hate me so much?"

"I didn't. I didn't even talk to her last night."

Sully grins and pokes me in the arm.

"Joke, Lizard."

Sheila calls me Sweet Komodo, or Gecko, or Whiptail. Skink, if she's mad at me. But just plain Lizard? Never. I like it.

Sully and I wash up together at the spigot. She douses her face and shakes it dry, wiping her sleeve across her eyes.

"How old are you, anyway?" We stroll through Pieville. "You look like quite the young lizard."

"Fifteen."

"Ooh, very tender meat. Fifteen!"

I think she's yelling my age to the world, but the door stamped with number fifteen zips open.

"What?"

The raspy baby-crow voice stops us both. A girl with a fluff of white-blond hair zips out the slice door. Her coveralls just about swallow her whole.

"Sully and the Lizard here," says Sully. "Who are you?"

"Rasta Lyn Shorlen, reporting for duty."

She salutes me, not Sully, and Sully laughs out loud.

"Rasta, my friend, with that voice you should be working for SayFree Radio. We'd all line up to comply, even Captain Lizard. Join us for breakfast?"

The three of us walk the path together.

"Where are you from, Rasta?" Sully asks.

"Shyland, west side. You?"

"Twa Burbs. Lizard?"

"Shy North, inner sector," I say.

"That's almost local," says Sully. "Skizzer distance, anyway. Who goes to CropCamp unless they're A: local, or B: a loser? Present company excepted, of course."

"She just called me a loser," says Rasta. "But not you."

"I said, present company excepted."

"I think you were being polite."

"I don't speak polite," says Sully.

She shoulders me, a friendly bump that surprises me

19

sideways. I bungle into Rasta. She laughs and shoulders me back, although her shoulder's only as high as my rib cage. I knock into Sully again. They're laughing, and somehow I am, too. I've not had a playful bump-and-push in a very long time. It's a strange mix of scary and good.

"So why CropCamp?" Rasta asks Sully. "No good at academics?"

"Actually, I'm a math brainiola," says Sully. "But I'm inclined to defiance so my da's putting me under the Machete blade. He says if anyone can track me out of Blight, it's her."

"Machete." Rasta nods at the name twist. "Lizard, why are you here?"

I could say that Sheila is a fikety-fike. I could mention how I almost flunked post-decision gender training, or the whole low-comply at school problem. Maybe I should just tell them that I'm a komodo dragon abandoned by the saurians on planet human. Maybe I should just shut up.

"Because I am."

Rasta and Sully exchange a glance, and Rasta says, "Can't argue with that."

We crest the ridge and stop at the top. The sun filters through the trees on the boys' side and lights up the dewdrops so the green nubbins of plants glitter with light and color. Beautiful as one of Sheila's paintings. Beautiful like the moon shadows and vape-scene, but with an entirely different palette.

"Whatcha lookin at?" A round girl with short dreds huffs up the path and stops to stand with us.

"Crops," says Sully. "We're fascinated. Bunch of burby kids dropped in the middle of agriculture."

"I'm not burby. My people are farmers. I'm a proud tradition."

"What's your name, proud tradition?"

"Tylee. If you all don't want to be farmers, why are you here?"

"Getting cleaned up and compliant," Rasta says. "Ready to be an adult, I am."

Rasta's voice hits Tylee the same way it did me and Sully, splitting a huge white smile across her dark-skinned face. As they talk, I walk over to the edge of the field and look out. Right there: That's where that guy stood. The crumple of clothes is gone now. I wonder where he is — or if he's anywhere. Maybe vaping is the best bender thing to do. Just step away from it all. When I get home, I'll talk to Korm about this.

The second gong rings.

"Chop-chop Lizard; Machete summons," calls Sully.

They wait for me so we can walk together. As if they're my friends.

CounCircle is a grassy oval next to the Mealio, bordered by shoulder-high neatly trimmed hedges. Boys enter from the east and girls from the west, in various raggedy postures of morning. A few boys are clean-shaven, a few still smooth-cheeked, and the rest have everything from heavy shadow to wispy whiskers. Some girls are neatly put together with eyeliner and tidy braids. Others, like Sully, are hair-spiked and sleep-creased. All of us wear the same beige coveralls except for the guides, who are in

21

light green. They direct us to stand at attention within the oval, facing Machete at the north end. Everyone looks more adult than me, except for maybe Rasta, and a small blond boy who could be her paler cousin.

Machete is back in charge. Looks like CropCamp is going to involve a lot of Machete talk. I watch and listen carefully. Hard to believe that she's the same person I saw rocking and crying in the night. I scan the comrade faces, hoping to see the bender and cut the night scene loose as a dreamscape. He isn't here.

Machete releases us with the "Come from One; live in the light; return to One" and we drop out of formation to enter the Mealio. It's large and open, with long tables set for breakfast. Counselors, teachers, and guides sit at the tables in back. Sully and Rasta and Tylee and I end up at a table with four guys.

"Look at me, getting lucky first morning first day."

A big, handsome guy sits at the head of the table. He leans on his elbows and gazes at Sully with his long-lashed eyes.

"I'm Aaron. Marry me after CropCamp, okay?"

"Don't you think you should take more time to look over the goods?" Sully says. "Maybe I look like a keeper on glance, but I've got flaws. Rasta here, she's flawless."

"Hello, Rasta." Aaron turns to her, flashing a grin that you know he practices in private. "I'm Aaron, and I'm interviewing women for a life of wedded baby-making bliss. Care to apply?"

"I think I'll go for the fellow on your left there," Sully says as Rasta's face goes to red. "He's got good bone structure and he'll make pretty babies."

"What's wrong with my bone structure? I'm telling you, it's solid." Aaron winks at me, of all people. "Do I need to show you?"

"Please don't," says Sully.

It's what we're supposed to do here — meet the opposite sex under controlled conditions and form unions. SayFree Radio is always talking about how stable camp-formed couples are, and how they either beat the low fertility rates or provide stable homes for adopted Blight babies.

We pass the food around, eggs and vegetables scrambled together with a tasty sauce. A river of flirt continues to flow between Sully and Aaron, and some of it is funny. The table titters with embarrassed laughter as tributaries of the flirtation trickle to the rest of us. Even the skinny pale guy with raging acne at the far end of the table.

Even me.

After breakfast, they divvy us up into six crews. I'm a Wednesday, along with Rasta, which means that we get Wednesdays off. Sully's a Saturday. Our Wednesday guide is Micah, a tall, dark-skinned guy with a beard attempt that looks like mud on his face. We follow him around on a grounds tour. He gives us our schedule, shows us the chart of compost and kitchen rotations, and passes out shower chits.

"After this," he says, "you earn shower chits in the power room. There are cycles and treadmills — shower chits cost a hundred cals. You can do that during your free time, before CounCircle, or between Block Four and dinner, or on your day off. Solitude after lunch and evening Social on the Quint are mando."

He issues our booktrons, water kaggis, and some heavy-duty scissor-clippers called secateurs. He shows us where to find spades and forks in the toolshed, and takes us out into the fields. The sun is higher now, and it pours like creamy sweet butter across my face and arms. I unzip the top of my coveralls, tilting my face up so the butter can spread to my neck, my heart.

The biggest fields are potatoes and cucumbers, primo crops for our sector. Organic farming is a big labor demand, so anyone who doesn't apply and qualify for an academic or specialty camp ends up in some kind of AgCamp, crops or livestock.

This potato field stretches long to the north. Checking my position from the tree line and the path to Pieville, I step over rows to where I think the bender boy was and drop to my knees to look for footprints. While I'm down here, I stroke one of the bold green plants popping from the dirt. Its little leaves are softly textured.

"Leave those be and listen," says Micah. "We'll have crop time this afternoon."

I stand, brushing off my knees, aware of everyone looking at me. Micah continues with his blattery-blat talk about soil type. Rasta leans in and nudges me with her shoulder, smiling. Micah keeps talking until the gong rings for lunch.

After lunch, Sully and Tylee and Rasta and I walk together to Pieville for Solitude.

"Struck a luck with Aaron on my crew," says Sully. "He's a pretty piece of work, especially when he shuts up. If I have to crawl around in the dirt all day, I might as well be following his bum. How do things look for the Wednesdays?"

"I'm not sure I like that Micah," Rasta says. "Saxem sounds like a lot more fun."

"He is," says Tylee. "He's got a mouth harp he played for us every time he changed subjects. At least you didn't get Lacey. Risa on Mondays said that she made them sit in alpha order and repeat back how to care for the secateurs."

We scramble down the steep slope, and the shade of the woods pulls us in with a cool breeze. We drop Tylee off at the first pie and head for the spigots.

"Lizard was petting the potatoes, and Micah acted like she was doing something dirty," says Rasta. "We're at CropCamp. I thought we were supposed to love the plants."

"Did you see that bender in the Pavilion last night?" Sully asks.

I jam my hands into my pockets, find the komodo, and clench it in my fist.

"He didn't even try to hide it." Rasta puts her hand on her cheek, fingers spread, and bats her eyes. Her mockery is a sharp poke to my stomach.

"Did you see how pretty his eyes were?" says Sully. "Greener than green. But I haven't seen him anywhere today. Have you?"

"He must've flunked PDGT big-time," says Rasta. "Maybe they made him leave. He screams bender."

My face is hot now. My eyes are down, down, down on the ground.

"Easy for you to say," says Sully. "What if everyone suddenly started telling you that you're a boy, and you have to act like one?"

I snap up to look at Sully. Nonbenders never say anything like that.

"But I'm not," says Rasta.

"Yeah, well, neither am I. We're the 95 percent. Lucky us." Sully glances at me. She's not fooled by the yellow ribbon in my hair. "My little cousin was born a he, and now she's a beautiful she. They tested her up before Grade One and she scored in the midthirties. Girl for sure. Transition complete by Grade Three, and she passed through PDGT in about six weeks. Easy for her. That guy last night is probably around fifty. I saw some of those midrangers in my cousin's cohort. They have it rough."

"Guess I never thought about it like that," says Rasta, thoughtful.

"That's because you don't have to. Benders have to think about it all the time."

"Sully, Kivali." Lacey startles us from behind. "Do you know the meaning of Solitude? You too, Rasta. Zip in there." She stands with her arms crossed until Rasta zips into her slice. Then she points at our pie and bossy-escorts us over there.. "Solitude. No chatter. Sleep or study, and do it quietly."

Chapter Four

I AM AMAZED. SULLY completely shut down Rasta's bender-bash before it even got started. I've never heard anyone do that. She did it without pointing me out in any way, although I'm sure she did it because of me. She must have, right?

I pace around my slice until I realize that Nona and Sully can hear my every move. Then I lie down on my cot, drumming my fingers on my stomach. What is going on here? Vapes? Bender defense? Skippy-happy feelings? Did Sheila have any idea?

Was it just yesterday, less than twenty-four hours ago, that I was skizzing along the roads with Sheila, refusing to speak to her? Waiting for the CropCamp joke to be over? Sheila's always said that the camps are barbaric. When and how did she learn that was wrong?

The gong rings. I thought I had plenty of time to tune in to Lizard Radio, but Solitude is already over. Back to the classroom and the crops, and then kitchen rotation, and then cleanup, and then dinner, and then our daily Cleezy dose of alla-One lecture and meditation to be sure that we're on spiritual track, compliant in community, and happy about it.

Sheila and I go to the bare minimum of Cleezies — just once a week. Sheila says that it's too gov-based to be a true religion. Korm says it's pure poison. She doesn't follow any regs at all. Sometimes Korm's ways look good to me, but she and Sheila both say the underground has an underbelly that nobody wants, not even Korm. It's better than Blight, though.

Blight is full of defiants and defectives of all kinds. SayFree Gov took a whole city, surrounded it with a biosensor fence, and chucked all the problem people in there. They throw the benders and samers and general defiants in there with the violents, and once you're in, you don't come out. There's no gov or structure at all. The only ones who come out are the babies who are born there. No one under the age of eighteen lives in Blight. I keep hoping that something will happen before I turn eighteen to make it easier for me to comply. Until then, they can't put me there.

After Cleezies we head over for Social on the Quint. We don't actually have to socialize at all. We just have to be present. I lie back and look at the sky and listen to Sully and Rasta and Tylee and a couple of Monday girls joke around. When the sun drops low, we all walk down to Pieville together. The last strands of daylight leak through the pine tops, and the other comrades drop off one at a time until it's just me and Sully.

"Home sweet slice." Sully stops with her zipper halfway up and flicks her eyebrows at me. "Time for a bit of jazz-off."

My heart thunks like a rock dropping in soft sand. Nobody

jazz-talks. Not out loud, anyway. Not that I've ever heard. Sully laughs.

"Lizard! Nervous? The plant-petting sensualist? Those jazzy sweetbits of Machete's landed smack in my biz, and then I spent all of today watching Aaron's pretty bum."

I point at Nona's slice and put a finger to my lips. Sully grins.

"Hope I don't offend my piemates with alla that. I'm a healthy almost-eighteen, and my mind drifts jazzwise. I can't help it."

She zips into her slice and leaves me standing in the deepening dusk. I wipe my sweaty palms on my coveralls, round to my own door, and zip in.

"You listening, Young Lizard?"

With only fabric walls between us, her every movement ripples the walls of my slice.

"No!"

"Ah, come on, I like it when you listen."

She lets out a little sigh-moan. My stomach does a slow sort of roll that it's never done before, and my knees feel strangely watery.

"Yeah, do it like that." Sully husks her voice down, and it lands smack in my biz. "Mmm-hmm, that's real good. Ooh, baby, you know I love that!"

Then she laughs out loud.

"You okay over there, Little Lizard?"

My face is so hot, I think it might combust. Footsteps approach outside, followed by a zip-zip. The curfew gong rings.

"Hey, look, Nona's home! Lizard, should I launch an encore?"

I close my eyes and shake my head.

"I'll save it for later. For you."

"Sully, that was curfew gong. I would appreciate your silence."

Nona's voice sluices over us both like ice water. After a frozen pause, Sully speaks again.

"Good night, Nona, my comrade. I feel your love and I return it manifold."

Next day in Block Two, Rasta and I move down a long row of potatoes. Four or five plants have sprouted from each mound, and they need to be thinned, so we pull out everything but the two strongest, healthiest in each group. We will feed the cities, one potato mound at a time. We work side by side for a long time, mostly not talking, occasionally looking up to brush hair aside or wave at a gnat. The soft soil kisses my hands. The sun worships my back. The breeze strokes my cheek like a whisper-touch of the finest fabric.

"You like this plant stuff, don't you?" Rasta asks.

"Yes."

So far I like a lot of things about CropCamp. It's much better than school or anything else at home. If I can fit in here, maybe I can step out of low-comply and never worry about Blight.

"My da figured a summer outdoors would be good for me. Plus, he was afraid if I went to something more interesting than crops, I'd get sucked into the cultural melee."

"What's that?"

"I'm not exactly sure. I think he's just scared of losing me.

Like if I really like camp, I'll turn into Lacey and never go home again."

"You as Lacey. Ha."

I scoot over to the next row. I like thinking about how the little green plants make food for us. At breakfast Sully said that she didn't care one thing about potatoes, except please pass some more because those are good. Rasta and I move to the next row.

"The hardest part here is how lonely it is."

"Lonely?" I say. "We've got people on top of us all the time, every moment, all day long."

"Not at night."

"I hear every move Nona or Sully makes. I even hear them breathing."

"But we're all walled off in our own little slices. And during Solitude, too. At home I sleep in the same rounder with my auntie and cousin where I can roll over and touch them, or whisper in the dark. And besides, you're all strangers. No offense, Lizard — I like you a lot, but I just met you."

Rasta sits back on her heels and wipes her wrist across her brow. I imagine her at home, a baby crow-chick with family feathers fluffed all around her.

"Lizard!" Micah yells from the edge of the field. "You've got DM this morning."

He taps his ticker and jerks his head toward Machete's office. I stand, brushing the dirt from my coveralls. Marks from the earthy dampness circle my knees.

"Good luck." Rasta squints up at me. "You've got Machete, right? You think she'll give you another one of those candy things?"

Jazzy sweetbits.

"Move it, Lizard," calls Micah.

I move it, heading for the office building and my first decision-making session. Sully says that the hard cases get Machete. Rasta has Ms. Kroschen, and Tylee has Mr. Mapes. I guess I'm a hard case. I press my hands into my jittery stomach and try to deep-breathe the nerves away.

When I reach the gravel lot, I turn three-sixty and sniff the air. Leaves murmur softly overhead. The granite boulders hulk on either side of the entrance, and beyond that the driveway leads out to the other world. If I can get along with the director, maybe I'll really be okay here. A chippie scutters around the corner of the main office building. The front door opens, and Machete steps onto the porch.

"Come in," she says.

The soft soles of my frods hit the worn wood of the porch steps. Machete looms over me, holding the screen door open so I have to duck beneath her arm. I pass into a cool, darkish entry hall.

"In there, have a seat."

She points to the open door on the right. An armchair angles in front of the big solid dark-wood desk. The chair is surprisingly cool and soft. I burrow in as Machete settles behind her desk.

"I've heard the others calling you Lizard," she says. "Why is that?"

Her tone's not sharp, but the question comes with a force and a poke, knocking us immediately off the safe doorstep of small talk.

"Just sort of a joke," I say.

"Do you like the nickname?"

"It's okay."

"What do they call you at home?"

"Kivali."

Even as I say it, I hear Sheila whisper *komodo* in my ear, as if she's standing right behind me. I reach in my pocket for reassurance.

"What's in your pocket?"

"Nothing."

I let go of the komodo, cross my arms over my chest. The komodo is private. Nobody but Sheila and Korm have ever seen it.

"What would you like me to call you?"

"Kivali," I say.

"Kivali it is."

She picks up the Deega from her desk and traces a finger on the screen, reading it over. Then she sets it down and leans forward on her elbows. She snaps her brown eyes to a lock-in with mine.

"You're a midrange bender, score fifty-two. You chose not to transition, and you were low-comply throughout post-decision gender training. Apparently not from lack of ability to learn, as your academics are consistently high, although group participation ranks at the bottom. You score top of the charts on physical skills — agility, balance, strength — but you refuse to play on any school or community teams."

I look down at the soft, worn slabs of wooden floor, the dark lines in between. This Machete, she says things right up front. That's not bad. Better than the school gov worker who sneaks around setting traps with nice words.

"Do you know what this tells me?"

Yes, I know. Potential, intelligence, ability. All wasted if I won't engage with my peers, participate, and better myself and those around me. Such a shame that I was abandoned, fostered by a low-comply artist who can't meet state standards with any consistency, but that's no excuse. The opportunities are there, and it's up to me to take advantage. I've heard it all before, but somehow I can't make myself be what they want me to be.

"You're an independent, and you either can't or won't disguise it. That kind of independence can be a powerful asset or a dangerous liability. Which is it for you?"

I raise my eyes to meet hers. Independence. It's just about the only thing that Korm and Sheila agree on. Korm says compliance is a sign of weakness, and I shouldn't even obey her or Sheila. Sheila says it's crucial to be independent in your mind, and just as crucial to be smart about when and where you act it out.

"Kivali, you've had a rough start." Machete's voice gentles down. "Abandoned and fostered. Midrange bender. It's a difficult path. I imagine that your peers have not been kind. Any problems with your comrades here?"

I shake my head. Does she know about the peer problems? About that day?

"I always keep a close eye on our younger campers. You're the youngest in this session by more than six months. I think you're ready, though — despite the concerns that your guardian, Sheila, had about you coming here so young. She's very anxious."

Sheila, anxious? Sheila doesn't do anxious. She meditates, she paints, and she carefully decides when and where to act.

"She'll be relieved to hear that you're adjusting well. The separation is difficult for parents, usually worse than for campers. This is especially true when the adult is asolo, without a spouse to help ease the transition. That dynamic creates an unhealthy interdependence between guardian and child, which can interfere with adjustment. Of course, I do update her regularly, and you'll have your once-weekly inflow from her waiting in the ayvee pod tomorrow."

"What goes in your updates?" I ask.

"Notes on your academic marks and overall observations about your adjustment. And of course, any behavioral problems, but I don't expect those. You're far too bright for that. Anything spoken here in our DM sessions is, of course, entirely confidential, even from Sheila."

I nod.

"How do you feel about the separation? Do you find it difficult?"

"I see why it's necessary," I say. "It helps us to develop independence and bond with our peers in community."

Machete smiles. She recognizes the quotation from the CropCamp infodoc. I did read some of it.

"Yes, it does," she says. "But how do you feel about it?"

"I feel okay."

"Over the years, I've found that many campers who were loners in their child-lives have an exceptional maturity and keen intuition. Almost like an uncanny intuitive guide."

She cannot possibly know about Lizard Radio. It's private in my head. Sheila wouldn't have put it in any of the Deega records, would she? Even as un-Sheila as she's been lately, I don't think she'd do that.

"You're exceptionally gifted, Kivali, in all aspects. Your community will benefit greatly from your talents once you learn to share. You have the potential to be a real leader."

I look up and fully meet Machete's gaze. Her eyes are deep, warm.

"I'll enjoy these sessions with you," she says. "I hope that you'll come to trust me, to work with me, and to expand your considerable capacities for the benefit of us all. Do you have any questions?"

"There was a boy," I say. "The first night, in the Pavilion. I haven't seen him since."

She doesn't look away. She doesn't even blink.

"Very observant. But then, he's visibly a bender, so of course you would have noticed him."

"Where is he now?"

"Sometimes, camp and comrade are not a good fit. That was the case here."

"What happened to him?"

"I can't tell you that. Each comrade's privacy is precious, even those who are no longer here. That's all we have time for today." Machete pushes her chair back. "We'll meet every Tuesday morning, but you can request extra sessions. If you have any problems at all, please come to me."

I stand, shoving my hands in my pockets, finding the komodo.

"I'm involved in every corner of CropCamp," says Machete. "We'll get to know each other quite well. Meanwhile, think about my question: is your independence an asset or a liability? We'll talk about it more next week."

She walks around the desk as she speaks, steps past me, and opens the door. In order to go through, I have to pass under her arm again.

Chapter Five

I FIND RASTA STILL in the potatoes. The crumbly dirt gives my knees a soft place to sink into.

"So? How was it?"

I shake my head and jam my fingers into the ground up to my knuckles. Machete didn't tell the truth about the bender in the moonlight, but she also didn't lie. I like how she talked about independence. Different from Korm or Sheila, but with shades of both.

"My da said we need to talk to each other," says Rasta. "He said we need to keep each other's inner sparks alive. Did she throw water on your inner spark?"

I shake my head again, pull my hands out of the earth, and begin thinning the row next to Rasta's.

"What did she do?" Her voice hushes down to a raspy whisper.

"Nothing. She was fine."

"So what's wrong? Something's wrong. I can tell."

"No, nothing's wrong."

We work in silence for a while, and I replay the DM session again and again. I cannot figure Machete out. She's nothing like the school gov worker. She seems to understand things the way that Sheila and Korm do. But then how can she work for SayFree? How can she be a camp director? And is the bender boy really the first vape from her camp, *ever* ever? Or does she cover them up? How could she cover it? When someone's gone, they're gone.

"Lizard, will you be my strong alliance?" Suddenly, Rasta is right next to me, in the same row. "We'll tell each other everything that happens. So one of us can't lose our inner spark without the other one knowing."

"No."

"Why not?"

She tips her head. Not offended, just curious. I take a deep breath, sit back on my knees, and give her my coldest flat-eyed lizard stare. If I'm going to be working with her all the time, she might as well know.

"I'm a bender. Midrange. No T."

She squints one eye.

"You don't seem bendery."

I hitch a move away from her, digging back into the plants.

"Wait, don't be mad. You just seem like a girl to me. I never would have guessed if you didn't tell me."

Like giving me a hand to help me up and stepping on my chest at the same time. I continue digging. Pull out the weak plants, toss them in the bucket. They'll go to the compost bins.

"I mean, not that there's anything wrong with it. I know some people are born that way so you can't help it — I mean, ahhh, I don't know what I mean. I'm just stupid."

I move to the next mound. She follows, scooting along on her knees.

"I hate it when I'm stupid. I'm sorry. Really. I like you."

"Why?" I don't look up. "Why don't you go be allies with one of them?"

Rasta sits back on her heels and looks down the field. Rory and Dakota are talking to Micah. Lyddie crawls down a row about halfway between us, a row over from Tuvik. "No." She shakes her head. "No, I don't think so."

"Why me?"

Rasta takes off her cap and runs her fingers through her feathery white, baby-fluff hair.

"Something about you, Lizard. I can't quite say what it is yet, but my da would like you. I'm sure of it. He's an excellent judge of character, and so am I."

I don't know anything about character, and I've never had an alliance, strong or otherwise. I'm still not sure what she means by it, but I'll not let a bender bigot anywhere near my inner spark.

"The bender guy." I watch to see if she makes that mean mocky face again. She doesn't. "I asked Machete about him. She said he's gone."

"Maybe he vaped."

I sharp a look at her. Was Rasta up there that night, too? Did she see him vape? She doesn't give anything away, just keeps plucking little plants out of the ground while she talks.

"My gram vaped. My da says one morning she just wasn't there. No body, nothing. Just blip, vape, gone. He says my gram was too wise and beautiful to stay on this earth, too exceptional. I never met her. It happened before I was born."

"But hardly anybody vapes from camps. And never from this one."

"That's what they *say*." Rasta tips her head up and sideways, nodding at a slant. "But how do we know?"

"Well, where does your da think they vape to?"

"Depends on his mood. Sometimes he thinks the gov kills them. Other times he thinks they get transported to some alien universe. Da's a bit of a nut sometimes."

"Lizard, Rasta," calls Micah, "Finish that row before lunch. Or at least before July."

We start moving again, passing each other as we hit the mounds one after another. Neither of us speaks till the end of the row.

"So will you?" Rasta asks.

"Will I what?"

"Be my strong alliance? I don't care that you're a bender. In fact, I like it."

With her big gray eyes and pointy chin, she looks like an elf. A very serious, committed, earnest elf.

"Maybe," I say. "Just for tries."

She holds her hand up, fingers spread and curved. I touch my fingertips to hers.

"Strong alliance," she says.

I give a quick nod, but I don't say it back.

Chapter Six

WHEN THE LAST BLOCK of the day ends, I run down the slope and trot back to my pie. It's all quiet — I'm the first one down from fields or classes. I drop my secateurs off in my slice and continue along the path that goes deeper into the woods. I want to find somewhere private, if there is any such thing in CropCamp.

The only pie past ours is Lacey's one-slice, about fifty paces beyond on the left. The path continues after that, and I follow it until I reach a fork. The left trail is clear, and the right one is sketchy, barely discernible. I take the sketchy one. Brambles and ferns stretch across trying to trip me up. I step over a fallen tree into a small open space where the path ends. Thin barky tree trunks surround me, stretching up to a piney canopy. The floor is soft brown needles. I kneel down and sniff. They smell hot and bakey, a cooked version of the delicious tang in the air.

I stand and scan to see how private it is, and I catch a movement of pale green in the distance. Lacey. I'm not as far from her slice as I'd thought. I head back to the fork, stepping quiet and moving slow so she won't notice me. I take the more defined path and continue deeper into the woods.

I haven't tuned in to Lizard Radio in two whole days now. I can't remember the last time I've gone that long. For sure not since Sheila first took me to Korm. That's been — let's see — seven — no, almost eight — years ago. After that horrible day when I came home from school with a cut under my left eye and a real-life fear of violents and Blight. I was scared to poke a toe out the door after that.

I never really told Sheila what happened, but I refused school for a while. She set it up so that I could mostly use the Deega from home. I still had to go once a week, and I fought it every time. After a few weeks of that, Sheila took me to Korm.

They'd been friends in the way-back, but Sheila had lost track so it took some looking. Korm doesn't live in a flat like regular people — everything about her is clandy and hush. Sheila knew someone who knew someone who told her where and when to find Korm.

That first day, Sheila introduced me, and I really truly couldn't tell if Korm was supposed to be a he or a she. She was big-shouldered and she smelled male and her voice was low-deep, but she had a mountain of hair stacked high on her head, and she wore a flowing skirt and moved like a woman.

She circled, looking me over. She was full of grace and power like a big prowling cat. I wanted her to choose me. She put a hand on the back of my head and said, "I'll take this one."

"Kivali, do you want to stay?" Sheila asked me.

I nodded.

"I'll be back in one hour."

Sheila closed the door tight behind her. The basement room was bare, floored with mats. Muted light came in through the two small rectangular windows. Candles on the floor cast flicker and looming shadows. Korm stood on her knees in front of me so that we were about the same height. Her hands were enormous but they danced and flowed as if they lived a life apart from the dark room and the musky smell.

"Everything we do together is secret," she said. "Even from Sheila."

I shifted, backed away a bit. Sheila had warned me about adults with secrets.

"If the secrets feel bad, we'll stop." Korm always heard my nervous thoughts, right from the first day. "You know right from wrong," she said. "Just trust yourself. Fact is, you are a bender, and I am a bender, and we know things different from everyone else, even Sheila. She says that you go on trance-missions. Is that true?"

I nodded. That's what Sheila called it when I used her meditation techniques. Only I went a lot further away than she ever did, and after that day at school I started doing it all the time. I think Sheila was scared I'd trance out and never come back.

"And you call it Lizard Radio?"

Sheila shouldn't have told Korm that. It was private, between her and me.

"It's okay," said Korm. "Trance-missions are good, whatever you call them. Now tell me who you are."

"I'm Kivali Kerwin."

44

My voice was tiny and tinny next to Korm's.

"That's your name. Now tell me who you are."

I shook my head. I didn't know what she meant.

"Don't think," she said. "Just tell me. Who are you?"

I liked that she asked *who,* not *what,* so I gave her a good answer.

"I am a lizard."

That made Korm smile. And when Korm smiled, the candles danced and the air floated soft and warm around me, and I relaxed. Much better than the last time I'd said *lizard.* That was at the market a couple of years earlier. A little girl asked if I was a boy or a girl, and I said, "I'm a lizard." Sheila hugged me so hard, she almost broke my neck, but then she said, "Next time, say *girl.*"

I didn't say *lizard* again until Korm. Not until Sully.

I continue on the wide path through the woods. I'm surprised that it keeps going — I had no idea that CropCamp spread so wide. I keep thinking I'll run into a fence or a sign. Micah said in orientation that the borders are marked with bright yellow signs so we won't cross the boundary biosensors accidentally. Biosensors are expensive, and they're usually only at sector borders, but all camps are enclosed with them for safety. No one can go on or off the grounds without transmitting bio-ID.

There's a break in the brush ahead on my right and I slow down, expecting I've hit the end. But no — the path opens into a perfect little grassy area surrounded by a grove of huge trees. These trees aren't piney. They're huge, with thick trunks stretching up into a canopy of leaves so dense, you can't tell which

45

branches go with which tree. They hold the grassy area in close and the green mirrors itself up and down and all around like it's a whole different world. I suck in through my nose. The smell is different, too. Muskier. Deeper. This is the spot.

I slip off my frods and set the komodo on one, so it can be out in the air and the woods and watch me. I barefoot to the center. The long grass is softly green, giving my soles cushion to spring from. My foot comes down on something sharp. It's an acorn. I put it in my pocket and close my eyes, bringing myself into myself.

Before you can be what you are, you must be all things.

I slow my breathing, pull the air in and around me. Pull the green of the grass up through my soles and into my blood. Feel everything and me, and me and everything, and steady and center.

Then I speak to myself in Korm's voice.

Be a rock.

I find the rock in me. Granite, like the boulders by the camp entry. Warm in the sun, cool in the night, rain pounding and snow covering soft and still in the depths of winter. The wind touches me in all seasons. I invite the wind to blow across my surface, and then I leap into it and become the wind, whipping through the trees and carrying the weather. Far below, a tiny spark glows. I swoop down and blow on it until the fire blazes, and I am the fire, howling and spitting light to the skies until the skies begin to rain. The water meets the fire in an explosion of steam, and I am the steam, hot into cold. I meld with the drops, dripping and swirling, splashing and crashing inside and out, running over the rock. The rock. I am the rock.

I open my eyes and look around the grove. I've always loved the way that Korm talks about nature and takes me through visualizations, but the depth of green here is so much more than anything I could imagine. Not just green for my eyes, but green in every textured sense, inside and out. I'll come here every day after Block Four for some Lizard Radio time. Except for Mondays, when I have kitchen rotation. All the other days.

I lie flat on my back, close my eyes again, breathe deep. I miss Korm. I miss her so much. But here in the grove, her voice holds me. *Now you can be what you are and go where you go. Just remember where you came from.* I lie back, close my eyes, head into trance-mission, and—

Gong.

Really? My free hour gone already?

I have ten ticks to clean up and get to the Mealio. I drop the komodo in my pocket with the acorn, strap on my frods, and take off at a run. Pounding the earth, sucking in the air, fire in my heart and blood rivers rushing through my body. There's nothing in the world that feels as good as Lizard Radio in the great non-imaginary outdoors.

As I thud up to the pie, Sully comes around to my side.

"Lizard! Where were you?"

"Taking a walk."

"That's not walking. That's running. Why do you look so happy? Having a bit of clazzy-jandy in the woods?"

"We're late," I say.

"Fike the fiking gongs. Two days of it, and I'm gonged out of my head. We should steal that thing and hide it somewhere. Want to help me?"

"Sure. After dinner. Come on."

I start up the path at a trot, and Sully jogs next to me.

"You're speedy," she says.

I charge up the slope and wait for her at the top, bouncing on my toes. I've been off-balance around Sully since that first moment when I said "lizard time" out loud like a six-year-old. But now I've found my feet here, and I've found the Radio. I've got my balance. Sully scrambles the last few steps to the top and stops with her hands on her knees, huffing.

"Go ahead. Don't be late on my account. You run like a fiking bunny rabbit."

"Come on," I say. "We'll fast-walk it. Better two of us late than one alone."

Machete sees us come in. She looks right at me, but she doesn't say anything. Sully and I split up, finding two open seats at different tables. I settle in my seat and look over at her, and she grins. I smile back, because how can I not?

Chapter Seven

"LIZARD! I THOUGHT YOU were going to muffle that gong."

"Lizard is a Wednesday. Let her sleep in."

That shuts Sully up. Nona hasn't addressed either of us since Monday morning, not one time. A tick or two later, my door flap opens and Sully pokes her head in, eyebrows stretched to the sky.

"She likes you," she mouths, pointing to the wall that I share with Nona.

I shake my head.

"How was your DM with Machete?" she asks out loud. "Did you get chopped?"

"Not really. I'll tell you about it later. I want to sleep some more."

Sully laughs and mouths, "You like her," pointing from me to Nona.

I wave her out and try to go back to sleep, but the birds are too loud. I only have one shower chit, barely enough to get wet, so I decide to go pedal some watts in the power room.

By the time I cycle and shower, Block One gong is ringing. On days off we're allowed to skip CounCircle and breakfast, but we have to be at the Study Center for Blocks One and Two. We have study sessions and rotate in and out of ayvee pod and DM sessions. Rasta quizzes me on the seeds and plants and soil types and SayFree tenets from the first two days, and then it's my turn for MaDa inflow.

The ayvee pod is a little room at the far end of the Study Center. I shut the door behind me, and it takes me a moment to realize what's missing. Noise. For the past three days, any time I've been indoors it's been full of talk, especially the Mealio. And the outdoors talks constantly, what with the crickets and birds and chirpy things in the night that Tylee claims are tree frogs. Insects whir and buzz, and the leaves and branches whisper back and forth, and animals scuttle around, and all the noise is everywhere. This ayvee pod has a ceiling, and walls, and ninety-degree angled corners, and no comrades and no wildlife or wind. Quiet.

I find the chip marked KERWIN, punch my code in, and hit PLAY. Sheila's face appears on the screen, filling me with a mash of feelings. I cross my arms, holding myself in close. She starts right off with her cheery-chipper CropCamp-will-be-fun tone. Her refresher course is rigorous and good, helping bring her work up to state standards. Such a good summer for us both — me in camp and her in the refresher course.

Who is this person? This is not Sheila.

Fike to the state standards, I'm an artist. You can't dictate art. Where's that Sheila? The one who first taught me to trance-mission? The Sheila who hates cams and won't have one in the house? She either bought one or went to the community center to make this. Her face fills the screen as she moves closer to the cam.

"Komodo. You're learning to be a good comrade and citizen, and you'll do that just right. Remember who you are. I held you in the baby days but I can't hold you now. Everything is changing. Nothing will be the same. We all have to learn and live and grow — you too. Me too."

The screen goes blank. Her inflow only lasted two ticks. She couldn't even be bothered to talk to me for the full five allowed ticks. Where the fike is my very own Sheila? Again, I scan my memory of the past two weeks.

It wasn't just the CropCamp rah-rah. One moment she treated me like a five-year-old, calling me "sweet gecko" and watching my every move. The next, she was abrupt and distant: "Things change, Kivali," and "Everyone has to grow up sometime." Almost mean, even. And back to "sweet gecko" five ticks later. She was so un-Sheila-like that it was easy to ignore the CropCamp stuff and treat it like a joke or a phase or something.

Also, Korm chose the same two weeks to go absent. Totally absent. She often goes absent for a week, but rarely for two. Does she even know that Sheila skizzed me off to CropCamp? Those two, they don't talk to each other unless they have to.

I take the earbuds out and hit PLAY again. The words don't sound like Sheila at all. I want to see what her face and body say.

Her gaze is cast slightly to the side, until — there. Right there. Her eyes flick directly to the cam, full on.

I stop it, reverse, put the earbuds in and listen.

Remember who you are.

Then her eyes shift ever-slightly away again. I freeze the picture.

"Well, that's the question, isn't it?" I ask the komodo. "Who I am. Only the lizards know."

I was maybe a day old when Sheila found me on the sidewalk outside her flat, wrapped in a yellow T-shirt with a cartoon lizard on the front. She says that I could've been dropped cosmos to terra, hatched or cloned, or dumped by someone with a secret. And because Sheila begged and fought and filled out the docs and petitioned, they let her foster me. Even though she's asolo, never been married. She had to shape up her work and register for flatchecks and do all sorts of stuff that she didn't want to do.

"Why?" I love the story. I've made her tell it a million times. "Why did you?"

"Because you were tiny and alone, because you looked right into my eyes, because I thought: *What if this one changes everything?* And once I thought that, I knew that I had to fight for you."

I put the komodo back in my pocket and watch the whole thing again with earbuds in. It's subtle, the eye shift. I'd never notice if I hadn't watched without sound. Maybe it means something. Maybe nothing. The green leddie over the door buzzes. My ayvee time is up.

———•———

I have all of Blocks Three and Four free, so I head back to the oak grove. I miss Sheila, the real Sheila. I don't want secret messages. I want her to be herself. Also, I want her to tell Korm that I'm away at camp. She should know. Doesn't matter what I want, though. I'll only see five ticks a week of any Sheila, fake or real or enigmatic, for another two and three-quarter months.

Since I have plenty of time, I follow the path past the grove to see where it goes. It gradually narrows, and after I've walked a ways, a splash of yellow emerges in the distance, eye-high. As I draw closer, the red lettering becomes clear:

CROPCAMP BORDER

BIOSENSOR BOUNDARY

Checking right and left, I see the signs spaced maybe one hundred paces apart, so you can't cross without knowing. The biosensors read your DNA and flash your info on a Deega somewhere, and the gov knows that you've passed. Korm says the biosensor lines are expensive and don't really cover the entire boundaries. She says the underground has been gradually mapping out the biosensor gaps.

Surely there are gaps here — but probably not on the path. Probably off in those thickets of brush. Not that I want to find out. I wouldn't have anywhere to go. I turn and head back.

The grove is cool and shady. I kick off my frods and put the komodo on watch, plant my feet in the middle, and breathe toward rock, but I can't feel it. When I was eight and Korm told me to be a rock, at first I couldn't do it. I think it really only took a couple of weeks, but I was a child, and it seemed like a million years before Korm was satisfied with my rock.

I had no patience. Korm had endless patience. It took months of study for me to move from rock to wind, and to fire, and to rain, and finally to begin my study of lizard. Lizard came quickly, because it's true, what the school gov worker blatters on about — when I focus, I learn fast.

I just need to focus. I close my eyes and listen for Korm's voice, but Korm is farther away than Sheila. I can't seem to draw breath past the midway mark in my lungs. I can't get deep.

My mind jitters around in circles. Crops, the Mealio, Machete's office, Sully, Rasta, studies, Cleezies. I can't find my razor-focus. That's what Korm calls it, and she can always help me find it, but she's not here. I lie down on the soft grass and watch the leaves against the sky.

Remember who you are. Kivali Sauria Kerwin. Does Sheila mean that I should focus on my lizard self? She used to make up bedtime stories about the saurians dropping me on her sidewalk. As far back as I can remember, she's called me lizard names. I like to believe in the stories. At least they're some kind of explanation.

Most people figure that since I'm fostered, I must be from the Blight Baby Nursery, but I'm not. Sheila has an ayvee of me from before I could walk, and I've seen it. Blight babies don't get fostered out of the nursery until their second birthday so that everyone can be sure they're certified healthy. And then there's a big long waiting list — it's hard to make babies, and even harder to get one if you don't make it yourself. Like Sheila always says, it's a miracle that they let her keep me.

I roll over and pick up the komodo and set it on my forehead.

"Lizard-dropped," I say. "You and me."

Since I was a tiny kidlet, I've been waiting for the lizard chitter and moan and shifting shadows to clear up and tell me exactly what to do. I thought that might be happening when I heard "Go to the fields" so clear in my head. I thought my Lizard Destiny was about to be revealed.

That night has already taken on a distant fantasy-flavor. Like Lizard Radio. It's so real when you're in it, and then later it's something else. Something maybe dreamed or maybe coincidence or maybe nothing at all.

At home, there's always Korm to make Lizard Radio real again. Here I have to do it myself. Maybe I haven't focused enough. Maybe if I tune in right now, and remember who I am, the saurians will speak. I close my eyes and breathe deeply and get quiet.

All I see behind my eyelids is Sheila shifting her eyes to look into the cam. *Remember who you are.* I don't remember learning to trance, but she's told me the story almost as many times as the found-on-the-sidewalk one. She accidentally left the SayFree broadcast on one night when I was three. I dove under the kitchen table and started up a holler-waller loud enough to make the neighbors call in.

Sheila turned off the radio and came under the table with me. She thought that I was too young to learn her meditation technique, but she tried it anyway. Breathe in slow, two, three, hold; breathe out slow, two, three, four. *Look at the shapes on the backs of your eyelids — see them there? Breathe in, two, three, and hold; breathe out, two, three, four. See them shift? Watch the show, two, three.*

I immediately calmed down. Sheila said she'd never seen anyone trance so quickly and so completely. She said it was like I'd left and gone somewhere far away, leaving my breathing body behind. It scared her, and she jostled me back. When she asked me where I went, I told her that they talked to me.

"Who?" she asked.

"The lizards," I answered.

"What did they say?"

"Secrets."

That's when Sheila started calling it Lizard Radio. I wish I could remember that first time myself. Maybe I knew lizardspeak back then, and I understood the secrets. Or maybe I said "secrets" because their whispery lizard language was secret from me, too.

When I tune in now, it's like I'm just on the brink of understanding. Like if I could move one twitch closer, I'd get it all. And somehow, even with the not-understanding, I understand it better than anything. It's more than imagining, less than state standards. Fluid and ethereal, gentle and encompassing. It's not that I actually see lizards, but I feel them and I hear them, and every lonely or sad or scared feeling disappears.

A chippie scrambles nearby. I open my eyes, and the komodo

slides off my forehead into the grass. I can't find the signal. I close my eyes again and try to make it happen, but that never works. It's like staring at a pinpoint of light in the darkness — you can't see it unless you turn and look sideways, because of the rods and cones and retina. Lizard Radio is like that. You have to listen sideways or it doesn't work.

I put the komodo back in my pocket and breathe some more. Even without Lizard Radio, it feels good to breathe here in the grass with the oak leaves dancing overhead. Tomorrow, I'll come back here and find the rock. Korm says that sometimes we go in with our minds, and sometimes we have to access the signal through our bodies. Tomorrow I'll start with rock and find my focus, and I'll tune in fully. Tomorrow.

Chapter Eight

THE NEXT DAY SULLY snags me right after Block Four, before I can slip off to the oak grove.

"Come with me," she whispers.

We take the main path past our pies, and I think that she's discovered the oak grove, too, but she stops abruptly just past Lacey's turnoff. I run up on her heels and stutter-step back.

"Tonight." She moves in so close our bodies almost touch, and whispers. "Leave the Quint right after mando Social. Meet at our pie."

"What for?"

I whisper, too, although no one's around.

"Gong destruction, maybe? Sabi from Thursdays called it. Very clandy. Stroll away from the Quint — casual — we'll leave one by one so the guides don't notice."

I've met Sabi. She's got icy eyes and spikes of static.

"We who?"

"You, me, Rasta, Tylee. A few others, I think."

I don't want to miss anything that Sully and Rasta and Tylee are in on, Sabi or no. I'll stay on the edge and leave quick if things go to bad.

Nona is the first to leave the Quint that evening. She always leaves as soon as it's allowed. She spends every second of free time zipped up in her slice. I leave a few seconds after, trail her down into Pieville, and circle our pie to stand outside Slice Twenty where no one can see me. I wait for the others, nervously fiddling with the komodo.

They show up one by one, and we gather in a quiet huddle. Me, Rasta, Sully, Tylee, Risa from Mondays, and Jyana from Thursdays. Sabi arrives last and walks past, waving at us to follow her.

We drop back to single file. I stay at the end, glancing occasionally over my shoulder. Sabi takes us on the narrow right fork to the little piney opening. After a lot of looking around and holding her finger *shh* to her lips, she signals us to sit, and everyone does.

"What do you think?" Sabi kneels, sitting on her heels so that she's just a bit higher than the rest of us. "Good spot, right?"

"Good for what?" asks Jyana.

"A hangout spot."

It's nowhere near as good as the spot that I found, but I'm keeping the oak grove to myself.

"Beats the fike out of Social," Sabi says. "They think if they force us into the same place every night, we'll all make friends. No go."

"That's not very come-from-One-return-to-One of you, my friend," says Sully.

"No. It's all a big robot factory. I say we blow it open."

Complete, total silence.

"You sure know how to put the fun in the social, Sabi."

Sully breaks the tension, and a breath of nervous laughter moves around the circle.

"You want to go play whuck-chuck like a good little comrade?" asks Sabi. "They're trying to drug and hypno us into total compliance, make us slaves to work in their fields. I say we revolt. Anyone with me?"

"Revolt with what?" asks Sully. "Our secateurs?"

"Ha." I don't believe in Sabi's smile, but I take an easier breath. Sully is keeping things sane. "The secateur revolution. That's funny, Sully. I'm just joking, you know. I wouldn't mess with SayFree. Too powerful."

"Joke about SayFree if you want, but my fam is better off." Tylee never has a single spike of static, and she's a little bit mad. "Everyone except the Blighters, and we're all better off without them running free on the streets. What's wrong with good behavior and safety? If you don't like manual labor, you could've studied harder and gone to FinanceCamp or Techno or any of the others. It's not slavery. Besides, everyone needs good food."

"Serious, you're so serious," says Sabi. "I just think we need to break loose a bit now and then. Isn't anyone else tired of doing what we're told all the time?"

"Me, I am," says Sully. "I don't know if I can handle this three-month-sing-along song."

"I'm a little tired of the big group thing, too," says Jyana. "I've been leaving the Quint early the past two nights just to get away from that guy Rory. He sits by me in the Mealio, in Cleezies, and the Quint, everywhere."

"So meet here whenever you feel like ditching the sing-along song," says Sabi. "And we don't tell anyone else about it, right?"

I meet Rasta's eyes. *Strong alliance.* We'll talk about this later.

"I'm good with that." Sully leans back and stretches out. "Check the sky. Pretty."

I lean back, too, propping on my elbows and tipping my face up to the purpling sky.

"We should play ha-ha," says Risa. "Any of you ever play that?"

"Oh, yeah, we did that on one of our school trips," says Tylee. "It was hilarious. I mean, it's just a kidlet game, but still. Here, Risa."

She lies down and pats her stomach. Risa pillows her head there.

"Come on, Sully."

Sully puts her head on Risa's stomach, and looks at me with her eyebrows raised, so I lie down, too. We end up in a zig of bodies zagging across the clearing, and Tylee teaches us the game, which is basically trying to say the correct number of *ha*s while your head bounces around on someone else's stomach.

"Ha," says Tylee.

"Ha-ha," says Risa.

Silence.

"Sully! Say ha-ha-ha!"

"Too much like a sing-along song."

"Fine, be that way. Ha-ha-ha-ha, Lizard."

I don't do it, either, but Rasta does, and her raspy baby crow ha-ha sets Sully off. Sully's laugh jounces my head, and I laugh, and that makes Rasta's head move, and she laughs harder. A current of breath and laughter runs from one body to the next, leaping from skin to skin, connecting us in a head-bouncing zigzag.

I can't quit laughing. Nothing is all that funny, but the tension release turns into a physical thing, and everyone is laughing and I'm part of it and tears start leaking out, and my head keeps bouncing on Sully's stomach until she groans and says, "Stop, it's killing me."

The laughs slowly die down, just a giggle and bounce here and there. The sky hushes and dims around us. Darkening treetops are etched against the sky, and the pine needles are soft beneath us.

"Are those chirpy things really frogs?" asks Risa.

"Yes," says Tylee. "Little green ones."

"Star pop!" Jyana points up. "Wish."

Sully touches my forehead, brushes her fingers over my brow. My heart chunka-thunks.

"Never get to see anything like this sky in Twa." Sully speaks casually as her fingers set every nerve in my body on high alert. "Is there even a name for that color?"

She strokes my ear, and her touch zooms into my chest, my belly, and my biz. I can't move, and I can barely lie still — I have no idea what to do. Should I pet Rasta's head? Is everyone else doing this?

The air is perfectly still, not a breath of wind. Sully softly massages my ear, and that area she's touching, that explosion of nerves and pleasure, becomes the only thing in my world. She gently rubs up to the tip, and I close my eyes, trying to steady my breath so that no one will hear it shaking.

Suddenly, my head slides off Sully's stomach with a bump. I open my eyes to a powerful flash of leddie beam coming toward us on the dusky path. The leddie stops and shines over us like a spotlight.

"You're all on culpa. Anyone who isn't sliced in the next five ticks is looking for an expul."

Chapter Nine

LACEY AND THE LIGHT turn abruptly and leave. We scramble to our feet. Nobody has a leddie, so we follow the distant bob of Lacey's along the narrow path, single file. The curfew gong rings. Lacey turns to her own slice without another word, and we continue into Pieville.

Sully and I stop at our pie as the others go on, and Rasta stops with us. Tylee doesn't. She can't get back to her slice fast enough. The three of us huddle on the empty Slice Twenty side.

"I think we'll be okay," whispers Sully. "The gong never rang until we were on our way back, so technically, we weren't doing anything wrong. We were on free time, and nobody said that we couldn't be in the woods during free time."

"Nothing wrong except Sabi wanting to overthrow the gov," says Rasta.

"Sabi's a semiautomatic," says Sully. "No one but us was there to hear it, though. Unless . . ."

She tips her head toward Nona's slice. Rasta nods and backs away. Sully softly shoulder-bumps me as she passes. I stand still and listen to the zip-zip of her door. And to the tree-frog chirp and mosquito whine. And to my own pounding heart.

I wake up Friday filled with dread. Fiking Sabi is going to land me with some horrible foster who will make me T and won't let me listen to Lizard Radio. And then I'll end up in Blight, and it'll be full of cold-eyed staticky Sabi types with nobody to stop them and no escape. You can bet that there aren't any gaps in *those* biosensor boundaries.

I'm so shaken, I don't even notice that my komodo is missing until the next morning when I roll over and look at the shelf. The acorn from the grove is there, but the komodo is gone. Then I remember that I dropped my coveralls and slid into bed without putting it on guard. I check my pockets, and it's not there, either.

I pull the coveralls on in a panic and hurry back along the narrow path. Everything shines deep green in the slant of morning sun, a-sparkle with tiny glistening drops. By the time I get to the little open space, my pant legs are soaking wet. The komodo greets me from a patch of rusty pine needles. One front leg raised like always.

I throw myself on the ground next to it. I touch the spot between its eyes and then hold it in my fist, rolling onto my back. My pulse picks up with the memory of Sully's fingers last night. That feeling spreads through my body again. *Time for a bit of jazz-off.* I can barely breathe. What if Sully was right here again, right now? With her hand in my hair? What if—

The wake-up gong rings me into the real-time day. I stand

and kiss the komodo. So relieved that I found it there waiting for me. I hurry back to my slice and set the komodo on the shelf, next to the acorn. No more pocket-carrying, not here. The coverall pockets are too loose, and I crawl around on the ground all day.

"Stay here." I touch the tip of its nose. "You'll be safer."

I run up to CounCircle, feeling half-naked and fidgety without the familiar metal shape in my pocket. Plus, I'm still undone by the echo of Sully's fingers on my ear and the stew of trouble Sabi put us in.

As we file from CounCircle into the Mealio, we meet eyes, shrug shoulders. Nobody's said anything to anyone about our culpa. We're on tiptoe, heads down and mouths shut. Everything stays unnervingly normal all day. During free moments, we agree to lay low in our slices. We show up everywhere exactly on time. After Cleezies, I'm on my way out the door when Lacey puts a hand on my shoulder.

"Meet at my slice in ten ticks," she says. "Ms. Mischetti's order."

Sully jogs up next to me.

"Here we go."

My nerves are already exploding, and Sully's voice touches shivers up and down my spine. She is not like anyone I've ever met. I glance down at her fingers, and ear tingles shoot all the way to my toes.

"Culpa at the worst," she says. "She can't expul all seven of us. It'd ruin her cert percentage."

We half-trot down the steep part of the path. Maybe we'll be okay. Like Sully said last night, we didn't actually break any rules.

"Maybe she'll make an example out of me," she says.

"Why you? It wasn't your idea."

"She'll probably think it was, and that might not be a bad thing. Boot me now. Save us all a lot of trouble."

"Why would you say that?"

I don't mean to get shrill, but she's scaring me. There's none of that jokey-Sully I'm-a-bad-influence thing in her eyes.

"My own da says I'm bound for Blight. He'd know if anyone does. I'm cut from his cloth, and that's not a fabric you'd want lying around your camp."

"If Sabi got us expulled, I'll kill her." Tylee comes up behind us. "I never should have gone. I knew it was a bad idea."

Rasta is right behind Tylee, so I'm left uneasy and unknowing about the fabric of Sully's da. The four of us head back to Lacey's slice together. As we pass my slice, I give the komodo a secret, silent nod. I wish it were with me.

Machete is waiting. She signals us to sit in the little clearing there. We're in a tight arc, Sully to my left and Rasta on my right. The other three arrive soon after with Lacey behind them. Once we're all seated, Machete starts to pace around us. Lacey leans on a downed tree, arms crossed.

"You're quick." Machete stops in front of Sully. "Most camps don't start with curfew breaks until at least the second week."

"We didn't curfew-break," says Sully. "Gong hadn't rung yet."

"We were about to leave," says Sabi. "If Lacey hadn't been

there talking to us, we would've been back in our slices by the gong."

"Lacey?" Machete turns to her. "Is it true? Was it before gong?"

"They never would have made it by gong." Lacey glares at Sully. "They weren't on their way back."

"So it's a technicality," says Machete. "We can't prove it one way or another, so there will be no culpa."

A sigh of relief passes among us. Three culpas make an expul.

"But Lacey, since you did such a nice job of rounding up this little group, I think I'll take the opportunity to explain some things."

Machete walks again, pacing clockwise. I resist the urge to swivel and keep her in sight.

"My job is not just to record culpas and scores. My first and foremost job is to keep you safe, and to teach you how to keep yourselves safe. Part of that job is to recognize strength and enhance it. What I see here is a unique power cadre. I see brains and intuition, connection and influence. I see steadiness and strength and creativity. I don't want to lose even one of you."

She continues to pace around us. It's been cloudy all afternoon, and the woods settle to a dusky gray. Machete stops in front of me, and I swear I can feel her foot on my tail. I stop breathing but I don't look away. She shifts her eyes a tick to my left.

"Sully. Do you find your days here uninteresting?"

Sully doesn't answer, but she doesn't look away, either. She's practically begging to be blamed. The air vibrates between them.

Machete slowly nods. As if she and Sully are making an agreement. Then Machete resumes her circular prowl.

"I understand your need to bond. Highly predictable, that those of you with some extra lumens seek one another and take a little lark. Form alliances."

Rasta's breath hitches.

"You're each finding and testing your personal capabilities, the reach of your influence. Discovering the intelligence and imagination and personal potency that set you apart. You could explore more productive ways to apply your leadership. I suggest inclusiveness of your comrades in the future — it'll be better for them, and for you, too. I appreciate this opportunity to have a clear visual on where our potential power base lies so that we can all work together."

A chill falls across the gathering, and my limbs begin to stiffen. My teeth would chatter if I let them.

"You'll all have your DM sessions with me from here on out. Rasta and Tylee, check the rosters in the morning for your schedule changes. Return to your slices now, and consider the best possible ways to use your leadership and unique talents for the benefit of the wider citizenry. I realize that you were just on a lark, but the ways in which we choose to have fun say a great deal about us. With power comes responsibility. We will explore this further in DM."

She turns and leaves. I stand, and my knees crack. I offer a hand to Rasta. Lacey still leans with her arms crossed, watching as we file back out to the main path. I don't breathe easy until we're back at our pie. This time, Tylee stops with me and Rasta and Sully.

"That was a big zoom-zoom," says Sully. "Machete's selling. Who's buying?"

"Me," says Tylee. "I am. From here out, I'm staying with the pack. She made a mistake about me. I'm not any power cadre."

"Guess you'll hear about that in DM," says Sully. "Rasta?"

"The whole thing made me cold," she says. "Chilly to the core. How about you, Lizard? What did you think of it?"

In the relief of non-culpa for me or anyone else, my attention has wandered back to Sully's fingers on my ear. I'm glad that it's too dark for anyone to see my face flush.

"The Lizard speaks not," says Sully. "Maybe we should all take Lizard lessons."

"I'm for that," says Tylee.

Rasta and Tylee leave me and Sully on the dark side of the pie. She turns to face me.

"Sorry I got you in trouble," she says.

She reaches up, and her fingertips are a kiss of cool on my hot cheek.

"Good night," she whispers.

Chapter Ten

THE GONG RINGS, AND the first thing I think of is Sully's touch cool-branded on my cheek. Sully doesn't holler because it's Saturday — her day off. I miss her on the way up to breakfast, and I miss her at lunch. I miss her all day long. I mean to tune in to Lizard Radio during Solitude, but instead I think about Sully. I think about her fingers, warm on my ear, cool on my cheek. I listen for her breath through the synthie wall.

After Cleezies, I sit on the grass with Tylee and Rasta. Sully is over on the edge of the Quint with Aaron. They're laughing. I pull my secateurs out of the holster. I open the blades, take a rag from my pocket, and start digging the grit out from the hinge joint. Saxem runs notes on his instrument, and a group of Tuesdays and Thursdays shout through a whuck-chuck game on the other end.

"Do you think Machete will tell our MaDas?" asks Tylee.

"Of course she will," says Rasta. "My da is not going to like this."

"We didn't actually do anything wrong, though. And we didn't get a culpa."

"He told me to keep my head down. He said, 'Do not attract attention in any way, for anything.'"

"Power cadre meeting and getting Machete for DM definitely counts as attracting attention," says Tylee. "But that's the end of it for me. I'm not risking my future for a ridiculous ha-ha game in the woods."

I glance over my shoulder. Aaron has Sully's hands pinned behind her back. She twists and kicks his feet out from under him. He takes an exaggerated fall and lies spread-eagled on the grass. She puts a foot on his chest.

"I'm heading pie-wise." I turn back to Rasta and Tylee. "See you tomorrow."

I skirt the whuck-chuck game and the little circle around Saxem. The sinking sun pours its last half-clouded rays across the fields, heightening the green. Not a breath of wind stirs on the humid air.

I stop off at the privo. When I come out, Nona is just outside, waiting.

"I didn't tell on you," she says.

"No?"

"No." Her eyes are rocky-hard fissures. "I know that none of you like me, but at least make it for the right reasons."

She marches off and zips into her slice. Footsteps come up behind. I turn, and there's Sully.

"What was that about?" she asks.

"She didn't tell on us."

"Says she."

"I believe her."

I imagine Nona listening, slitted eyes shifting from my voice to Sully's.

"Okay then, me, too. Come for a walk with me, would you? I need to talk."

"Why not talk to Aaron?"

I almost cut my own tongue on the sharp blade of my words. Sully stops and cocks her head with a grin.

"Jealous? No need to be. He's a toy. Come on. I need a real friend."

The sudden softening of her expression, the asking in her eyes — it reaches inside and loosens the tight place in my chest. I point into the woods, away from Nona's ears.

"We don't have much time before gong," I say as we walk. "We can't get caught out late two nights in a row."

"I know. We never have much time before some gong."

The humid night air presses down on us. We continue around a bend, out of sight of Lacey's slice. Sully stops and leans against a tree trunk, arms crossed. I'd like to see her dark form in the deepening green under Sheila's paint brush. Sheila can take any visual and amplify it until you can't stand the beauty.

"I'm looking at the end here," says Sully. "My whole life I've been headed toward Blight, but it always seemed like a long time away. Now it's smacking me in the face, and I'm not ready."

"What do you mean, smacking you? We got clear, not even a culpa."

Sully slides down the trunk. I sink to cross-legged, facing her.

"Machete came down hard on me in DM today. Told me that she rarely expuls comrades, but sometimes has to sacrifice one for the sake of the others. Said she's not going to let me take a bunch of innocents down with me."

"That's not fair. Did you tell her it was Sabi?"

"Of course not. Wouldn't help, anyway. Machete's out to chop me. I'm a repeater and she knows it. I got expulled from AstroPhysCamp and then a RepeaterCamp. My da yanked money strings to get me in here, last chance. I turn eighteen in August."

"You'll have to mind the regs then. No more messing around. She can't expul you if you do everything right."

Sully shakes her head, looking down at her hands.

"Lizard, I'm hardwired to go wrong. Genetic defect, and not much help from the parental people."

"What do you mean, wrong? You don't seem wrong to me."

"When I was a kid, I could skate through everything. People laughed, let stuff go. But the camps are different. I can't do it."

"You have to. You can't go to Blight."

"I know. They'll eat me up and spit me out there. I guess it'll have to be underground."

People are always threatening to underground but it's not so easy. I know because of Korm, and she says it gets harder all the time. Even if Sully could manage it, I'd never see her again.

"I'll help you comply. We'll cert through together, we will."

Sully picks up her head. In this moment, meeting her eyes in the fall of night with the memory of her fingers in my hair, I'd do anything for her. She smiles, but it's not a happy smile.

"You're lured in by my jazz-wise wiles, right?"

"Wrong." I stand, brush off my bum, swallow the vague taste of lie. "We have to get back. Gong will ring any second. You need to be more careful. We both do. Come on."

I turn toward the pie. Sully stops me with a hand on my shoulder. She pulls me around to face her, tucks a lock of hair behind my ear. Her touch blasts my skin, jazzes through my blood, liquefies my legs. Our faces draw close, and then closer.

Dark envelops me, sweet and rich, no vision and no sound, just the electric velvet sensation of tender skin meeting skin, Sully's breath in my mouth, her hand on the back of my neck. I lose time and form the way I do in the depths of Lizard Radio.

Then Sully draws back. Not far. Just enough to put space and air between our lips and our hearts.

"See," she whispers. "I'm nothing but trouble."

I shake my head, and she puts her hand on my cheek, holding my face still.

"This is exactly what Machete means," she says. "Corrupting innocence."

Her fingers trail slowly across my skin as she turns. I move to follow, and my lizard skin splits, first at the chest where it can't contain my hammering heart, and then across my face, undone by the new chemical wash rising to the surface. It peels down over my hips, melting in the heat, scaling off of my knees. I step out, leaving it in a dark crumple on the ground, and I follow Sully.

Chapter Eleven

I LIE IN THE DARK, wide awake and open-eyed. Clippity-clop heartbeat and shallow breath. My stomach has taken on a life of its own, spinning and dipping in a tilt-o-swirl. I'm skinless. Raw and open and naked to the world.

A tree frog calls. Again. And again. Scratchy solo chirp in the night. Finally, another answers. Back and forth. Chirp — pause — chirp. There is no moon. There is no wind. The trees are silent.

Back around decision time, they warned us about midrange benders becoming samers. Especially if they don't T. I was only ten. I didn't like boys or girls. I didn't much like anyone. I planned to be asolo, like Sheila or Korm. Never thought for a second what that might mean. What I'd miss.

I can't be a samer. It's bad enough being a bender. I won't be a samer, too. I just won't.

But what's this feeling, this twist and drop in my gut, this surge through my chest and the shake in my fingers and breath? Is this what people mean by falling in love? Because it feels like a fall. It's the same stomach-drop half-sick feeling. Velocity, no control, everything in a twist. It's incredibly disturbing. I might never be able to eat again. Or sleep, either. All I want is that fluid electric connect. I run the full-sensory memory through my body, over and over again.

The chirpers go silent. A light flashes, and I jerk up in a panic, listening hard. Did someone see us? Any jazz contact is grounds for expul. Samer jazz contact, that's fifty culpas and ten expuls all rolled into one. A low rumble moves through the trees, and I let my breath out.

Not a leddie. Lightning. Now I smell storm, and wonder how I didn't notice it before. I lie back down, force my eyes closed. Squinch them tight. I suck in the deepest breath that I can manage, move my lips as I count, search for familiarity, for peace, for the Radio. But the only thing on the back of my eyelids is a cinematic stereo replay of Sully sensation.

I put my finger in my mouth, run it around the inside of my lips where her tongue ventured and her breath touched. What is Sully? How can she shake me like that? The pie walls ripple as the treetops begin to twitch and shiver. I've always loved the dark and the magic that rides on a storm wind, dancing with lightning. But that was with the protection of a lizard skin, real or imagined.

I zip my window closed. As I get back in bed, I grab the komodo from the shelf. I curl the familiar metal curves and sharps into my palm and put the fisted lizard to my heart. I feel nothing. No comfort, no connection. Everything is different now. One dusky twilight moment changed it all.

Thunder cracks through the grumble, and I pull the covers

over my head, wrapping myself into an unprotected ball of human shiver. Irregular drops of rain chase the front of the wind and smatter on the fabric walls. The drops call in reinforcements, and the storm throws itself at me. It hammers on all sides, trying to get in. Flash and crash, louder, closer, everywhere. The storm is on me and in me, crack and bash. Every rumble, every thrash of wind and every howl moves through me as if I'm not only skinless but formless.

I sit up and the cot is a juggernaut flying through space, a swirl of sensation and emotion. I shallow-pant, staring wide-eyed at the flashing light, waiting for the explosion of lightning to split me open. It goes on and on, faster and faster, top speed, flash-crash after flash-crash.

And then flash-pause-crash. And flash and rumble. More space, more breath. The light stops stabbing my eyes and gentles to an irregular shimmer. The thunder crashes and complains through the trees, across the fields, and away. The wind dies, leaving behind a steady rain.

I manage a deep inhale. My breath shakes all the way in and all the way out. My eyes are wet, my throat thick and swollen, my chest compressed. I hear nothing from the other slices. Maybe Sully is scared, too. Maybe she's been waiting this whole time for me to come to her, be with her. I throw off the blankets and pick up my coveralls from the floor.

Another light flashes. A small light. This time it's a leddie beam, moving on the path outside.

"Everyone okay in there?" Lacey calls. "Did you stay dry?"

"Yes." Nona's voice is so flat, so earthly, so regular. "Dry."

"Lizard? Sully?"

I strain my ears for Sully's reply. Nothing. My heart beats faster. Where is she? Why doesn't she answer?

Slappity-slap, against my slice wall. I jump.

"Lizard!" Lacey's voice is sharp. "Are you okay?"

"Yes," I manage.

Lacey slaps the synthie again on Sully's side.

"Sully?"

"Whuh?"

"You okay?"

"Mmm."

Her voice is full of sleep. Even without the storm, how could she sleep?

I drop my coveralls and slip back into bed. I stare at the dark. I might never sleep again.

Chapter Twelve

BUT I DO SLEEP. Or maybe I just drift through muted sensation for a few hours. Either way, the sun is in my eyes. I unzip my window. The trees drip with sun-dazzled green. A light breeze touches my cheek. I feel everything.

I step into clean boxers and reach for a shirt. I can't imagine the day. How will it be? How will Sully be? Does she feel all of this, too? No. Not like this. She probably kisses people all the time. People like Aaron — and at that I stop, T-shirt halfway over my head.

Has she? Has she kissed Aaron like that?

I drop my shirt and sink to my cot, face in my hands. I'm so far over my head, I can't even see the surface. Maybe she kisses lots of people. Maybe that's what she means by being bad. But wait — Aaron isn't allowed on the girls' side. They have no privacy, never. So it can't happen. But maybe Sully wants it to. Maybe she'd rather.

The gong.

"Morning, comrades!"

Sully hollers, the same as every morning. I finish dressing and walk around to her door. She zips herself out, turns, and faces me.

"Hello, young Lizard."

"Hello."

My face is fiery hot, and my voice doesn't even sound like me.

"Lizard, Sully! Did you survive the storm okay?"

Rasta trots over from the spigot, carrying her toothbrush and towel.

"I slept through it until Lacey came and banged me awake," says Sully.

"You *slept* through that?" Rasta's voice cracks. "I thought we were all going to die. Lizard, did you sleep?"

"I didn't sleep."

I look directly into Sully's eyes as I say it, wanting her to know. She winks, and sensation flash-floods through my body. Sully is a sweet-fisted miracle, and her every breath hits me like a hurricane.

With a bird-tip of the head, Rasta checks me, and then Sully. I drop my eyes to the ground. My feelings threaten to leak out my pores and spill everywhere.

At the privo, I close the door. My stomach is shaking. That wink from Sully. Does it mean that she's thinking about our kiss? Or maybe she's just playing it breeze, showing me how? I try giving a Sully-style grin to the privo wall, and it stretches my face in an odd way.

"Lizard, are you coming out of there, ever?"

I walk up to CounCircle with Sully and Rasta and Tylee,

who joins us on the way. I do not watch Sully's every move, and I do not listen to Sully's pitch and timbre for every tiny clue. Not much, anyway.

As we get up from the breakfast table, Aaron tiptoes behind Sully and puts his finger on his lips to shush us. He covers Sully's eyes, and she smiles, and my stomach sinks. Aaron's hands are so big. They cover her face. His shoulders are so wide. Sully turns and punches Aaron in the ribs, and he doubles over as if she's mortally wounded him.

"Our first shiny Sunday at CropCamp," she says. "No class, double fields, and double Cleezies. How lucky can we get?"

Aaron's cave-tunnel dark eyes glow as he straightens, flashing his toothy smile. Tylee and Rasta and I follow them out of the Mealio. Aaron has a way of walking like water tumbling over rocks. If I T'd, could I walk like that? Would my shoulders be that big? Is it too late to transition?

I take a side trip to the privo, try to settle myself down. I'm late to Sunday morning Cleezies. Machete hasn't started to talk yet, but everyone's all settled on the Pavilion benches. Rasta, Sully, and Tylee sit together. I meet eyes with Nona in the back row and look at the empty spot on her left. She nods. I make my way back there, pretending not to see the others' quizzical looks. Nona doesn't say anything to me. We don't even look at each other.

Machete leads us in the chant: *Come from One. Live in the light. Return to One.* The voices blend to a melodic hum. It circles around my throat, squeezing. I look down at the rocks, shocked at the stinging behind my eyes.

"The thing that causes us pain in our lives," says Machete, "is our insistence on our uniqueness. Our belief that we're different, separate, each the center of our own little universe. As you grow into adult community, contemplate the paradox of separation from the One. Of course we're all different — that's the challenge. When we mistake difference for separation, whether we think we're better than the rest or worse, we find trouble. Study the ways in which you hold yourself separate. See where the pain is. Then study the feeling of being together. Seek your peace."

She nods to Saxem beside her. He stands and begins plucking the strings. A soft slow run of individual notes dances across the rocky floor, gradually building into something so complex, I can hardly believe that it comes out of a single construction of wood and wire. The sound comes from inside and out, from the trees and the rocks, a floating transport of melody.

"Close your eyes, and breathe deeply."

Machete's voice is low, barely carrying over the music. I close my eyes immediately. I breathe in the notes and the rocks and the circle and Machete's voice.

"All the way in, hold, then all the way out."

Just like Sheila taught me. And Korm. My breath still shakes a bit. The music quiets down to a delicate run of individual notes, and Saxem begins to sing.

> *We all come from the One. We separate like drops of rain, like flakes of snow, like crystals of ice. We melt and return. We run to the river, run to the sea.*

Crashing waves and trickle of stream, rushing in the light of life. We come from One, we return to One.

The melody and words flow with the images. He taps the wooden body of the instrument three times, and then starts again. Other voices join him. Everyone sings. I open my eyes. Some comrades still have eyes closed, others open. The surround of melody vibrates deeply in my chest, playing my heart like an instrument. I sing, my voice so intertwined with the others that I can't hear myself as separate.

What if I really am from the One? No saurians, no lizards, just human like everyone else. Not a dragon. Just Kivali, killing myself with daydreams, holding myself separate, causing my own pain.

The song comes to a slow stop, and we all hold silence. Machete speaks again.

"We have a slower, more relaxed day today. Move with your comrades in the fields. Observe the ways in which you hold yourself separate, the ways in which you think you're unique. How do these separations serve you? How do they hurt you? We meet again tonight at the usual time. Come from One."

"Live in the light."

"Return to One."

The fields had been dry, and they sucked up the puddles, but the soil is still wet. Rasta and I plant spinach. Squatting is too hard so we just crawl around on our knees, and our coveralls and gloves are filthy muddy. She matches my silence, and we work easily together. She calls me Lizard. She knows that I'm a bender. All my life, I've thought these things matter. What if they don't matter?

My Grade One teacher turned me in for gender testing, and I scored fifty-two. If I'd come in at fifty-three or higher, transition to boy would have been mandatory. Hormone blockers would have started right away, with surgeries and male hormones coming later. But anywhere from forty-eight to fifty-two was midrange, and therefore iffy. *It's your choice,* they said. *You're free to choose, but if you don't pass post-decision gender training within three years, we make the choice for you.*

I had to choose by my tenth birthday. By that time I'd been learning with Korm for almost two years. She'd helped me with the fear, helped me live in the world with the Radio as my guide. Korm won't teach anyone on artificials, not even hormone blockers or boosts. Sheila is opposed to all medical intervention. The choice was mine, but I was a child. Now, far away from the advice of Sheila and Korm, I'm beginning to understand the consequences.

PDGT three times a week was hellish as they tried to train me into something properly female. Approaching thirteen I was the oldest kid there, still not getting "girl" right — and not wanting to. One of the kinder trainers pity-passed me. I'm not sure why.

I saw plenty of kids like Sully's cousin come and go, passing through PDGT in six weeks. If I had T'd, I would've passed much faster. They would have been teaching me to be like Aaron. I'd be bigger now, and broader, with a deep voice.

I wouldn't be Sully's piemate, though. I might be a flirt toy in the opposite-side Pieville — if I were lucky. I wouldn't be able to hear her breathe in the night, and she wouldn't shout me awake every morning.

Every choice sets off a world of possibilities.

Every choice cuts off a world of possibilities.

I glance over at the cucumbers. Sully is midfield, picking with Aaron. I don't think that she's a samer. Maybe it wouldn't be so bad to T. It's too late to do it by the regs, but I've heard there are other ways.

In evening Cleezies, we again lay our palms open and receive a morsel.

"We call them kickshaws," says Machete. "They are the taste of camp, of completely sheltered camaraderie and the freedom that comes when all are safe."

Sully stands on my left, and my entire left side vibrates and tingles. Apparently I have extra Sully-sensors planted on my human skin that go crazy every time she's close by. I want Sully's touch more than I want the kickshaw, and I want the kickshaw a lot.

"Choose a comrade with whom you have not yet spoken," says Machete. "Choose by eye contact, and stand face to face. Do this without words, now."

Sully moves away, leaving a hollow of empty space on my left. Someone taps my shoulder. It's the small blond boy, the one who looks like Rasta. He's soft-skinned, and his curls form a ring of gold around his head.

"Now," says Machete. "Enjoy together."

The boy reaches out and sets his own kickshaw on my lower lip. I pull the sweetness in. He lifts the kickshaw off my palm and puts it in his mouth. We stare at each other, not quite chewing. Prolonging. My eyelids weigh heavy but I can't look away. He has become beautiful. He glows in the firelight. His eyes are half-lidded. I feel me and him at the same time, as if I'm both of us. The kickshaw dissolves, beautiful kickshaw, spreading down my throat and around my heart. Bits of crunch hide in my teeth, and I dig them out with my tongue. So does the beautiful boy. The delicious drape of group silence holds us all close. I find a whole new world in his dark blue eyes.

"Return to your seats, please."

He nods at me, and I smile in return. We shuffle back across the rocks, and I miss him until Sully lands next to me. My left side lights up again, and my chest churns with a new cascade of longing. Nothing in my life with Sheila prepared me for any of this.

"It's been a good first week," says Machete. "As we come to know one another better, we can begin our true work together. Please return to your pies with no conversation. We conclude our Sundays in absolute silence."

We file out the door. Nobody speaks. I'm not complying; I just am. I'm alla the One. We move like a slow-spreading liquid into the dusky dense green, and the sky, low and purple, holds our hush. Me and Sully, and the blond boy and Rasta and Tylee and even Nona and Lacey and Aaron and Micah and Sabi and everyone. We are us. I love us.

Sully walks shoulder to shoulder with me. CropCamp is good. So good. If my life at home were like this, I wouldn't care about Lizard Radio. I'd only want this.

Chapter Thirteen

I JERK OUT OF a deep sleep, disoriented and groggy. I've been dreaming again, and I find it unnerving. Sheila says that I don't dream like regular people because of Lizard Radio — it serves the same function. Maybe that's true, because since I've been here and not tuning in, my nights are a whirligig of images and voices. I wake to a whisper of dragon claws and an aching aftertaste.

I blink at the dust motes in the slant of morning sun. The birds are on a crazy holler fest, like they can't believe the sun has risen again. My heart hurts. I close my eyes and look back, trying to trace the details of the dream-story.

The komodo wasn't silver, and it wasn't small. It was a full-size, fully alive Komodo dragon, and it walked with Korm in a barren shadowed world. No birds or trees, no people. Just Korm and the dragon and me, trailing behind. The only sound was the dragging of the dragon's claws each time it lifted a foot. No matter how fast I walked I was still behind, separate, different. I called out, and they heard nothing.

No wonder people talk about dreams all the time. It's like living a whole other life behind the sleep curtain. You wake up, and it's still all over you. I turn to face my real-world komodo. It stares at the door. I pick it up, sniff it. No smell. No movement. It's an inanimate metal toy. A symbol.

Sheila gave it to me on Decision Day, my tenth birthday. For growing past my fear, she said. For keeping my core self intact. From the moment I opened the box, I have carried it with me always. I was never apart from it until I came here. Here, it spends its days on the shelf, waiting for me to come back.

It's so beautifully crafted. The artist captured everything Komodo — the skin, the claws, the curve of the powerful tail, even the unique movement. It is the lizardest of the lizards. *Keeping my core self intact.* Keeping myself separate.

The gong rings.

"Hellooooo, CropCamp!" Sully yells.

I set the komodo down, and the day begins. Jokes and a tangle of nervous-happy skitter with Sully up the path. At CounCircle, we have a brief morning meditation. In the quiet, the dream-dragon's claws scrape again in the back corner of my mind. I don't like it.

Come from One. Live in the light. Return to One.

I speak the words together with my comrades. We file into the Mealio for a good breakfast, in community. My job is to learn, and to work in the fields, and to live in the light. Be a good comrade and citizen. Even Sheila said that in her inflow. She did.

After breakfast and before Block One, I run down to my slice. I pick up the komodo and look it in the eye.

"Everything is different here," I whisper to its pointed face. "I can do it without you."

I crawl to the door, unzip from the bottom corner, and poke my head out. Look and listen. Nobody's around. No one but the birds and that chippie over there, perched on a fallen log.

I hold up my fingers in front of my face. I appreciate the rounded, short-cut nails. Using that human hand, I dig a hole just outside my door. The dirt is hard-baked, and it packs in under my nails. I let the komodo help me, using its sharp metal snout to scrape deeper to where the earth is cool and soft. Once we've formed a rounded hole, as deep as my fingers are long, I set the komodo at the bottom. It looks at home there, a watch-dragon in the darkness, taking care of the underground while I live in the light.

"Stay here," I whisper. "Guard my door."

I cover it. First a layer of damp, cool dirt that will feel good on its lizard skin. Then a dry, dusty layer. Then pine needles, carefully scattered over. I fuss with the pine needles, moving and smoothing them so that they look normal, untouched. I stand and wipe my dirty hands on my coveralls and head for the spigot.

Nona steps around the pie, suddenly blocking my path. She must have been right there, just out of sight, spying on me. Listening in. Anger sparks in my chest.

"Can I talk to you?" She bitter-spits the words, and they're sharper and hotter than my anger. "I know it's a lot to ask, but would you sit next to me at a meal sometime, and maybe say a few words to me? Act like we're friendly?"

Her narrowed eyes are shiny, a little bit wet. Her voice, for all of its heat, is slightly strangly.

"Ms. Mischetti says I'll get a culpa if I don't start connecting with community. She says I have to engage. I can't risk a culpa in the first month."

"She'd give you a culpa for that?"

"Yes. She would. Will you do it?"

"Um, okay. Yeah. I'll do that."

"Tell all your little friends that I asked you to. I don't care. That way you won't risk your standing by having them think that you like me. But please, try to make it look real when Ms. Mischetti's around. Just once in a while."

She steps back into her slice. I wait.

"What are you waiting for?" she asks.

"You. So we can walk up together."

Chapter Fourteen

IN BLOCK TWO, RASTA and I swelter in the cucumbers. Sweat drips in my eyes. I forgot my gloves, so fresh dirt chunks up under my fingernails and seals into the creases of my hands. Rasta has her gloves, so she pulls back the prickly leaves and I tug the cucumbers loose. It's best to pick them small — whoever picked this row last time didn't do a good job. Some of them are bigger than my hand. I toss them thunkety into the bucket.

"I've been dying for a chance to talk to you alone," says Rasta. "It's a strong alliance thing."

She straightens onto her knees, takes off a glove, and pulls something out of her pocket. A light brown nugget. A kickshaw.

"Where'd you get that?"

My voice pitches loud, and we both look for Micah. He's over on the tomato green talking to Saxem.

"Where'd you get it?" I whisper.

"Last night," she says. "I pocketed."

"How'd you do that? Didn't your partner notice?"

"No. I partnered with some Friday guy, and he wasn't even

looking at me. I think he was looking at Lacey's bum. Who did you partner with?"

"That Monday boy who looks like you. Rasta, why'd you do it? Didn't you want it?"

"Of course I did. But maybe Sabi's right, maybe they're drugging us."

"Sabi's lunar."

"Maybe, but that doesn't mean she's wrong. Don't you think it's a drug? I mean, doesn't it make you feel different?"

"Good different. I like it. What are you going to do with it? Do you want to give it to me?"

Rasta laughs and shakes her head. She puts it back in her pocket, and we scoot down to the next plant. I kind of want to tackle her and grab the kickshaw.

"Rasta. Why am I your strong alliance? Why not Tylee, or Sully?"

She sits back on her heels and gives me the bird-tip of her head.

"For one thing, I know that you won't tell."

"How do you know? I love the kickshaws. I might even take it away from you."

"No, I trust you. You've got a way about you. My auntie, she says that we all have different vibrational frequencies, and they resonate or they don't. I like Tylee a lot and she's honest and true, but she has a different pitch. And Sully . . ."

I so much want to know what she thinks about Sully. Does

everyone think she's amazing? How can they not? I can't even see straight when she's around.

"You can see the light around Sully from a mile off, and everybody's drawn to it. Me too. But it's like — I don't know. Like she knows that it's there, and she turns so you can see it from the best angle, but in that turn you can't see what's behind the light. Whereas you, Lizard, it's like you've got some high-rev power and don't even know what you've got, so you don't show or shield any of it. And it vibes with me, and that's why I trust you."

I've seen behind Sully's lights. Back in the woods, she let me look without anything shining in my eyes. I can't tell Rasta that, though. Strong alliance or no, what's between me and Sully is private.

"So why do you like me?" she asks.

"It's your voice. It makes me happy every time you talk."

"Everyone says that about my voice." She's disappointed. "That's an outer, so it doesn't count."

"Yes, it does. It's not just the sound, it's what you say with it, and how. It's — I guess it's like your auntie says. Frequency or something. Without the inner, your voice would just be unusual. Not — special."

A very small, shy smile. She scoops out a hole, puts the kickshaw in, and covers it over. I pat the top of the mound, flattening it with my palm so it looks different from the other dirt.

"I'll come back for it," I say. "When you're not watching."

Rasta pushes my hand away, laughing. She digs the kickshaw

back up, tears it into tiny pieces, and mixes the pieces with the loose dirt.

"No, you won't," she says. "Kickshaws are not good."

The next day, Sabi is gone. At breakfast, Tylee tells us that she never came back to Pieville after Social. The girl guides, Katrina and Shari and Lacey, came to clear out her slice before first gong.

"What'd she do?" Rasta asks.

"Do?" says Tylee. "She didn't need to do anything. She just had to be her Sabi self. That's plenty for expul, don't you think?"

"Sabi's nearly eighteen," says Sully. "Straight to Blight. At least when I get expulled, I'll know someone there."

I don't care one thing about Sabi — I'm actually relieved that she's gone — but I will not let Sully leave CropCamp. No, no, no, no.

I have my second DM session that morning. Machete's door opens, and she fills the frame. I duck under her arm, and the cool of the building falls all around me. She directs me to sit again in the cushy chair across from her. Probably the softest thing in CropCamp. I curl into the deepest corner, enjoying the break from the fierce sun.

"So. You had quite a first week. How does it feel, as the youngest camper here, to be part of the elite power cadre in girlville?"

Be careful, Rasta said. *She's going to push around and find our weak spots. She found Sabi's somehow — got her to say or do the wrong thing and — wham, gone.*

She did that to Sully, too. Not the wham-gone, not yet, but pushed her into thinking it'd happen soon.

Pushed her to me. Dusky Sully in the woods. Sully's fingertips, Sully's laugh, Sully's eyes. Sully's mouth.

"Our friend Sully has taken quite a shine to you. Why do you think that is?"

I snap up to meet Machete's eyes. Can she see what's in my head?

"We're piemates," I say.

"Proximity. Nona Raglisch is also in proximity, and that hasn't put her in Sully's path. So I'm wondering — what's in it for Sully? She's almost three years older than you. What do you think that she could be getting out of this?"

Machete slices right to the core of my own questions.

"We often befriend someone who has what we lack. What do you think Sully lacks?"

Nothing. Sully lacks nothing.

"It's easy to see why you admire her. She's bright, charismatic. But Kivali, you arrived here with independence as your outstanding characteristic. The question I left for your consideration last time was whether that independence is an asset or a liability. Independence without initiative is just reaction, rebellion. Did you initiate that little gathering the other night?"

Machete eases back in her chair and gazes at the square glass of the window. Outside, the heat shimmers.

"Or did you just go along with everything that Sully suggested?"

"If you think it was Sully's idea, why did Sabi get expulled?"

"Sabi made decisions, and those decisions had consequences. We're here to talk about your decisions."

"Ms. Mischetti, what's in the kickshaw?"

She grins so broadly, I can see all the way to her back teeth. She leans forward on her elbows.

"Now I'm seeing the real Kivali. You're the first camper in this session to put that question out loud. I answer your question with a question. Why do you want to know?"

"I've never had anything like it."

"No, I don't imagine you have. You partnered with Emmett. He's the next-youngest CropCamper. I was pleased to see you two make acquaintance. You'll be good for him."

"But what's in the kickshaw?"

"You. You, and me, and Emmett and Tylee and Sully and Jyana and Lacey. All of us."

She continues to smile. I stare at her.

"That's not the answer you want, is it?"

"No."

"You need your own answers, not mine. You need to know yourself deeply, and learn when and how to apply that self to the good of the greater community. I tell you that the kickshaw contains community. You say that you've never had anything like that. That's something for you to think about."

"How can I trust you if you won't give real answers to my questions?"

She smiles again, and nods.

"Excellent question. More for you to think about, along with the ongoing question of independence. Here's my most important question for you today: are you a leader or a follower?"

I'm not either. At least, I don't think I am.

"Neither is superior," she continues. "But they carry different responsibilities and different types of power. Once you decide which way you want to interact with the world, with your community, I can help you develop your skills."

I look out the window. I've never felt anything as comfortable as this chair. It holds me in a soft, cool calm. Since losing my skin, nothing's been calm. The wind blows right through me. Every time I see Sully, my stomach practically goes into convulsions. I could fall asleep in this chair.

"Kivali." Machete speaks softly. "Remember: if anything gets too big for you, too overwhelming, you can always come to me. I might not know the answers, but I can help you think through the questions. And our sessions are entirely private. By law."

What I really want to know is, why *does* Sully pick me over everyone else? Or does she? She can't possibly like me the way that I like her — that's too much. But if she does — what do I do with that? How do I get through the next eleven weeks of feeling like this? And what happens after?

"It's a lot to handle at age fifteen, all these new feelings." Maybe Machete has a peephole into my skull. "All these changes and decisions. That's why most parents hold their children until seventeen. Even then, it's difficult. You're extraordinary, and I want to see you do well. Anything you need, you let me know. If you do well, we'll all do well."

Her clement gaze strokes my cheek, wiggles through cells of skin and bone to find my thoughts. Gentle. What if I trust her? I might. If I meet her eyes, I'll say things out loud.

"As you think about leadership and initiative and community this week, remember the strengths you arrived with, the very things that draw Sully and Rasta and the others to you."

A shiver runs somewhere along the crease where my physical self and my feelings hinge together. I blink back the rising wet in my eyes.

"You may go now if you like."

I'm not sure I can. Maybe I don't want to.

"Or if you like, you may stay here and rest a bit longer."

I want to. I do. But she doesn't like Sully. She wants to expul her. I can't stay here. That's like going over to the other side. I uncurl my legs and stab my feet onto the floor, straightening my knees.

She does not stand and make me walk under her arm. She stays at her desk. I look in her general direction as I open the door, but I don't meet her eyes.

"Thanks," I say.

"You are very welcome."

I believe her. Without my skin, I believe everybody. I walk through the cool entryway, open the screen door, and step onto the sun-blasted porch. The heat embraces me, holding me from every angle.

Chapter Fifteen

MACHETE IS RIGHT. I'VE just been going along with things. Maybe that's why Sully acts like nothing happened between us. Maybe she thinks that I think it's no big deal. How can she know how I feel if I don't tell her?

The gong rings after Solitude. Sully and I walk up the path together. I'm so nervous, I can't breathe right. Am I going to do it? No. No, shut up. Yes, do it. Hurry, do it now, before she splits off with the Saturdays.

"Sully," I say. "Meet me back at our pie after Block Four?"

"Sure," she says.

Easy as that.

When the gong rings to end Block Four, I run down from the fields. I stop at the spigot, wash my face. Run for my slice, grab my toothbrush. Brush my teeth. Put my nose inside my coveralls and sniff. I don't want to stink. I think I'm okay.

I wait on the back side of our pie in a wild fidget. My heart should calm down and stop making me sweat. It won't. Our precious free time ticks away. Where is Sully? Maybe she forgot. Maybe she doesn't want to come. Maybe something better came up.

Finally, finally, she saunters down the path. I wrap my arms around myself to keep from running over and grabbing her and shaking her and yelling, *Where were you? What took you so long?*

"Hey, Lizard," she says. "What's up?"

I turn and start walking into the woods. I hope that movement will settle me down. My armpits pour cold sweat.

"Where are we going?"

She trots up alongside me. I pass the fork and continue on the main path.

"Again, the Lizard speaks not," she says. "It's a surprise? A CropCamp hike?"

I want to be in the center of the oak grove. I want to set the soles of my feet on that patch of grass. Maybe in that place, I can find enough solid ground inside me to speak with initiative. Not be such a follower. We walk in silence, and I forget everything I had decided to say. The grove is farther back than I remember. Nothing from those first couple of days seems real anymore — Lizard Radio speaking in the night, the vaping bender, the grove. All that was before Sully.

Finally, the path opens ahead on the right with a breath of space and light. I don't face Sully until I am planted in the dead center of the grove. She comes more slowly behind me, looking up at the trees.

"Sweet. How long have you been stowing away this secret spot?"

"Since that day we were late for dinner." My voice works. "We need to talk."

"Okay." Sully nods. "You're mad about the kiss, right?"

"No!" I can't stand on my shaky legs anymore. I drop to sit on the grass, and Sully sits cross-legged, facing me. "No, not mad. I feel . . . I don't know. Like I'm nervous all the time. Like I don't want to eat. Is this normal? Is this what people feel?"

I can't look at her. Half my guts are splat on the ground between us. I might as well put out the rest.

"Sully, are you a samer? I mean, would you ever be one?"

"Lizard." Her voice is so soft, I dare to look up. Her eyes are dark—not lit up, just warm. Deep warm, deep true. "I don't know what I am. I like some boys, and sometimes I like girls. You're kind of both."

She looks down, shakes her head.

"Marrying someone like Aaron, that's what I'm supposed to want. I'm even trying to want it, but it's just not working. I've got damage. That's a long story you don't want to hear, and it might not even matter. Chicken or egg, it's in me now. I can't make myself fit here or anywhere else."

This is the Sully I love. The Sully who lets me see her. She doesn't let anyone else see her this way. Not Aaron, not Rasta, not anyone.

"I feel like that, too," I say. "All the time, all my life. Sometimes I think that I'm really not from here."

"What do you mean?"

I take a long blade of grass and start to pull it apart, one green thread at a time.

"My foster, Sheila, she found me."

"Found you?"

"On the sidewalk, newborn. Nobody ever figured out who put me there or why. The only clue is that I was wrapped in a yellow T-shirt with a picture of a lizard on it. That's why I have the thing about lizards."

Sully leans in, all listen and no speak. Have I ever been listened to so closely? I don't think so.

"Sheila gave me Sauria for a middle name. It means lizard. When I was little, she used to tell me that the saurians dropped me here to save the world."

I drop my head and find another blade of grass to shred. I sound like such a little kid. *Dropped me here to save the world.* It keeps reverberating in the silence of the grove. I wish that Sully would say something. Finally, I look up. The intensity of her gaze turns everything inside me to hot liquid.

"I knew that you were special the second I heard your lizardy voice. Me, I'm all grandiose blah-blah-I-don't-belong-here, but you might actually be from somewhere else."

"I think it's just a story that Sheila made up."

"Here I am jazzing around in your biz, throwing you all off everything, and you're probably some kind of lizard superhero. I'm an idiot."

"No, you're not! I mean, if there's anyone here who's special, it's you. You're not like anyone else, ever. Nobody else can make me feel like this. It's — I don't even know what it is. But it's so big. So much."

Sully shakes her head. She looks down again, breaks a twig in half. Puts the pieces together and breaks it again. Then she looks in my eyes.

"You and me, we're friends. No more jazz. It'll just drag you down with me."

"No, don't say that! I feel you everywhere. All the time. Since you kissed me, it's all I can think about."

She looks at me with such sympathy, I can hardly stand it. I don't want sympathy. I want that super-gravity force to pull us together again. I want her to want it like I want it.

She stands, gives me a hand, and pulls me up. I want her to put her hand on my neck again and pull me in, but she's still all sympathy. She likes me, but she doesn't feel like I do. I cross my arms, look at the ground. Sully reaches out her finger and catches the tear that spills over my lower eyelid. She puts her finger in her mouth.

"Tear of Lizard. Probably has magical powers."

She sucks on her finger, and I can't breathe.

"You need to understand about me," she says. "I am truly not good. I will do the wrong thing every time. It's a genetic defect, passed pure from my da."

"You are good. I can see it."

She shakes her head, no, no, no. Stares into my eyes and lets me see her in there, behind the lights, behind the flash, into that lonely secret place where she truly believes that she's not good.

She puts her hands on my shoulders and draws me in close enough to set my entire body on electric fire. She reaches into my hair, close up to my scalp, and shakes my head gently back and forth.

"You are so irresistible," she says.

My knees almost unhinge.

"For once in your life, Sullivan." She's not talking to me anymore. She's not even looking at me. "Do the right thing."

She resists. She takes her hand from my hair, and her eyes, those eyes that say so many things her mouth doesn't say, she takes them away from me. Turns. Walks out of the grove. Leaves me shaking, skinless and alone, with the vibration of her body still shimmering through me. I sink to the grass.

It hurts. It hurts like nothing has hurt since that eight-year-old day in the school yard. And like that day, I can't understand why I hurt so bad because nothing is broken. But still, it hurts so much.

The tears come fast and hard, harder than they have since that day. Once they start, I can't stop them. I shudder and sob and it's almost like a watery vomit, the way the tears rip themselves up and out of me. I cry until my eyes go dry, until I'm empty and silent. Finally, I roll over and look at the sky and touch the earth beneath me.

I am not eight. This is nothing like that, and I can't cure it by pretending to be a lizard. It's time to get real. Sully does not feel about me like I do about her. She is my piemate, and she is my friend. That's it. That needs to be enough.

But she said that she likes boys *and* girls. *You're kind of both.* She said that. So why wouldn't she like me best?

I shouldn't have talked about lizards. It made me sound not-sane. Or too kidlet.

I sit up, brush myself off, and trudge out of the grove. The gong rings. I trudge faster so I won't be late for dinner.

Chapter Sixteen

RASTA PULLS ME ASIDE on the Quint that evening.

"Lizard, what did she do to you?"

Can everyone here read things right off my face?

"You've hardly said a word since your session — was it awful?"

Oh, she means Machete. Not Sully.

"She was okay," I say. "But she blames Sully for the power-cadre thing."

Rasta tips her head. Did I say *Sully* in some different tone of voice?

"She talked about leadership and initiative." I rush on. "And about making decisions and stuff. You know, decision-making."

Rasta's head stays tipped. I should tell her — no. She wouldn't understand. If it were her, she'd tell me. But I'm not her. I'm just not.

"You like her," she says. "I can tell that you do. But Lizard, be careful. Something about her just feels wrong, even when she sounds right. Do you know what I mean?"

Machete. Not Sully. Machete.

"What do you mean, wrong? Wrong in what way?"

"The kickshaw way. Feels good, so you relax and don't notice that it's wrong."

"But Rasta, maybe the kickshaws *are* good."

Rasta looks off to the reddish west. Quiet. When she speaks, it's barely over a whisper.

"I think I might throw up in her office tomorrow."

"No, you won't. You'll be fine."

She sighs and lies back on the grass. She holds up her hand.

"Strong alliance, right?"

I touch my fingertips to hers. I don't say it back, and I don't meet her eyes. Of course she notices. She notices everything.

It's Wednesday morning, and Sully doesn't holler me awake. Maybe she's being considerate like Nona asked her to. Her feet move across the floor, rustle zip-zip, and gone. No movement in Nona's slice, though. Nothing at all. I doze a bit, then blink awake again. Somebody moans.

"Nona?" I whisper. "Is that you?"

Another low moan. I pull coveralls on, slip outside, and stand at Nona's door. She never opens her windows. Never. Not even when it's sweltering hot.

"Nona? Are you okay?"

It's a fresh morning, full of bird tweedle. A gentle breeze wafts over my skin. Nona moans again.

"I'm coming in."

I unzip the door. Nona is huddled beneath the blankets.

"Are you okay?"

Clearly not. A sheen of sweat glistens on her face, and her skin is papery pale. Her eyes are halfway open, and for a heart-stop tick I think she's dead. But dead people don't moan. I put a hand on her forehead. Coal-hot.

"You have a fever. I'm going to get someone."

"No!" She moves, grabbing the pant leg of my coveralls. "No."

"But they'll come looking when you don't show up."

"I'm okay," she whispers.

I sit on the edge of the cot. She shivers so hard, it makes the whole cot shake. I go next door for another blanket and throw it on top of her, tucking it under her chin. She grabs my pant leg again and stares into my eyes, like she's begging but I don't know for what.

"Where's Donovan?"

I lean closer. Her whisper barely has any breath behind it.

"What?"

"I want Donovan."

"Nona?" No response. "I'm going to get someone."

She doesn't protest this time. I run up the path, into the crowded Mealio, and I find Katrina, the Friday guide.

"Nona's sick with a fever, a bad one. She's down in her slice."

Katrina nods, goes to Machete's table. I leave the Mealio after breakfast without meeting anyone's eyes. The depth and force of an unguarded Nona unnerved me. Her fever shivers shook into my very cells.

———•———

"About your escapade last week."

Sheila is on the screen with her hands fisted, chin tilted up, angled toward the cam as if she's about to start marching off the screen, right into the ayvee pod with me. She's wearing that crazy head-scarf with the yellow flowers, the one that she used to wear to make me laugh while she drilled me in PDGT exercises.

"Kivali, you must comport yourself in the manner of a young citizen. You must comply with the regs. You are there to learn, and to assimilate, and to become an integral cog in this great wheeling nation."

What, exactly, did Machete tell her about Thursday night?

"You must not lose your focus. You must not risk your future. You must take full advantage of this opportunity, and you must not waste it on shenanning. Listen!"

She raises one fist with her pointer finger straight up. I hit pause. She freezes in the rinkety-dink pose.

Soon after I started PDGT, SayFree Radio came on one night while we were cleaning up after dinner, and instead of turning it off, Sheila threw down the dish towel, pointed one finger straight up in the air, and yelled, "Listen!"

Then she grabbed my soapy wet hand, pulling me with her in a march around the table.

"I listen to SayFree—I don't think," she chanted. "Love me some SayFree, rinkety-dink. SayFree talker is a big dumb fink." I started laughing and tried to pull away, but she yanked me along behind her high-stepped marching.

111

*"I speak for SayFree, I'm missing a link. Can't hear
me now, I'll write it in ink. In a few more years, I'll
be extinct. I smell worse than the pee of a mink.
Yup, it's true, I very much stink. I'm a twikkery
fikery finkety-fink."*

She kept going until she didn't make any sense at all, and we both
fell on the kitchen floor laughing. Since then we've called SayFree-
speak rinkety-dink, and neither of us needs to say a word. We just
point up. I kept pointing up a few weeks ago whenever she talked
about CropCamp. She acted like she didn't notice. I'm so relieved
to see her do it now. That's the real Sheila.

I hit PLAY. The screen blinks, and she's in a normal stance,
hands in her pockets, head-scarf gone.

"It's early summer still. I think of you when I wake and wonder what you do between the up and the down. I mean, when
you're not breaking rules and wreaking havoc and generally
bringing shame on the family name."

She moves in close again, even closer than before, so that one
eye fills the entire screen. Individual lashes and etchings on the
skin, and deep warm brown with glimmers of gold surrounding
the black center.

"Sweet komodo. Gorgeous gecko, my lovely lizard. You must
be brave, and you must be smart. I wish I could hold you in my
arms like I did so long ago, but you're way too big and you'd break
my elbows. I picture you every single day, and I draw your face
when I miss you too much. You know where I live?"

She moves back, her face and body coming into view again. She bams her right fist in the center of her chest. The thud comes through on the mic, loud and clear.

"I live right here. You can always find me."

Her lip stud curves up, and her eyes dance unspoken words. Then the screen goes blank. I pull air into my lungs, a lot of it. All I can hold. I let it out slow. I can actually feel her. I thud my own chest. *Right here.*

I punch PLAY again. Why *did* she send me to CropCamp? I don't think it's because she's dying of some disease. She looks plenty healthy. Maybe she knew that it would be good. But how could she know? She couldn't know that Sully would be here.

"Gorgeous gecko," the ayvee Sheila says again. "My lovely lizard."

I'm not really a lizard. Sheila knows that, right?

Chapter Seventeen

NONA DOESN'T TURN UP all day, and she's not in her slice when I go down that night. I worry that she's been sent home for sickness, or maybe expulled, so I'm relieved to hear a zip-zip the next morning before gong. I wait until Sully goes to the privo, and then round to Nona's door.

"Nona? Where've you been?"

"Quarry. For sick people."

Her voice is its usual flat tone, minus the fever-quaver.

"Are you okay? Feeling better?"

"Yes. Better."

She opens her door and hands me my blanket.

"Hope you didn't freeze last night. Don't worry, there's nothing contagious on it."

She's still pale, and her closed-up slice smells of fever. I take the blanket and she starts to zip the door, but I reach out and stop her.

"You said something yesterday when you were in the fever."

Her face is carefully expressionless but color deepens on her cheeks.

"What did I say?"

"You asked for Donovan."

"Do you know him? Donovan Freer?"

She is still careful with her face and her voice, but a trace of that fever-longing shakes through. I shrug and shake my head.

"I was delirious," she says. "You don't need to check on me anymore."

She zips the door in my face.

The next couple of days pass in the new normal. CounCircle, breakfast, ag class, crops, Solitude, crops, citizenship class, dinner, Cleezies, Social on the Quint, sleep. Nona doesn't have any fever rants. Rasta survives her DM with Machete without throwing up.

I am doing okay with Sully. At night I sleep a few paces from her. In the day I see her light. I have two and a half months left with her. I will soak it up. I won't waste one second of this time in her presence trying to force something that can't and won't and probably shouldn't ever happen.

So I study, and cycle for shower chits, and weed and plant and cull and tend. I say "return to One; live in the light," and I play whuck-chuck on the Quint. I don't tune in, and I don't go to the oak grove. I toss the acorn out into the woods where it belongs. I give a courtesy nod to the komodo each time that I step over it, except for when I forget. I am human with the humans. I joke around with Sully, and I look away when she and Aaron flirt. I try not to replay every moment alone with Sully in my head all day long. Mostly I am not successful, but I try.

I wake Saturday with cramping in my guts and I hurry for the privo. I feel worse as the morning goes on. Reddaze never agrees with me. When we get out to the fields in Block Two, I curl in the grass alongside the greens. Just for a tick or two. Just to let the sunbeams stroke me until I feel good enough to work.

Micah boot-toes me awake.

"Lizard, what's the matter? Are you sick?"

I drag myself up to a sit. He squats and looks in my eyes. I've never been up close to Micah, never seen past the muddy face-hair. His eyes are brown, and kind.

"Go take a rest," he says. "You look like hell."

"It's just reddaze. I'll be okay."

"Get out of here. I'll see you in Block Three. Don't skip lunch."

I push myself up against the heavy humidity. I wave to Rasta and trudge toward the pine ridge. Halfway down the path, I remember that it's Saturday. Sully's day off.

My feet lose some of their cement, and I catch a quick face-wash at the spigot. Sully has Machete this afternoon. I can help her think about what to say, how to get on Machete's good side so she stays here for sure. We can go back to the grove, lie in the grass, look up at the sky, and talk. Nothing wrong with that. It's too hot in my slice, anyway. I'll rest better back in the grove, in the breeze. With Sully.

Five steps short of the pie, I stop.

"Sully!" I whisper. I move forward a few steps, tap on the fabric. "Sully, it's me, Lizard."

Not there. Cramps squeeze my innards again, and every part of me is dripping sweat. I'll go back to the grove anyway. It'll be nicer back there. Micah said to take a rest; he didn't say where. I meander along the path, deeper into the green. I really should come back here more often. It's so beautiful.

I walk quiet-quiet, no sound. Set my frods on the earthy path, not disturbing the birds or the chippies. I come to the opening, turn right. Stop. My stomach hits the ground.

Sully. And Aaron.

She's lying on top of him. Pressed body to body, in a way that I haven't known enough to want until right now. She looks up, and our eyes lock for an instant that goes on for hours inside of me.

I turn and run, pounding away from the grove. I zip into my slice, close the window tight, and dive into my cot, pulling the covers over my head. I'm soaked in sweat, and I'm surrounded by the smell of myself, and it is not good. Cramps seize my entire body.

The grove scene is locked on the inside of my eyelids, and I'd give anything to un-see it. Sully's face. Aaron's hands in her hair. My grove, holding the two of them in deep green as if they belong there. And behind that, the shadow of me spinning lizard tales. A ridiculous, deluded child. No wonder she resisted.

I'm not special. Not to the saurians, not to Sheila, and

definitely not to Sully. Who falls in love with a bender who thinks she's a lizard? Nobody, that's who. I bet I was a bad kisser, too. I'm sure that Aaron is a good kisser. At least he didn't see me. I don't think so, anyway. I'm not human or lizard. I'm less than both, not enough of either.

I avoid Sully for the rest of the day, and she makes it easy for me because she's never where I am. I sit with Nona at dinner. By myself at Cleezies. I leave the Quint right after Social and walk down with Nona. She doesn't ask me anything, and I don't ask her anything. I hole up in my slice for the night, trying not to breathe too loud. Whatever I am, it's all wrong.

Chapter Eighteen

SULLY DOESN'T HOLLER ME AWAKE. I stumble through the day with my head down, taking care of business, earning shower chits, doing an extra kitchen rotation. I run into Rasta on the way to evening Cleezies, and we sit opposite Sully and Tylee.

"Sully's waving at you," Rasta whispers.

"I don't care."

I don't look at Rasta, and I don't meet her eyes. She can probably smell it on me. Not just the lie, but the shame, the freakishness. Why does she keep looking at me?

"I'm going to pocket again," she whispers.

I need that kickshaw. I'd never turn it down.

"Maybe you will, too."

I shake my head no.

"It feels good to resist. Try it."

Machete comes in, and we shut up. We sit through the Sunday reports from crews and a couple of songs and some supposedly funny stories. We act like civilized people when inside we're a bunch of starvers riveted on kickshaw juice. All of us except Rasta.

When Machete steps to the center, my spit pumps start working overtime. If I open my mouth, I'll be stringing saliva. Every cell in me wants that kickshaw. I want the taste, the texture, the sensation. I want it to slide through my cells and take away this horrible taste of otherness and failure.

"It's our third Sunday together," Machete says. "Now is when the real work begins.

"Our camps serve many purposes, but experiential learning is the most important. Unless you learn to properly apply the words of the booktron, the concepts are useless. Empty, lifeless words. This afternoon, we continue with a long-standing tradition of comrade instruction. Each week at Sunday Cleezies, I will call upon a comrade to deliver a spontaneous talk on a SayFree tenet studied during the week."

Machete scans the circle like a high-flying hawk on a search for prey.

"Today's topic is community cohesion through participation. Rasta, please step forward."

Rasta's body twitches next to me. For a moment, I think she'll refuse. But then she stands. Two spots of deep red ride high on her cheeks. Machete looms over Rasta, and when she speaks, her voice slices through the empath-hush of the circle.

"Rasta, will you please speak about Tenet Two and the common good?"

She steps back, leaving Rasta alone. I can't look and I can't look away. Of all people to drag up in front — why didn't Machete choose Aaron, or Tylee, or even me, for that matter?

"Tenet Two." Rasta's voice is a soft rasp. She clears her throat and speaks to her feet. "Tenet Two says that personal safety for all depends upon unity."

"And that means . . ." Machete prompts.

"It means that we have to keep the group in mind at all times. To remember that we come from One. A finger and a toe seem to be a long ways away from each other, but if you cut the toe and get an infection, it eventually affects the finger. Every action I take, I need to consider the effect on everyone, not just on me or my crew or even just CropCamp, but everyone."

"Very good, Rasta. Tell us, what does that mean for you personally? How do you apply that in your own life?"

Rasta clears her throat again. Eyes down.

"It means don't be selfish." Whatever magical chemical Rasta carries in her throat deepens. "I shouldn't ever use my freedom to do something that compromises your safety. Freedom comes only with safety. It's not FreeSafe. It's SayFree."

Silence walks the circle. Rasta's last words reverberate.

"Rasta, that's a beautiful interpretation." Machete walks back to the center. "Nicely done."

Rasta starts to move back to her seat but Machete drops a hand on her shoulder.

"Now comes your reward. Micah, the kickshaws, please. Everyone stand."

We all stand. Obedient, waiting, hands out while Micah roves the circle. He sets a kickshaw on my palm. Rasta does not look safe up there, and certainly not free. She looks sick. She'll gag on kickshaw in front of everyone. She'll never get it down.

"We all experienced feelings of empathy and camaraderie," says Machete, "when I asked Rasta to speak for the rest of you. She spoke well. Now, we all experience relaxation and delight together, as a community. Rasta, please lead us."

Rasta's cheeks blaze. Will she refuse? Not in front of everyone, surely not. She picks up the kickshaw — hesitates with it at her lips — then takes it in. The kickshaw sensation visibly washes across her face. Her color fades, and her shoulders settle. My own body melts and de-tenses.

"Now, everyone."

If I were better, I'd honor my strong alliance and do the right thing. But I want the taste. Even more, I want the ease that comes with following a strong leader, of being one of the all, living in the light. Safe.

I want to believe what Machete said, about all of us being in the kickshaw. I want Machete to be right.

"My da . . ."

Rasta sobs in the dusky pine light. I walk her down to Pieville, away from the people, back to the little clearing. First time I've been here since we gathered with Sabi.

"But Rasta, what could you do? You had to take it."

"He said, 'Don't stand out, baby.'"

Her words rasp out on a fresh tide of tears. Her da is a mythical creature to me, a paragon of love and courage and warm understanding. Fierce feathered wings wrapped around Rasta, holding her close and making her strong.

"He said, 'Keep your head lower than low.' So first I get caught in that stupid power cadre, and now I'm the *first* one to get picked out of the crowd."

"He'd be proud of you." I want it to be true. "You're braver than any of us, Rasta, and stronger, too. You did it just right. And tonight, it was good what you said. You did great."

She wraps her arms tight around her legs and bangs her forehead on her knees.

"I did what she wanted, like a puppet bobbling around. And then you all did it, too."

"It's not your fault, what we all did. We would've done it no matter what because we wanted kickshaw. Plus, that was so smart, that thing about SayFree and not FreeSafe. Did you think of that on the spot?"

"My da said it once."

"He talks to you about the tenets?"

"Of course."

Rasta's da grows bigger, giant-size benevolence and wisdom. Living in the system but still thinking, not just rinkety-dinking. Sheila never talks about the tenets except to make fun of them. We aren't any freer than Rasta's family, and I think we are way less safe.

"Nobody knew that I pocketed last week." Rasta picks up her head and stares at me. "No one but you." Her red-rimmed eyes drill into mine. "Did you tell?"

"Of course not! I wouldn't!"

"I don't mean Machete. I mean, did you tell anyone else? Sully, maybe?"

"No. I didn't tell anyone." I might have told Sully if other things hadn't happened, but they did, and I didn't. "Maybe it was just a coincidence that she made you go first."

"Made me get up in front of everyone and talk about participation? And then eat a kickshaw where everyone could see me?"

"Okay, maybe not a coincidence. Maybe one of the guides saw you pocket and told her."

"I don't think so. I think Machete is something bigger than any of us can understand or fight. I'm so scared of her."

"Rasta, I know you don't think this, but what if . . . I mean, what if she's good? What if she's really trying to help us?"

Rasta wipes her eyes and gives me a long look.

"Lizard. Don't. I can't stand it if you go there. Don't let her change you."

"I won't. I just — I don't know. She makes a lot of sense sometimes."

"That's what's so dangerous about her."

"Tell me more about your da. The things he says, okay? Please?"

"I should just shut up," she says. "So I don't get you in trouble, too. I shouldn't tell anyone anything, ever."

"But then you're letting her change you."

Rasta's head falls sideways in a baby-crow tilt, and she caw-laughs.

"Lizard, I knew that I picked right. You're the strongest alliance ever."

She wipes her face. I help her up, and walk her all the way back to her slice.

"Tomorrow is Monday," she says.

"Week Three."

"Week Three," she echoes.

She holds up her hand, and we touch fingertips. This time, I meet her eyes. She really is my strong alliance, and it's time for me to be hers and stop hiding things. I'll tell her what happened between me and Sully. I'll tell her soon.

Chapter Nineteen

FOOTSTEPS TROT UP BEHIND ME after Block Four. Sully yanks me around to face her with a force that startles me.

"Why the big icy chill? It's like living with two Nonas. You wouldn't even look at me in Cleezies last night."

"What do you care?"

My words spill shaky over us both, and she steps back. She looks down and rubs her hands over her face. Then she stretches her arms out, palms up in a half shrug, opens her face to me, and there are her eyes. Dark and warm, no lights and no jazz.

"Come on," she says. "Walk with me."

This Sully I cannot refuse. The secret Sully, the one she reveals to me in private. As I walk with her, my heart practically bursts into song. My heart is stupid. Sully doesn't speak until we're well past Lacey's slice.

"It's not what you think. It was his idea to have a little sneak-over on our afternoon off, and I couldn't say no. I mean, not without hurting his feelings, and —"

She stops abruptly. Turns away from me. Shakes her head, squares her shoulders, and turns back.

"The truth is, I asked him to come over here, and he found a way. And yes, I know better, and yes, I did it anyway."

Why? Why would she do that? And in my grove. *Mine.* I can't believe I took her there, let her see me. . . . Did she tell Aaron? Did they make fun of me there?

"Hey. Hey, hey, hey, come on now."

She steps toward me, hand out. I jerk away.

"If there's anything I'm not . . ." Sully looks down, shoves her hands in the pockets of her coveralls. "It's worth any of that."

How dare she talk to me that way? Her soft words slide through my ribs to my stupid, gullible heart.

"Fine," I say. "You want to get yourself expulled, do it."

I start back toward the pies. She runs around and stands in front of me. I look away. She jumps over to where I'm looking, right in my face. I look the other way. She jumps over there. She looks for the smile but she's getting nothing from me.

"I told you," she says. "Left on my own, I'll always do the wrong thing."

"Not with me, you didn't."

I do not want my voice to shake.

"Yes, I did, and I'm trying to fix it." She steps close, and I'm not strong enough to jerk away again. I cannot refuse her any more than I can refuse kickshaw. "You're the best friend I have here. Be my friend, okay? Even when I do it wrong?"

Hand on my shoulder, one cool finger on my neck. Holding me in and holding me out at the same time.

"That saurian stuff I told you, it's just a story." My voice shakes. "Something Sheila made up."

"Maybe. Maybe not."

Her eyes are so full. Mystery and warmth and jazz and light. I want her to pull me in, to say that I'm irresistible and mean it. I want to do the wrong thing because it's right and neither of us can stop ourselves.

"Come on," she says. "Let's go be good little CropCampers so they'll let us pick their cucumbers."

She takes her hand away from my shoulder, her finger off my neck, and she turns away from me. She does not feel like I do. She does not. My body pulses with a jumble-jazz of disappointment and wishing-wishing and wanting-wanting. And suddenly, clear as clear, Rasta's voice is in my head.

Don't let her change you.

The next morning, I wake before gong and stare at the sunrise rays leaking through the synthie ceiling. It's too late to not-change. They're all changing me, whether I let them or not. Sully and Machete, Rasta and Nona and even Lacey and Aaron. And the kickshaw. The dragon lies deep in the earth, and I'm a shake-up of skin and heart and biz. Nothing lizard about me.

I dress quietly, layering with a warmer and a cap against the morning chill, and zip out soft and slow. I creep past Nona's and Sully's doors, through the sleeping Pieville, and up to the fields.

In the middle of the potatoes, I kneel and push my fingers into the cool, damp earth. The sun tips yellow heat over the treetops, and I face the day. Live in the light. Return to One. Just like everyone else.

It's disappointing, actually. For all the pain of being different and separate, it's been a good fantasy. Baby komodo dropped from the cosmos, listening to the saurians on a secret radio, waiting for my moment to rise and make my move. It's sad to let that go, but it's time. It's called growing up.

At CounCircle, I look around at the faces. They don't look as old as they did only a couple of weeks ago. They look like me. The circle collapses, and we head into the Mealio. Sully is in the crowd ahead of me. I move closer, hoping to sit with her at breakfast, hoping to show her how human I am.

"Hey, pretty boy."

She reaches up and tweaks Aaron's ear. He puts an arm around her, something between a hug and a headlock. I override the pain twinge by pounding the lesson to myself. *She does not feel like I do. She doesn't.* Grind it in. Make it real.

I will not tell Rasta about me and Sully. I need to forget about me and Sully. I step back and bump into someone behind. It's Emmett, the blond boy I shared kickshaw with. He smiles just enough to dent his dimple.

We walk into the Mealio together. I take a seat across from Nona, and she nods. Emmett sits next to me, and Tylee and Rasta join us. I pass Emmett the eggs. He pours juice in my glass. Tylee mentions the rumor of a three-Sunday-weekend in early July.

Emmett bumps his knee against mine. His eyes hold a soft and gentle shade of kickshaw. Nice, but nothing to jelly my bones.

In my DM session with Machete that morning, his name comes up again.

"A friendship with Emmett will be good for both of you."

"Why?"

"You tell me. You picked him for kickshaw last Sunday."

Did I pick him? I thought he picked me.

"Kivali, you seem distracted. Or distant. There's a change over you. Has something happened?"

Almost involuntarily, I meet her eyes.

"Have you given thought to last week's question?"

Which was what?

"Leader or follower, Kivali?"

Oh, that. Well, that's gotten obvious over the past few days.

"Follower," I say. "Isn't that what we're supposed to do here? Follow all the regs and do what we're told? If we don't follow, we don't get certed."

Machete nods. Pauses. Watches me.

"Do you see me as a leader?" she asks.

"Sure, of course. You're in charge."

"But I follow the tenets and the edicts of the SayFree Council and GovCentral. I answer to someone, always."

"So you're a follower?"

"Kivali, would you like to be a leader?"

"It's easier to just do what I'm told."

"Yes, of course it's easier. But does it come naturally? Do you like it?"

I'd like it fine if I knew for sure who to follow.

"What if you could have it all?" asks Machete. "Ease and community, *and* your independence? Most people move happily with the herd. I don't think that's true for you. As a leader, you would carry influence. Not to maverick off on your own but to work with others, to work with what is, to exert your strong will and clever mind for the good of everyone."

"You mean, to make them change the regs?"

"Who is *them*? *Them* is you, and me. We're all in this world together. If you allow yourself to truly be a part, there is no *them*."

But there's always been a *them*. *Them* makes me go to school, and make a decision, and attend post-decision gender training, and get a camp cert, and comply with state standards. . . .

"Kivali, you can be a decision-maker, a leader, an influence in the *us*. I see that potential in you. But you'll have to truly join us, and let go of the idea of *them*."

"Ms. Mischetti, who is Donovan Freer?"

Machete flinches — just the tiniest twitch. Then she pulls the blanket of authority and leadership — of *them* — back over her face and her features.

"Kivali, I'd like you to tell me more about your home life." The change of subject is so obvious. "Do you enjoy school?"

I play along but my mind is on rapid fire. Why did I ask that? I didn't plan to — it just came out. The name clearly means something to Machete. She asks banal questions, and I give empty answers until my time is up.

"We had a miss there," she says as she stands. "You startled me. I responded from the startle, rather than the truth. Donovan Freer was the bender boy that you saw at orientation, the one who left and won't be back."

The bender boy! *That* was Nona's Donovan Freer?

"It's important that you and I be truthful with each other, Kivali. We both need to be responsible. An irresponsible leader can do widespread, irreparable damage. Neither one of us wants that. Now get on back to the fields — we've gone over our time."

Chapter Twenty

I FINALLY MANAGE TO pull Nona aside from our pie that night, a few minutes before curfew gong.

"Tell me about Donovan," I say.

She does the same flinch-and-cover as Machete, but instead of pulling power she pulls a deep breath and looks me in the eye.

"I thought you didn't know him."

"Machete told me that he's the guy who was here the first night and then gone. I saw him."

Nona relaxes. It's subtle, but it's there.

"He really was here, then," she says. "I thought maybe I dreamed it."

"He was here," I say. "He vaped, that first night. I saw it, almost. I saw him, and then he was gone."

Nona's mouth makes an *o*. Then her face softens.

"He did it," she whispers.

"Nona, who is he?"

"We were kidlets together. He was my best friend. We had a bad time, both of us. We stuck together."

"Why you? You're not a bender."

"You don't have to be a bender to have a bad time. It's easy for you. You get along."

"Only here."

"I'm telling you about Donovan. He didn't want to T, and no matter how much PDGT they rammed down his throat, he kept coming up Donovan. He flunked, so they took him away. Put him with a foster in another sector. I didn't see him after that. Not until here."

The gong rings, and she immediately heads for the pie.

"Nona, wait!"

She stops, shakes her head no, and zips into her slice. I stand alone in the dark. What else don't I know about Nona?

The next day, I enter the quiet of the ayvee pod, put my chip in, and hit PLAY. Sheila's face leaps onto the screen. She rambles on through three ticks, then four. It's all rinkety-dink. At four and a half ticks I hit PAUSE and study her image. Her eyes angle down to the right. This is the longest inflow she's done, but she hasn't looked at the cam once. I'd rather have a half tick of real than all of this blattery-blat.

I punch PLAY to finish the inflow.

"My beautiful Kivali-dragon, I miss you every day. When you come home, you can teach me about potatoes and cucumbers and spinach and all the other things you're learning."

I'm reaching to turn it off when the Sheila image turns fully to the cam, and I catch my breath.

"Remember. No matter what happens, beware the fly pepper."

Her lip stud rises when she smiles, and the screen goes blank. I watch the last bit again, and then again. She always says, "You have to learn to tell the fly shit from the pepper." When I was a kidlet I used to get mixed up and call it fly pepper. And then she'd fall to the floor covering her head and yelling, "Fly pepper! Fly pepper!" Sometimes I'd do it, too, and we'd both laugh like lunars. It no longer seems funny.

After lunch, the sun blazes a direct ray on our pie, and my slice is a steam bath. I can't even draw a deep breath, and I pour sweat with every movement. I make the slow-tickiest of all exits. No runaround allowed during Solitude, but even if I get caught, Machete won't expul me over this. I doubt she'd even give me a culpa. For whatever reason, she likes me. She thinks I'm a leader. My independence is an asset.

I barefoot along the path. Still hot, but better than steaming in that sweaty pie. I ease past Lacey's slice and take the right fork. The little clearing is perfect — all shady with a breath of breeze.

I sink down to the pine-needle carpet and stretch out on my back, inhaling the deep hot scent of the pine needles. I roll over and press my skin to the ground. The earth and my heart beat in rhythm, and the treetops murmur sweetness overhead, shifting the shadows. It feels so good to relax, turn off my brain, listen to the trees, and drift.

Something nips the rim of my ear. I startle and collide with a human body, lengthwise over mine.

"Shh-sh-sh, it's okay. It's just me."

My body knows Sully's smell and touch before I'm even awake.

"Why is the lizard sleeping in the woods?" she whispers in my ear. "Culpa-worthy."

She rolls away and props on an elbow alongside me. I drop my face in my arms, close my eyes again. Sun heat, Sully heat. Her presence still completely shakes me, no matter how much I want it not to. She puts a hand on my back.

"Lizard. What's wrong?"

I shake my head, face hidden.

"S'okay. Don't talk."

Hand in my hair now, rubbing, fingers down to my scalp. Setting off small, soft explosions in my stomach and my biz. Off-guard and human-skinned.

"Don't."

I push her hand away and sit up, scooting back against a tree. Draw my knees up and wrap my arms around them.

"Come on, Lizard. Don't be mad. I'm not jazzing you, I'm just—"

A stick cracks, and we both freeze. Nona clumps fast along the narrow path, not even trying to be quiet.

"Lizard, Lacey knows you're out," she puffs. Her cheeks are high red. "She's looking for you. When you weren't there, she took off. Probably to go tell Machete."

We scrabble up as Nona lumbers off. She looks like someone

just learning how to run, like she's never done it before. Sully grabs my arm.

"Can we trust her?"

"What's not to trust about that?"

I pull my arm free and take off after Nona. We all three arrive back at the pie together and dive in with a chorus of zip-zip. I try to slow my breathing. Wipe the sweat from my forehead, rebraid my hair, and wait. Eventually, footsteps approach.

"Kivali?"

I step up to the window screen. Machete and Lacey stand just outside my slice.

"Where were you a few ticks ago?" Lacey asks.

"Privo."

"Kivali, come with me, please."

"I checked the privo," Lacey says to Machete as I zip out. "Checked every stall, and the showers, too."

"I guess you missed her, then," says Machete. "Thank you, Lacey. I'll take over now."

I follow Machete. Eyes watch from behind slice screens as we pass the pies. The air presses heavy. We climb the steep path, and sweat runs down my ribs. My stomach is wet, and so is the back of my neck. Did Lacey see Sully on top of me? That'll make it an expul for sure, no matter how much potential Machete thinks I have. But what about Sully? Why didn't Machete get her, too?

Stepping onto the shaded porch gives instant relief from the heat. Inside, it's cooler still. Machete leads me into her office and closes the door behind her. I go directly to the comfy chair as she sits at her desk.

She leans forward, eyes full of concern, and I don't have a chance to pull together any excuse or explanation before she speaks.

"I'm afraid that I have some bad news. Your guardian, Sheila, has gone missing."

A sudden chill clammers my sweaty T-shirt to my skin.

"What do you mean, *missing*?"

"She didn't show up for her refresher course on Monday. Nobody has seen her since Sunday morning."

"But I just saw—" I point toward the Study Center, the ayvee pod.

"She made that on Sunday for a Tuesday delivery. Kivali, do you know where she might go? She has no associations on Deega other than her art coordinator. Do you know of anyone else? Friends? Acquaintances?"

I shake my head. Korm isn't exactly a friend. Besides, Korm doesn't officially exist.

"She hasn't crossed any sector borders, and no body has been found."

Body? *Body?*

"I know that this is a shock, but please try to focus. Any ideas you have, any at all, might help us find her."

The shivers start somewhere in my stomach and spread across my body. I draw my feet up on the chair, hugging my knees. Clench my teeth so they won't chatter.

"There's food in the fridge," says Machete. "Half-finished work on her desk."

"They were in our *flat*?"

"Of course we were in your flat. Everyone wants to find her safe. It's not *they*, Kivali. It's *us*. We're together on this. We all want to find Sheila."

I pull my knees in closer.

"Kivali, I'm so sorry. It's a terrible thing, a frightening thing." Her voice glides into a smooth melt, like Cleezies, like kickshaw. "You'll need your community now, all of us, to help you through. Especially if this turns out to be a vape."

The word hits my chest like a concrete block. I've believed that Korm will vape one day. But not Sheila. Not ever Sheila. I look out the window and inch air back into my lungs. Then I turn to Machete.

"Is it you?" I watch carefully for a flinch or a look-away. "SayFree? Did you take her?"

Machete slowly shakes her head back and forth, meeting me eye for eye.

"Vapes are not the gov, Kivali. I would not work for a gov that vapes its citizens. I would not be an *us* to such a *them*."

I don't think she's lying. Machete doesn't need to lie. If she doesn't want to answer, she just asks a question back.

"Then where is she?" I whisper.

"We don't know."

I close my eyes. Don't look. Don't breathe.

"Kivali."

What if Sheila is gone? Really, truly gone forever? I don't care if it's an honor. I don't care if it's a privilege for the wise and the good. I don't want Sheila to be gone.

"Kivali."

It's a huge effort to open my eyes. Machete holds out a kickshaw.

"You need community," she says. "You need us. Take this. Let us help you through."

Kickshaws are not good. But what if they are?

I uncurl my legs, set my feet on the floor. Step up, take the kickshaw, put it in my mouth. Close my eyes. Sensation flows over me, but I don't feel good and happy. Just tired. So, so tired.

"You'll want to rest in the Quarry." Machete stands, puts her arm around my shoulder. She wants to protect me. "It's quiet and cool downstairs. No one will bother you there. You can barely hear the gongs."

Yes, quiet. And cool. That's what I want. Sleep.

Chapter Twenty-One

I WAKE TO SOFT SEMIDARKNESS. The Quarry room is quiet and cool. I'm on a cot with my coveralls still on, blanket over me. Gray light filters through the high row of small windows. Dusk or early morning? I can't tell. The bed is much softer than my cot. Feels like floating.

Something happened. Something bad. I don't feel bad, though. The bed is good. Everything is okay. Sleep. Rest is good.

"Sheila?" I can't see anything. I thrash my arms in the darkness, trying to swim clear to the light. "Sheila?" My voice is shrill, frantic.

Then I remember. My heart races but there's nowhere to go, so it crashes against my ribs like a wild pony trying to escape its stall. I put my hand on my chest, trying to soothe it. I'm wide awake. I have no idea what time it is. Calm down, heart. C'mon, easy. Shh. Settle. Deep breath in, two, three.

My breath shakes all the way in. Out, two, three. Yes. That's better. In, two, three. I close my eyes. Out. Deep inhale and — there! A faint, distant chitter. The lizards sound like home, like comfort, but the signal is shaky. I reach out, trying to grasp it and hold it and pull it close, and then it is gone.

"Kivali."

It's full daylight. Machete hands me a glass of water. I sit up, blink awake. Peel away the strands of hair sweat-stuck to my face. The room is large and square. Three beds line one wall. The other two are neatly made. The high rectangular windows are made of thick, opaque glass. They let in light but not clarity. The far corner is curtained off, and I have a vague memory of using the privo there.

"Kivali, how do you feel?"

Machete has pulled a chair up next to me.

"Did they find Sheila?" I ask.

She shakes her head. I drain the water glass. I am so dry.

"She's been missing five days now. It's officially been designated a vape."

I don't plan to throw the water glass, but it flies through the air and crashes impressively against the opposite wall. Machete doesn't flinch. I lie back down and stare at the ceiling. If I had another glass, I'd throw it.

"I know," she says. "Someone very close to me vaped, a long time ago. I know how you feel."

I don't look at her. She doesn't know how I feel. She knows how she felt. Maybe that was bad, and I'm sorry, but she doesn't know how I feel. Even I don't know how I feel.

"You need your community now more than ever," she says. "It's not good to grieve alone."

I'm not grieving. Sheila will be back. She just doesn't want to be found. She wouldn't leave me.

"I think it'll be good for you to sleep in your own slice tonight, and go back to classes and crops tomorrow. It's close to dinnertime now. You must be hungry."

I am very hungry.

"What time is it?" I ask.

"Four fifteen. Friday."

Friday?

"Yes." Machete reads my face again. "Grief can make a person sleep for a long time."

But I'm not grieving. There's no reason to grieve.

"Ease your way back into camp. Your comrades know that you've had trouble at home, but I haven't told them any details."

She walks me upstairs, past her office, and out onto the porch.

She gives me three shower chits.

"If you get overwhelmed, come right back. And check in with me after Cleezies — you'll want another kickshaw to help you sleep."

Yes. Yes, I will want another kickshaw. It will help me sleep.

The gong rings to end Block Four as I finish a luxurious three-chit shower. I'm sweating again by the time I get back to my slice. Nona's footsteps approach, and she zips in. Seems like there was something that I wanted to ask her, but now I can't think what it was. I sit on the edge of my cot, looking at my hands. My hair irritates me, clinging to my neck and cheeks, dripping down my back. I start to whip it into a wet braid, and then stop.

My secateurs are tucked in the holster on the shelf. I slide them out and release the safety catch so the blades yawn open. I pick up a lock of wet hair and saw through. It's not easy — the blades aren't meant for cutting hair — but the sharp pull on my scalp feels oddly good. Tears start in my eyes, and then recede. I grab another chunk of hair and snip and saw. I hate this long hair. I've always hated it.

"Lizard." A whisper outside my window. "It's me, Rasta."

I unzip the door, step back to let her in, and zip back up. It's an auto-culpa, being in someone else's slice with the door zipped, but surely they won't do anything to me right now, or to Rasta. Community and all.

"Help me?"

I hand her the secateurs and drop to the floor, sitting cross-legged.

She looks the question into my eyes. I nod. She sits behind me on the cot, lifts a lock and starts cutting. She tosses a wet clump on the fabric floor beside me.

"Keep going," I say. "Short all over."

My scalp prickles and burns as Rasta pulls and saws. I try to keep my head still.

"I'm hurting you."

"It's fine. Don't stop."

"Are you sure?"

I nod. She cuts. My head feels lighter. I close my eyes, surrendering completely to Rasta's yank and pull. They made me grow it out. I never liked how it looked or felt, but I couldn't pass PDGT until it was long enough to braid. I got less of the what-are-you looks and comments when I tied it off with a pink or yellow ribbon. I could walk into a public women's room without anyone screaming at me.

The day after I passed PDGT, Korm helped me celebrate by cutting off the long ponytail. Sheila was furious. *Korm overstepped this time. She should know better.* It made school worse than usual, and the school gov worker was not pleased. Visibly bending at age thirteen — people don't like that. Sheila convinced me to let it grow again. *A little extra hair, a silly ribbon. These things won't kill you. Other things might.*

A tear trickles down my cheek, and I brush it away. Rasta stops.

"Are you okay?"

"Yes. Keep going."

"I'm done. It's kinda choppy-looking, but I don't think I can do any better with these."

I run my fingers through. No tangles. No sweaty strands. It feels good. Better than good. It feels fantastic. My head is light and free. Not safe, but free. Rasta kneels and uses the side of her hand to brush all of the hair into a single clump.

"Machete said that you have trouble at home," she said. "What does that mean?"

"They say Sheila vaped."

Rasta looks up with big wide eyes.

145

"Vaped?"

Footsteps rustle outside. I ram my finger against my lips.

"Lizard?" It's Lacey. "Ms. Mischetti asked me to check on you."

"I'm trying to sleep." I don't have to fake the irritation in my voice. "Can you just leave me alone?"

"Sorry. I'll be back at dinner gong to walk you up."

We barely breathe for the next few ticks. I get up quietly, unzip my window, and check. No sign of Lacey. Rasta slips out.

"I'll be in my slice," she whispers. "Stop and get me on the way to dinner, okay?"

I don't close the door behind her. Instead, I brush away the pine needles in front of my door and carefully dig away the first layer of loose dirt. I search with my fingertips for the hard metal edges. A sudden fear seizes me. The komodo is angry. I feel it. It will bite me.

I take a deep breath and exhale, shaking the fear away. If the komodo chomps, I'll pull it out dangling from my finger. I will apologize for putting it out of sight, for hiding away the one tangible thing that I have from Sheila. I will gentle it back to me.

I dig deeper with fingernails and secateurs, searching for the familiar shape. The komodo is not there. I use the blade tips to dig the hole wider and deeper, to scrape down and down, but I find no dragon in the dark and the dirt. Where can it be? Who could've taken it? Nona? Did Nona see me bury it?

The predinner gong rings. Footsteps approach on the path from Lacey's direction. I grab the clump of hair, put it in the bottom of the hole, and quickly cover it. Toy dragons don't vape. I just didn't look closely enough.

I stand, wiping my dirty hands on my coveralls. Lacey stops short, eyebrows drawn at my choppy hair.

"What happened to you?"

I don't answer. Lacey's eyebrows go up, and she shrugs.

"Well, come on. I'll walk you up to the Mealio."

She's on a special community-care mission from Machete, but it doesn't mean anything. If Machete expuls me, Lacey will be the first to heave my duffel out of Pieville. I stop at the spigot to wash up, and Rasta joins me.

With Lacey right behind us, we can't really talk. When we get to the Mealio, Emmett appears on my other side as if he's been summoned. He and Rasta flank me through dinner like twin guardian spirits. I don't know what makes Emmett think that I want him there, but I do. It's just how he showed up the other day, in the middle of Sully's flirt with Aaron, perfect timing with his angelic dimple-smile.

He doesn't seem to notice my choppy hair, but others do. People stare and look away. Sully gives me a nod and a solemn smile from across the Mealio. Everyone obviously knows that something is wrong. I wish they didn't know. I hate everyone looking at me.

It gets worse in Cleezies.

"We gather here for three months," says Machete, "and the rest of the world continues on. Sometimes while we're here, difficult things happen at home."

My stomach curls in on itself. No. What about confidentiality, what about privacy and discretion?

"When they do, it's more crucial than ever that we come together as a community. This is where we learn to support one another outside of our insular family units, to be with the One, and stay together in the light. We create communal safety.

"Your comrade Kivali — Lizard, many of you call her —"

She's doing it.

"— has had some difficult news from home. A terrible loss. I ask that you support her, that you hold her in the One, that you consider her more deeply and more carefully than you ever have. She needs us all right now, and we need her."

I wish that I had another glass to throw. I'd fling it at Machete's head. She signals Saxem, and he plays a tiny two-fingered tune. She tells us to close our eyes, and everyone does. It's a relief to get their stares off of me.

Machete tells us to breathe deeply, and at first I won't. I glare at her, but she closes her own eyes. She counts the breath, and I fall into rhythm with everyone's in-and-out without meaning to. I breathe with my comrades and watch their shuttered eyes, and the frantic skittering beneath my ribs begins to settle. All of us, in, two, three, and out together. I let my own eyes close.

In the quiet, behind the safety of my eyelids, glimmers of real pain spark and crackle. Maybe Sheila is hurt and alone somewhere. Maybe I should leave camp and try to find her. I don't want to. Where would I look? And where is my dragon? I can't leave here without the komodo.

Saxem's music continues to weave around me, and the pain and uncertainty flares, fades, flares again, melts, sharpens, pulses. If I still had my lizard skin, this wouldn't hurt so much. Or maybe it would hurt more. Maybe Sheila's disappearance would rip that skin right off and leave a gaping mortal wound. Here at CropCamp, I've built up some human endurance. I'm not alone.

Machete brings us slowly back into the Pavilion.

"Before you open your eyes, please think deeply." She speaks in that warm, swirling kickshaw voice. "If you were experiencing sharp pain, fear and grief and uncertainty, how would you want your comrades to treat you? Think about that. Then think even more deeply, not about yourself but about what you know of your comrade Kivali. How do you think that she might like to be treated? What would keep her safe? What would make her feel held in the light of the One, now more than ever?"

There's a long pause, and I can feel everyone thinking about me, and I hate it. I don't want anyone to think about me, not ever. I hold my breath, dreading the moment when they all stare at me.

Rasta nudges me with her shoulder. Emmett puts a toe on my instep, a foot caress. I barely slit my eyes open. I look for Sully, spot her on the other side of the circle. She nods at me. No jazz, just warmth. Nobody else looks at me at all, and Machete is right. They are keeping me safe. Holding me in the One. Comfort and care wash over me. These comrades, they are not vague murmurings that come and go in the dark. They are real, and they are here, and they are with me.

149

I like CropCamp.

I like having Machete in charge.

I like being part of the One, living in the light.

Maybe Sheila and the dragon left because they knew that I'd already left them.

Chapter Twenty-Two

I LEAVE THE PAVILION with Rasta but Machete calls me back, and I remember her kickshaw promise.

"What does she want?" Rasta asks.

"She's giving me a kickshaw to help me sleep."

"Don't take it," Rasta whispers. "At least not right away. You can save it for later."

A half moon hovers over the treetops as comrades stream to the boys' and girls' sides. I go back to Machete while Rasta waits.

"How are you?" Machete asks.

"All right."

"You cut your hair."

"Yes."

"Did it help?"

"Help what?"

Machete smiles, and puts a hand on my shoulder.

"Kivali, I admire your courage. I'll get Katrina to trim that up for you tomorrow. Meanwhile, take this, and get some rest tonight."

She hands me the kickshaw, and I put it in my pocket.

"I want to wait till I'm back in my slice," I say. "I'll take it there, when I'm alone. That way I can feel the community around me all night."

I'm doing what Rasta wants and what Machete wants, both at the same time. Can't get better than that — unless I can get Sully in on it, too. Machete nods and squeezes my shoulder.

"Good night," she says. "I'll expect you on regular schedule tomorrow, but please know that you can come to my office at any point. We can talk if you'd like, or you can have some alone time in the Quarry. Meanwhile, talk to your friends. Let them help you. And stay checked in with me. I'll help you through this."

I nod, and return to Rasta.

"Good job," she says once we're well away from Machete. "Now I think that you should give it to me."

I put my hand in my pocket, and for a split second my fingers think they will find the komodo. Instead, they find the kickshaw, and the touch alone makes my mouth water.

"But I want it," I say.

"I know. But maybe you can try the night without it. Just try. I won't rip it up and bury it. If you really need it, pretend that you're going to the privo, and whisper outside my slice, and I'll give it to you. I promise."

We skid down the steep part of the path and approach Rasta's slice. There's no one else I'd trust with a kickshaw, but I know that Rasta won't take it. When we get to her pie, she holds out her hand. I hesitate.

"You'll keep it for me, right? In case I change my mind?"

"Promise."

She takes it and holds up her other hand. We touch finger-tips, and I walk back to my slice with crow feathers wrapped around me. I stop at Sully's door and whisper-call.

"Hey, Sully."

"Hey, Lizard. You okay?"

I want her to come out and look deep into my eyes and ask again. I want her to pull answers out of me, to find all that I'm hiding from myself. The chirp of tree frogs carries on the dense, humid air.

"Yes," I finally say.

"Good."

I wait. She doesn't come out. I want the kickshaw. I turn back toward Rasta's pie and almost knock into Nona.

"I am sorry for your loss." She doesn't whisper. She doesn't care if Sully hears. "And I'm glad that you got back in time."

Seems like years ago that Sully and I were scrambling back to our pie, thinking that we were in trouble.

"Thanks, Nona. And thanks for warning us."

"You're welcome. I owed you."

"For what?"

"For doing what I asked, enough for Machete to believe it. You're decent, and I appreciate it."

She turns and zips into her own slice, leaving me in the dark. I don't think she stole the dragon. I don't think she would do that. And I don't need the kickshaw. Not right this minute, anyway.

Back in my slice, I find all my pink and yellow ribbons and begin to saw through them with the secateurs, which are gritty and dull from cutting hair. I cut and tear the ribbons to shreds, and then I slow-zip my door open and sift through the loose dirt and hair, feeling for the komodo. I still can't find it, although the hole is now almost twice its original size. I dump the ribbon shreds in with my shorn hair and cover it all over again with pine needles and dirt.

Then I drop my coveralls, and spread out on my back in my boxers. It's way too hot. I slept all day; there's no way I'll sleep tonight without kickshaw — but after two days of fog, it's good to have a clear head.

Where is Sheila? *Come on, breathe. Out. In.* What does it really mean, vaping? And who does Machete know who vaped? Besides Donovan Freer? Tomorrow I'll tell her how I saw him vape, and that I saw her see him vape. Then she'll tell me what vaping really is. She must know, and it's important that she and I be truthful with one another. She said so.

Also tomorrow, I'll dig around in that hole in full daylight and find the dragon. I can be here and be in community and have my dragon, too, can't I? And Sheila? Sure, I can. Tomorrow. For now, just breathe, two, three. . . .

No gentle murmuring this time, no vague shadows. Image after image hurtles my way, flashing through the heavy, humid darkness behind my eyelids. The visuals are louder than Lizard Radio ever was and more solid than any dream has ever been.

Donovan Freer steps into focus. His burning green eyes sear

through me, and then he spins away. He reaches up and pleads with the skies.

And then he's Korm, pleading with the skies.

Then the moonlit field is empty — but no — there's someone coming from the boys' side. It's Aaron, creeping on all fours in the night. He is a cat, but he is Aaron. He leaps up and catches a bird, rips it apart with teeth and claws. He turns to me and smiles his easy jazzy smile. His shiny white teeth drip with blood. I turn and run, and I end up in Korm's basement meeting-place.

The tiny silver komodo is in the back corner with one foot raised, inanimate. I take a step toward it and then stop. The komodo grows before my eyes, swelling to full-size living flesh. It leaps across the room in two bounds, a fury of teeth and claws and hot fetid breath. I fall and whimper and crawl away, crawl back to consciousness, shivering in the dark. A dream. It was a dream.

Rasta is right. Lonely in our slices. I need kickshaw. I should get up and get it from Rasta, but I'm afraid. The dragon is mad, maybe too mad to be gentled back to me. I cannot step over its dark lair, not even for kickshaw.

I close my eyes and finally drift in the direction of sleep. Korm meets me there. She sits in the middle of the oak grove, stroking the back of a little green gecko, no bigger than my thumb.

Tokay, it croaks, looking at me. *Tokay.*

"This gecko." Korm strokes the tiny lizard from tip of nose to end of tail. "This gecko can hold eight times its body weight with a single toe. Did you know that?"

Of course I know that. I studied geckos in my first year with Korm. I know their environment, defense and reproduction, their distribution and habitat. I open my mouth to recite but not a word will come out, not one sound. Korm leaps up and stares at me with the fiery green eyes of Donovan Freer.

"You didn't know that, did you, Kivali? There's a lot that you don't know, isn't there?"

She squats and puts her index finger under the gecko's chin. It crawls up her arm as she straightens, and comes to rest on her shoulder. They both look down at me. Korm shakes her head, disappointed.

"Go tell that to your One," she says.

Chapter Twenty-Three

I WAKE WITH A sick heart. The air is dense and silent. No birds, no tree froggies, no Sully hollering. The gong rings. It's Saturday. The sky is gray. I don't know anything. I pull coveralls onto my already-sweating body, hit the privo, and wash up. Then I stand next to our pie and wait for Nona to emerge.

She steps out, nods to me, and zips her door closed behind her.

"Do you know where vapers go?" I ask.

"Do you?"

Who does she think she is, Machete?

"Come on, Nona. Just tell me, okay? You seemed happy about Donovan vaping. Where did he go?"

"Lizard!" Rasta comes bounding from the privo. "You did it! You made it through the night."

Nona presses her lips together and shakes her head slightly. Rasta looks at her, then at me.

"Did I miss something?"

Again, Nona shakes her head. After an awkward moment, I turn and start walking. Rasta, strong alliance as always, shrugs and walks with me. Nona walks on the other side. There's no horseplay with the three of us, none of the tumble-and-ease we have when it's Sully. But somehow, that's all right.

At morning CounCircle, Machete looks at me meaningfully. I nod: yes, I am okay. Once I get Nona to tell me what she knows, I will definitely ask Machete some direct questions and get some direct answers. Emmett joins us for breakfast. He sits across from me and doesn't say anything. I like that about him very much.

Katrina catches me as I'm getting up from the table.

"Ms. Mischetti told me to fix your hair."

She carries a Mealio chair outside and motions me to sit. She has a spray bottle, a towel, a hand mirror, and sleek, shiny scissors to clean up Rasta's and my hack job.

This haircut is nothing like the secateurs cut, or like the time Korm chopped off my ponytail. Katrina starts by putting the towel around my neck, tucking it into the collar of my coveralls. She combs her fingers through my hair, starting at my forehead and traveling to the base of my skull. I close my eyes. She sprays a cool mist from the bottle and uses the comb to lightly rake water through my hair. A drop trickles behind my ear, and she catches it with the towel. She runs her fingers close to my scalp, pulls a lock out, and snicks the scissors. Another lock, another snick. Dark wet tufts fall to my shoulders, my lap, and to the ground.

Katrina's touch is like Sully's, minus the heat and jazz and plus some extra cool-glowing warmth. No one has ever touched my head so gently. I close my eyes, but it's not Sully I see on the insides of my eyelids. It's Sheila.

158

Was she gentle like this when I was a baby? I can't remember. Sheila's kind and measured, but not what you'd call gentle. Not like this. Maybe if I fall asleep with Katrina's hands in my hair, I'll wake up and everything will be okay, today and on into forever.

"There." Katrina's voice startles me, and I open my eyes. She ruffles my hair and hands me a mirror. "Looks much better, don't you think?"

My hair is like Aaron's, a bit tidier and minus the sideburns. No scraggle or strand. I run my fingers through, and it feels unbelievably good. I feel more bender and more lizard and more comrade, all at once. My head is so light, I can't get over it. Like I'm free from a binding mask.

"So much better," I say. "Thank you."

She pulls the towel out from my collar and passes it over the back of my neck, roughing the itch away.

"You'd best get going." She snaps the towel, and hair clippings waft on the air. "I took longer than I should have."

I take off at a trot past the fields to get my booktron and secateurs. The sky is textured, with one level of gray shifting over another. I open the trot to a run, and the air fills my lungs and my heart picks up its pace as if it's headed for home. If no one were around I might skip or gallop. But it's still Block One, and the Saturdays and Thursdays are in the cucumbers. Sully pops to her feet and trots over to intercept me. Always happy for an excuse to get out of the fields.

"Hey, Lizard. Look at you — nice haircut!"

She reaches to touch it, and I knock her hand away. I

dance around, my fists up. "Come on." I poke toward her jaw, dance back.

She doesn't play. She takes a step back, looking at me.

"You okay?" she asks.

"I'm fine! Come on, hit me."

I punch her on the shoulder, and she rubs her arm.

"Can you stop that a second? I'm trying to say something here."

I ease back, still jouncing on the balls of my feet. She shoves her hands in her pockets, takes a breath that raises her almost up on her toes, and lets it out.

"I want to say that I'm sorry. About everything. Sorry that whatever bad thing is happening, you don't trust me enough to talk to me. I never should have played jazz with you. I wish that I could take it back."

I can't contain the ouch. She sees my flinch, of course, and she reaches fingers toward my face. Again, I knock her hand away. Her eyes pop wide, bare-naked and full of genuine hurt. She backs off, blinks as she turns away from me.

"Don't hate me, Lizard."

"I don't hate you."

"We're still friends, right? You and me?"

"Sure. Friends."

My voice comes out colder than I mean. With half a sad smile, Sully returns to the cucumbers. She doesn't look at me again. She wants to take back the moment when she made me human. I want to not care. Neither of us can get what we want.

———•———

I'm almost back up the path from Pieville when the sky opens. No sprinkles, no pitter-patter. One moment the clouds are heavy and low and quiet, and the next they dump everything they've got. I don't bother to run. I let the huge drops smatter my head and face. My hair drips in my eyes. By the time I get to the fields, the Thursdays and Saturdays have run for shelter. I arrive in the Study Center, drenched, just before the gong for Block Two. All the other Wednesdays are dry, but by the time we run to the tool-shed they're as wet as I am. My coveralls are heavy and dragging, and the chill of my exchange with Sully soaks into my skin and deeper.

Micah splits us into different tasks, and Rasta and I head for the corner with armloads of spades and hoes to clean. Rasta asks me something but I can't quite hear because the rain is jumping up and down on the metal roof. I lean closer, and she raises her voice.

"So what were you and Nona talking about?"

I can't answer her without yelling, and it's not anything I want to yell, so I shrug.

"You're the only one she ever talks to. I think you're the only one she actually likes."

I nod. The rain hammers on. Rasta and I use wire brushes to clean the spade blades. She doesn't poke any further. That's one thing about Rasta. She speaks when it's time to speak, and shuts up when it's time for silence. Maybe they taught her that in the baby-crow nest.

When we finally leave the metal-roof noise and walk in the rain again, she bumps up close to me.

"Maybe you could come to my house," she says. "After camp. My MaDa could foster you."

"They might still find Sheila." I speak quickly. "Just because they say it's a vape doesn't mean that it is."

Rasta meets my eyes from beneath the dripping bill of her cap. I have to look away.

At lunchtime, Lacey squats next to my chair.

"Ms. Mischetti asked me to see how you're doing. If you need anything."

"I'm fine," I say. "I don't need anything."

The rain continues. I'm glad to get back to my slice for Solitude and strip off my wet coveralls. I flop on the cot and close my eyes, and the next thing I know, the gong is ringing.

"Lizard?"

The voice is so far away. I wrench open my eyes. The zipper moves on my door, and Lacey pokes her head in.

"Ms. Mischetti says that you shouldn't miss dinner."

Dinner? Lacey leaves, and I blink at the ticker. They let me sleep through Blocks Three and Four. Why? Then I remember and wish that I didn't.

Water cascades during dinner, making the always-noisy Mealio even more chaotic. Emmett comes close as we walk out of the Mealio and speaks directly in my ear. His breath is warm, but I don't quite understand his words.

"Wait." We step into the corner of the Mealio until almost everyone is out. "Say it again?"

"Donovan Freer was my piemate."

I look over my shoulder. We are alone except for the few comrades on rotation, crashing dishes in the kitchen. Emmett continues in a whisper.

"I met him that first aft. I heard him leave his slice in the night. I followed him. I saw it happen."

"I saw it, too," I say.

"I know. I heard you warn him when the light came on. Did you see Machete?"

I drop to a squat like Machete in the field, arms over my head. I pop back up, and Emmett nods. We saw the same thing.

"It scared me," he says. "I ran back to Pieville, zipped in, and stayed. Saxem and Micah came before morning gong and took Donovan's things. They told us that there'd been complications with Donovan's registration, and he had to leave in the night."

"Have you told anyone else?"

"No one."

"Why me?"

"Because you were there. And because — well — I think that you should know now. Right?"

His long-lashed eyes look into mine. My own eyes start and sting, and I look away. The gong rings for Cleezies. We rush through the rain. I fall onto the wooden bench next to Rasta, panting, shivering anew with the dream image of Donovan begging to the skies, and then of Korm begging to the skies.

Machete stands to begin Cleezies. Her mouth moves, but the rain torrents on the roof and drowns her out. She shakes her head

163

and taps her ear, indicating that we should just listen. So we sit, comrades and guides and Machete and teachers and counselors, all of us in community. We listen as the water attacks the roof.

Rasta and I lean shoulder to shoulder, propping each other up. Even with all of that sleeping, I'm still so tired. I look down at the rocks and let my vision fuzz. Slowly, my eyes close, and the pounding rain surrounds me on all sides.

A curious vibration begins somewhere in my rib cage. A cellular chitter. As if Lizard Radio has set up a tower deep inside of me. The transmission is strong, and it increases in power, morphing my cells from the inside out. My nose lengthens into a snout, and my skin crusts into scales. I stretch out long and slide my belly along the rocks. My fingernails grow into claws and I raise my head, flicking my yellow-forked tongue, testing the air. My breath rasps, catching deep in my chest.

A bony jab strikes my side. I open my eyes.

"You're snoring," Rasta whispers.

Snoring? I blink awake to the chilly, damp evening air. No dragon skin, no radio. The boot-stomping deluge is over. Now the rain trots lightly back and forth on the roof. Machete signals us to stand, and I push myself up on two legs. I check my skin, my hands. No beads or scales. My fingernails are short. Machete releases us, and we pour out into the evening. Rain still spatters from the treetops, but the sky has finally emptied itself. The sun is an orange spotlight sinking in the west.

Rasta stops to talk with Tylee, and I don't wait for her because a hurricane of tears is rapidly rising from my gut, rushing up my throat. The intensity of dragon sensation in the Pavilion makes reality all the more painful. There is no Lizard Radio, there are no saurians, and there will be no rescue. All of that is gone now, truly gone forever along with Sheila and Korm and everything that I thought I knew. Dreams are dreams, and real is real.

The last rays of sunlight sear through the fabric wall as I fumble with the zipper and slide into my slice. My eyes hit the shelf, and the hurricane halts.

The toy komodo crouches on my shelf, left front leg raised.

I wrap my arms around my chest, holding in the bangety-bang of my heart. I stare at the komodo, waiting for it to move. It does not. Finally, I take one step forward. Then another. I reach out a shaky hand and touch its back. It does not move. It is inanimate.

I zip the door open and drop to my knees. The wet pine needles haven't been disturbed. I push them aside and dig through clumped strands of wet hair and shredded ribbon. I dig farther into the mud. Nothing. I cover it over and zip back in.

I wipe my muddy hands on my coveralls. The komodo is still in the same position. I reach out gingerly, take a step closer, and pick it up. It is clean. No dirt in its creases, no sign of being underground for two weeks.

I bring the komodo up close to my nose and look into its steely eyes.

"How did you do that?"

My breath shakes and my words quiver. The lizard speaks not.

Chapter Twenty-Four

IT'S HARD TO SETTLE down and sleep. Every time I close my eyes, explanations and ideas about the komodo's reappearance swirl through my head. I keep jerking up to be sure that the toy dragon hasn't moved. It hasn't. It's a quiet silver glint in the moonlight. Finally, long after CropCamp has settled, I manage to keep my eyes closed. I follow my breath in and out, and shadows begin to move on the insides of my eyelids. A soft murmur rises, and the Radio carries me to sleep.

The gong rings. I open my eyes. I don't know if I've slept or not. Was I dreaming? Or was Lizard Radio playing all night? It seems like both and neither. I reach for the komodo and cradle it in my palm. Stroke between the eyes as I've done hundreds of thousands of times since the day Sheila gave it to me.

I've now been at CropCamp for three full weeks, a lifetime and a flash. I set the komodo back on the shelf, get out of bed, and unzip my window. The air is light and clear. Blue skies and a skippy breeze. The birds sound so happy.

Maybe I dug the komodo out, and somehow made myself forget it.

Maybe I never buried it in the first place.

Maybe it crawled through the dirt up to the fields and feasted on the kickshaw that Rasta buried there, and then returned to me.

Every day, I know more of nothing.

One thing I do know — starting now, the komodo stays with me.

At morning Cleezies, Machete announces that today is Silent Sunday. We are to move through our chores and rotations without speech. The fields are still too wet to work, so we'll have extra contemplation and study time in our slices. Then at three p.m., we'll have early Cleezies. The grass should be dry by then, and we'll meet on the Quint.

Halfway through morning chores, I break off and go to Machete's office. She said to come to her if I need anything. I need information. I find Micah on his hands and knees in the office entryway, wiping down the floor. He looks up when I enter.

"Ms. Mischetti said that I should come if I need to talk."

He shakes his head and points at Machete's closed office door. He's taking this Silent Sunday thing very seriously. I roll the komodo over between my fingers.

"She said anytime. Because I have things going on at home."

His eyes are regretful, understanding. But still he shakes his head and points at the door again. Then he puts a finger to his lips: *shhhh.*

"Really?"

He nods.

I go back to my chore rotations, mopping the Mealio floor with Jyana. Since we can't talk, we just work. It's a big, wooden floor, and first we have to put all the chairs up on the tables.

Machete is not at lunch. Ms. Kroschen and Mr. Mapes are here, even though it's Sunday and they're usually off. Maybe Machete is finally taking a day off. Figures — the one day when I actually want to see her.

The komodo and I nap through the early afternoon, deep and dreamless without so much as a hum from Lizard Radio. The gong wakes me, and Machete welcomes us all to the Quint. She directs us to lie in a big circle, arms outstretched, hands linked. As I lie down, I push the dragon deep into my pocket so that it won't fall out. I reach out to Rasta, and she sets her hand in mine. My right hand is linked with Emmett's. Nona is on the other side of him, and Sully is on the other side of Rasta. Thirty-seven comrades. Thirty-nine at the start, now minus Donovan and Sabi.

"Today we enter a new phase." Machete walks around the outside of our circle. "Today and for the next week, we are in transition from the adjustment phase to the immersion phase. As of now, all inflows stop. For the next nine weeks it will be only us. You, your teachers and counselors and guides. All of us in cohesion and symphony. Working and learning together as you take your first steps into your future community roles, as workers, as comrades."

The unease that runs around the circle isn't quite audible, but it's palpable. I'm not so worried. I wouldn't have an inflow anyway, not until Sheila is found. The lizard came back. So will Sheila. The sky is broad and deep and blue with puff-clouds. The breeze blows across us. Nobody speaks or moves.

"This is your last week as children. Beginning next Sunday, you'll be fledgling adults. So in this, your last week as children, you must each give careful thought to the adult you want to become. The schedules change. You'll have at least two DM sessions this week. Cleezies will last a full hour, and curfew will ring thirty ticks after the close of Cleezies — so the entire Social time is mando, and there will be no free time after that.

"Today, as a celebration of the beginning of the end of childhood and a treasure on the threshold of change, you will receive double doses of kickshaw. And yes, as many of you have guessed, the kickshaws contain a drug."

The weight of Rasta's hand in mine increases as if the force of gravity suddenly doubled.

"And yes, the drug is more than a passing pleasure. The drug in kickshaw is an integral part of our culture, our peace, and our safety. We do not give it to children. You are no longer children. You stand on the brink of adulthood, with all of its impulses and dangers. With adulthood comes tumult and struggle. You have new power, and with power comes responsibility. Now is when you learn to temper and focus your power and responsibility. Now is when we teach you how to do that, in safety and community. Your parents and guardians know of this drug, of this practice. They use it themselves."

A circular gasp rises from the grass. I raise my head and look around. No one gets up; no one leaves. Where would we go? Our parents signed the docs and turned us over. Yes, Sheila, too. No matter where she is, she signed the doc. Does she use the drug? Does Rasta's da? We are pinned to CropCamp dirt with the weight of all that we don't know, all that we can't imagine or guess.

"I ask you to consider today's kickshaw experience with full knowledge. You will not lose consciousness, but you will lose coherence. That's why you are lying down, in solid touch with one another. We'll watch over you. The effects to your mobility and coordination will last for approximately two hours. Then, to give you time to absorb all that you've learned in the past three weeks and to begin your preparation for the transition week, we'll have a silent dinner. Then to your slices. No speech from now until first gong tomorrow morning."

Rasta's hand twitches. What if she jumps up? What if she bolts for the gate? Will they shoot her down? Tackle her? Force the kickshaw on her? Vape her?

I want the double. I want to feel the juices move down my throat and pulse through my veins. No matter how much I want to be fierce and true like Rasta, I am not. Machete wants to give us something sweet and good. She makes it so easy for us. We're flat on our backs, among comrades and friends, held by the alla-One. We have nowhere to go. The parents gave permission.

Micah places the kickshaw on my lips, and saliva shoots like a fountain. I part my lips and hold the extra-large morsel in my mouth, my pool of a mouth. The first swallow slides down my throat and the kickshine spreads. Rasta's hand burns in mine, body electric. Emmett's heat radiates sideways, and the connection on either side is so intense that my actual cells try to move first toward Emmett, then toward Rasta.

Sheila said that CropCamp would be good for me, and she was right. With or without the komodo, with or without Sully's jazz, I am better here. I am more a part of things than I've ever been, and for the first time in my life I have friends. Real friends. All of us, and all of the comrades in camps everywhere, all taking the same ride at the same time, one and the same, together. Whether the lizards speak or speak not, I live in a human skin, and I am with the humans.

The kickshaw's warm fluid spreads me in a puddle of earth. I suck in air, inflate my lungs. Color swirls and pulls me up and out of myself. Down below, my physical body morphs before my up-high eyes. Claws grow from my hands, but then they recede. Skin to scales and back to skin. Snout lengthens, shortens. My entire shape pulses and changes, misting from one to the other.

The other bodies shift, mostly in color. Sully pulses hot red, Emmett flows a deep green, and Nona's body is a sketch of charcoal, just an outline draped on the grass. Only Rasta looks like herself, unaffected. She holds the kickshaw between her teeth, refusing to touch it with her lips. Drool runs out the corner of her mouth.

How can she do that? How can she be that strong?

Lacey notices Rasta's resistance, walks over, and presses the kickshaw through her teeth and into her mouth. The outline of Rasta's body fades. A shimmer of deep purple light pulses between me and Sully. My body has lost all traces of lizard, but like Nona's, it has no color. Just a human outline.

Hours later, the gong rings. Rasta's hand twitches in mine. Emmett's fingers wrap around my other hand. I pull away and sit up, stiff-bodied. The Quint grass and the treetops are green, the sky a deepening blue. Still daytime. Nobody radiates colors, nobody shimmers or morphs. We all look like we look. Half-awake humans, coming up from under. I rub my face and yawn.

"Dinner in ten ticks," Machete says. "You must all be strictly on time. Remember, no speech. After dinner, you will go directly and silently to your slices. There will be no gongs tonight. Curfew begins immediately after dinner."

Curfew sounds like the worst sort of punishment. I want only to be close, to be touching. I want Emmett and Rasta closer. Sully is miles away, and I long for her to again reach out and touch my hair. How could I have knocked her hand away? Why would I do that?

All through dinner, I'm so aware of the separation. Each of us is locked up in our own bony skull, full of thoughts and feelings that we can't share. Nona and Sully and Machete and even Lacey and Micah — they each have an entire world inside of them, and I can't ever know it. I'm so completely alone. Even when Emmett bumps me, his skin and my skin keep us from really touching.

After dinner I go to my slice and pull the blankets over my head. I don't want to be separate. I don't want adult tumult. I don't want power, and I don't want responsibility. I want . . . Sheila.

My missing grief finally arrives. My eyes fill and tears spill out, dripping into my ears. My stomach and chest get in on the act with involuntary shudders and gasps. I huddle in a ball, and tears and fear erupt from the floor of my stomach, from the marrow of my bones. The grief shivers and wrenches and convulses me. It throws me on the ground, batters me in the wind, crashes into me head-on again and again.

"Lizard." Sully's voice. "Lizard, are you all right?"

"No speaking." Nona's voice is flat.

"But listen to her."

"She'll be okay."

"She doesn't sound okay."

Sully's voice is full of fear. Nona's is not. I cry harder.

"Lizard, should we get somebody?"

"Sully." Nona's voice smacks against the synthie walls. "If you try to leave this pie, I'll stab you with my secateurs."

Chapter Twenty-Five

SHEILA IS GONE. AFTER the night's wild grief ride, I wake in the morning to calm gray waters. She's gone. The komodo in my pocket is all that I have left from my childhood life. I cannot think about after CropCamp right now. I can barely think about this day.

Sully and I walk up to CounCircle together. The clouds moved back in overnight, layers of muted blankets. Thankfully, Sully is quiet. She doesn't mention my noisy grief in the night, or Nona's threat. Neither do I.

At CounCircle, Machete announces that a new schedule is posted in the Mealio. As everyone files in for breakfast, we clump around the bulletin board to see. My name is listed under Machete with DM on Monday, Wednesday, and Friday.

"Triples."

Sully points at my name.

Rasta wiggles in beside us. She arrived late to CounCircle with huge raccoon circles marking her elfin face. Her night had to be at least as rough as mine. Her da's betrayal must be killing her. I need to talk to her, about that and everything.

"I'm switched back to Ms. Kroschen," she says.

Aaron appears from behind, sets his hands on Sully's shoulders, and looks over our heads.

"I have Machete now? And look, three times a week!"

"Lizard, too." Sully points.

Aaron looks over at me. It's the first time we've looked directly at each other since the very first day. Unless you count my dream with the blood-dripping teeth.

"You and me, Lizard. Team Machete."

He holds up a fist. So different from the way Rasta holds up her spread hands to touch fingertips. Aaron smiles his easy jazzy smile, and I turn away. I'll not be part of any fisted alliance.

My first DM session takes me out of Block One right after breakfast, before I have a chance to talk with Rasta. I settle into the chair, leg curled under me. I study Machete's face as she reads something off the Deega. She looks different somehow. Maybe it's because she's not looking into my eyes, not speaking, not handing me kickshaw. Sitting there, she's just a person.

"Sheila didn't say that you could drug me."

Machete's eyes snap up, and for a brief instant, they are wide. Then they narrow, and her jaw juts slightly forward.

"You are here with full guardian permission," she says. "Just like every one of your comrades."

Her gaze is steady, but when I lick my lips I smell fear.

"I don't believe it. Maybe you're not lying, but you're not quite telling the truth."

She stares at me the way she stared at Sully that night outside of Lacey's slice. I do not look away. Sheila is gone. I have to find the fly peppers on my own.

"Kivali. This transition is difficult for every young comrade, and for you it will be harder than most. The loss you've sustained is terrible, and the timing is unfortunate. Everything must seem uncertain to you. But you're still responsible for your choices, every one of them."

Maybe. But when the komodo and I crawled out of the grief chasm this morning, we brought something new with us. I'm not sure yet what it is, but it's mine.

"Are you responsible for your choices, too?" I ask. "Every one of them?"

Again, Machete's eyes widen and then narrow. I'm poking a stick into a dark hole of danger, but for the first time, I sense something sensitive and afraid in there.

"You need to step carefully, Kivali. Don't let your past destroy your future."

"Why are you threatening me? What are you afraid of?"

I've gone too far. The stick and the hole and the teeth and the fear disappear in a flash. Machete smiles and leans back into the power of *them*.

"Sheila was a powerful force and a strong influence. She could make the untrue seem true, and the true seem untrue. She should have been honest with you."

"What do you mean?"

"There are some things that Sheila didn't tell you."

There's a lot that you don't know, isn't there?

I lick my lips again, and the fear I taste is my own.

"She did the very best that she could with you, but she had some mistaken ideas. You see, I know this because Sheila and I were once friends."

"I don't believe you."

My words don't fly out fast enough to cover my own eye-widening, and Machete, who is now leaning forward on her elbows, doesn't miss a thing.

"Oh, I think that you do. Why would I lie about that? Loyalty is a beautiful quality, but we must choose our loyalties carefully, and accept the truth when we hear it."

The leg curled under me pricks and stings. I concentrate on that peculiar feeling, zillions of tiny tingles. I don't want to look at Machete. If I look, I'll believe everything she says.

"You're so young." Machete's voice is now full of compassion. "Sometimes I forget how young you are. So much happened before you were even born, so much that you know nothing about. We were young and independent, too. We made our choices. You saw how Sheila lived. You see how I live now. She struggled to make a life. I bring my strengths to my community, and contribute, and live well."

Machete rises and comes around her desk. I uncurl my leg, dropping my tingle-dead foot on the floor. I stand and lightly stomp, backing so the chair is between me and Machete.

"Foot's asleep," I say.

"Kivali." Her voice is all kickshaw. "It's not fair that you have so much to deal with. It's too much, I know. It must feel as if you're utterly alone in the world now that Sheila is gone."

She steps closer and puts a steadying hand on my shoulder. She has never touched me before. There's no fear in her touch. It's all strength and gentleness. And she is sure of herself in a way that Sheila never was. She has the power of the gov behind her.

"Micah said that you came by yesterday when I was gone. I apologize for being unavailable. I think we need some more time together, the two of us. Come, you can relax in the Quarry this morning while I finish up some paperwork."

She could make the untrue seem true, and the true seem untrue.

Sheila? Or Machete?

Fly pepper or no, Machete is here, and Sheila is not. She wants to help me. I need her to want to help me. So I don't resist when she guides me out the door and down the hall to the Quarry stairs.

At the bottom, she signals me to slip out of my frods, and I have a vague memory of doing this before, years ago, the day that she told me about Sheila's disappearance. The day that Sully nipped my ear. Machete swings the door open, and I step through.

"You rest here," she says. "I'll check in on you before lunch, and we'll have some time to talk then."

She puts her hands on my shoulders again and turns me to face her. Her eyes are like her voice, chocolate brown, kickshaw smooth.

"Kivali, I want what is best for you. Now more than ever, your choices matter. Let me help you make them."

"Ms. Mischetti, may I ask you something?"

"Of course. Open communication is key."

"I thought that no one could vape from a camp. How did Donovan Freer do that?"

Machete's upper body twitches forward as if I'd punched her in the gut. She turns from me and leaves, closing the door behind her. I listen to her footsteps on the stairs. Another door closes above.

I reach out to the doorknob in front of me and check. The door is locked.

Chapter Twenty-Six

THE KOMODO SPITS STATIC from my pocket. Not audible, but plenty loud.

"I know." I pace a fast circle, climb up on beds to check the windows — they don't open — and check the door again. "I know."

We do not like being trapped. We don't like cages. Neither one of us. I sit on the edge of a bed, bring the little dragon out of my pocket, and set it on my palm. The inanimate lizard looks back at me without comment. I curl it into my palm and pace around again.

Sheila would have told me, wouldn't she? If she knew Machete? I don't know. There's a lot that I don't know.

As I turn to pace the other way, music suddenly surrounds me. I stop and turn in place, looking for the source of sound. There — a small speaker in the corner of the ceiling — and there, another. All four ceiling corners have tiny speakers. The music is soft and swirly and mild. It's — well, I suppose it's kickshaw music.

I pull a chair under one of the speakers and climb up, feeling around for a switch. The surfaces are smooth. Maybe it's a cam, too. I wave a hand in front of it, and hop off the chair to study the room more closely. The way they're angled, they see every part of the room.

I hide the komodo away in my pocket, and I fidget and pace with prickles of watching eyes all around me. Why, oh, why did I challenge her? I shouldn't have cut my hair. I should've just shut up like all the other comrades because now she can do anything to me. She can cage me forever. I could rot down here. Maybe she has Sabi hidden away down here like a wild dog. Maybe she'll set Sabi and the guides on me as punishment. . . . It will be bad. It will be worse than . . .

A full-blown picture explodes in my head, and it shakes me so much that I start to crawl under the bed — but no — the cams. I go to the privo and pull the curtain and crouch in the corner by the toilet, directly under the cam. It can't see me here. I wrap my arms around my knees, komodo clenched tightly in my fist, and try to stop the picture from playing, the picture of my always-dreaded future and past that I try to shut down, ignore, explain away, but there's no stopping it now.

That day in the school yard roars to life, bigger than ever.

   "It belongs with the girls."
   Shove.
   "Not with us. It's wearing boys' boots."

Shove.

"Well, we"— shove from Liam —"don't want it."

It still felt like a game, a bit of a game, even with Liam's icy eyes, a bit of push-rough-tumble, and I liked it — not this or that, just back and forth, like I was the ball and part of the game.

"Not ours."

Shove.

"Not ours."

Shove.

Then Liam caught me by the hood, wrenched the collar tight around my neck, and faced me toward the girls.

"What is it?" he yelled.

Then he laughed. And the girls I was facing, they laughed. And the boys behind, they laughed. Even Clare, who I thought was my friend. She didn't try to stop Liam. Neither did Niko.

"What is it?" yelled Amanda.

Not Amanda anymore, not Niko or Clare or Skyler or Jonas. Just a laughing swarm without smiles, pushing without hands — what IS it what ARE you what IS it what ARE you — and then I was on the ground and the voices blended and the boots kicked near my face, ice chips flying; and when I closed my eyes the terror roared in, louder than yelling or boot thuds, louder than anything, a roar so loud that it *drowned out the world until suddenly Sheila's words slipped beneath the roar and said,* Listen to your radio.

I squinched my eyes tighter and listened side-ways, and there!—*a whisper of whirr. I followed it through space to the place where I am me and that's all I need to be, where the sun shines warmth into my skin and the cool comfort surrounds me with-out human words, and I drifted forever, until forever ended and I opened my eyes.*

The kicking boots were gone, and I knew for a fact and true that I had no human friends. Nobody but Sheila. Just Sheila.

I shouldn't have worn the boy boots that day. Sheila used to let me, before Decision Day. I'd wear all boy clothes when we went to the other side of the city, and people thought I was a boy. Not even a question. I liked the game of back and forth. But after that day, it wasn't a game anymore. Nothing was.

That was the day when I truly believed the saurian stories. I was lizard-dropped, and only the lizards could save me. One day they'd come and help me do whatever good deed I'm supposed to do here on Earth, and then they'd take me away to the land of Lizard Radio where everyone is like me.

I really did believe that all along, tucked away in my secret insides. I believed it like I believed in Sheila, and then in Korm.

Now I have no Sheila. No Korm. I'll end up in Blight, and that day will go on and on and on, never-stopping, no gov, no SayFree, no regs, just the violents hating me for being me. I'll have nothing but a tiny silver toy.

I hold the komodo between my thumb and forefinger, shielded by my hand. We go nose to nose, and I search it for signs of intelligent life. The music stops abruptly. I scramble to my feet, jamming the komodo in my pocket as footsteps echo on the stairs. I run and land myself on a bed, trying to look as if I've been there all along.

Machete enters and closes the door behind her. She brings over a tray with a sandwich. She looks completely collected and Machete-ish, as if that last moment in the doorway never happened. She pulls a chair over.

"You must be terribly afraid."

She *was* watching me on cam. She knows that I was hiding in the corner.

"You're so vulnerable right now, and you have nowhere to turn."

She's so sad and so understanding, but the dragon doesn't trust her.

"Since Sheila disappeared, I've been doing some research on fostering regs. I've explored your options, and I think that I've come up with a solution that will work for all of us." She leans forward, elbows on her knees, hands clasped. Her eyes, looking up slightly, are earnest and warm and open. "I could foster you —"

Every breath of air sucks out of my cells. The lizard in my pocket is dead silent.

"— if you'd like that. You would stay here at CropCamp, and become a young guide until you're old enough to have more options. You'd receive your full agricultural education here if you like — you seem to enjoy working with the crops — or you could go to school. All of this depends, of course, on you cooperating so that you receive your camp cert."

She waits for me to speak. I cannot speak. My insides shift and recalibrate, unstack and restack. If I do as she says, I could live deep in the green and the skies, the crops and the oak grove. Days on end of that deep tangy smell and a home and comrades, kickshaw-flavored and under Machete's control. Completely human, completely safe. All I'd have to do is shut the lizard up. Forever.

"Kivali. I know that you had a rough time coming up. No disrespect to Sheila, of course, but there were some serious gaps in your guidance. I'm afraid that she indulged some of the very traits that make it hard for you to get along, hard to include yourself in the One. Is that true?"

That is true.

"Your comrades need you. I need you. You're exceptional, and I don't want to lose you. I'm willing to work very hard to help you, but I need you to work with me. I need you to commit to me, and to what we do here. I need you to make a firm decision."

My only other option is Rasta's MaDa. But is that an option? Even if they'd want me, would the gov let me go there? I wish that I could go home to Korm. Korm always speaks truth. Always.

"I can't decide until you tell me about Donovan Freer," I say.

A tinge of color rises up Machete's neck and across her face. I want to lick my lips and smell the fear again, but I hold perfectly still and wait.

"I will. You have to understand, Kivali. This is sensitive for me. You and I will talk more about vaping. But first, we need to settle some things between us. I want to teach you how to wield your power responsibly. I want to help you develop into a strong leader that your comrades can trust."

"I don't want to be a leader."

"But you are."

"Sully's more of a leader than I am."

"Sully likes power and knows how to use it. Your fear of power will, in the long run, make you a better leader."

"What about you?" I cannot stop the lizard from speaking. "Do you like power or fear it?"

Machete smiles. Not a big smile. Just a lip-tip.

"You also have uncanny nerve and interesting twists of perception."

"But do you like it or fear it?"

"We're talking about you, not me."

"But do you like it or fear it?"

Machete's eyes deliver one fiery knife-flick, and then she turns away. She stands and paces the room as I did earlier, several times around. I wait with a fast-beating heart. I'm holding power here, but I don't understand it. I fear it.

"Will you work with me or not?" she asks.

"Will you tell me the truth or not?"

Machete brings a hand up to rub her forehead, hard. Scrubbing it. As if she's trying to erase something. In the distance, the gong rings.

"We have a lot to talk about, but I can't do it now. I have to take care of some things. I'm afraid that I can't let you back out with your comrades, not until we have more time to reach an understanding."

"But you can't just keep me in here. Everyone's going to wonder where I am."

"I've told them that you're in the Quarry again. The stress of grief is too much, and you've fallen ill. You'll stay here until we can be sure that you're not contagious."

"Because what if I am."

"Exactly." Machete nods. "Because what if you are."

Chapter Twenty-Seven

THIS TIME, I HEAR the turn of the dead bolt.

I pace again, gripping the komodo in my pocket. The walls seem to have twitched closer together, pressing the air tense and dense around me. The music starts again.

I lie flat on the cot and draw a deep breath against the heaviness of my chest. The sharp corners of the komodo comfort my fingertips. I try to follow my breath to a place of clarity. I wish for the oak grove. I'd lie in the breezy grassy clearing, bask in the sunlight, and let it warm me inside and out. I'd relax there. Maybe I could tune in, or maybe Sully would come and find me. She likes the lizard in me. She's the one who named me Lizard. She believes in Sheila and the saurians. We'd lie in the soft grass and figure things out together.

Sully would run her fingers through my hair, and she'd pull me close, and my body would be so happy, every cell of my body, because it all feels so good. The sun, and Sully, and the birds in the oak tree overhead — it is very perfect. I've never been happier, never felt better. Sully's hand moves on my scalp, and suddenly, she grabs my hair hard and yanks my head back, her face right up close to mine.

"Kivali," she says. "We're all counting on you. Me, too."

My eyes pop open to the Quarry. No Sully. No grass, no birds, no sunshine. The kickshaw music plays on.

I do not like the cage, but I'm not afraid. The lizard is with me. I didn't have the komodo back in the school yard, but I have it now. And for some reason, Machete is at least a tiny bit afraid of me. Or of the lizard in me. Either way, it's good.

Hours later, the music fades into footsteps, and Machete enters without knocking.

"We have a problem," she says.

We?

Machete and I face off in the center of the Quarry.

"Your comrades are worried that something's terribly wrong with you. Three of them will come to visit this evening, and you will tell them about your distress, and the intensity of your grief." She glances down at my untouched sandwich. "And your upset stomach and your need for rest, and they'll be reassured."

"You want me to lie to my comrades?"

Machete walks over to the windows. "No need for you to lie." She speaks with her back to me. "In a position of leadership, you learn to limit what you say. You tell carefully chosen truths. This is one of those times. Until you're on more solid footing, and until you and I can find an understanding between us, throwing out untested truths and half-formed ideas to your comrades could cause tremendous harm." She turns to face me. "If you think it through, you'll see that I'm right."

I shake my head. I don't see anything.

"Kivali, I won't let you bring harm to the other comrades. I don't want to expul you, but I will. You'll leave here with no cert, and the gov will choose an appropriate foster for a CropCamp disciplinary expul. You don't want that."

"You'd expul me for asking about Donovan Freer?"

She turns away but not before I see it again, that flash of vulnerability. The moment where the power balance tips. It's brief, though. When she spins back to face me, her eyes are sharp and clear.

"I am offering you the kind of dedicated care and attention that I've given to very few campers over the years. Beyond that, I'm offering you a place to call home. Choose that, or choose to fight me and leave this place. One or the other."

You must be brave, and you must be smart. A sudden ache for Sheila pierces through me so sharp, it almost takes my breath.

"You have tremendous potential. If you decide, if you make a full commitment, then and only then will I answer all of your questions, because I know that you'll use the information with care. I'll teach you to step outside the lines and examine the ambiguity that troubles you. That's always been the problem for you, yes? Ambiguity? This and that? Not one or the other?"

Yes. No one has ever articulated that for me so well. Not Korm, not Sheila.

"I'm not asking you to lie to your friends. I'm asking you to choose the manner and content of your truth-telling carefully. Learn to understand that gray area so you don't fear it."

"Is that what you do?"

"Yes. Remember what I said at the beginning of CropCamp? If you leave here without a cert, it'll be because of your own choices. Kivali, you're one in a thousand, maybe one in ten thousand. Trust me, I've seen many young people over the fifteen years I've been directing this camp. If we lose you, it'll be a terrible loss."

The room reeks of fear — and not just mine. The air around Machete vibrates with it.

"Which three?" I ask.

"Sully. Rasta. Emmett."

Machete crosses to the door and stands in front of it, hands on her hips.

"I have a camp to run, and timing is difficult at this point in our program, but I've cleared my schedule for tomorrow. Directly after breakfast, you and I will talk through all of this and work some things out. Then you can move back out to Pieville with your comrades, and you and I will work together for your good and the good of the camp and community. I trust you, Kivali. I'm asking you to trust me."

"I'll tell them that I'm resting," I say. "But I'll also tell them that I'll be out by tomorrow at lunch, for sure."

Machete smiles.

"You know more than you think you do. You will be a pure pleasure and challenge to work with over the weeks to come."

"Wait." I stop her as she pulls the door open. "How did they get you to agree to a visit?"

"They asked. I agreed."

"That's a carefully chosen truth," I say. "If you trust me so much, then tell me."

Machete closes the door again and leans against it.

"They threatened a camp-wide sit-down strike if I didn't let them see you. Didn't even ask me — just came forth with the threat. I must say, I'm tempted to let it happen so I can see how they work it out, how they get everyone to cooperate. It'd be an interesting and informative exercise. But they needn't resort to threats to see their ill and grieving comrade. It's a perfectly reasonable request. Besides, I thought that they made excellent choices in the delegation."

I hold back the huge smile that dances up from my chest. It's not just me and the lizard. We have friends, and they are brilliant. Rasta's heart. Sully's leadership. And with Emmett in, of course Machete would say yes.

"What time are they coming?" I ask.

"After Cleezies. Fifteen-tick visit. No longer, because we don't want to wear you out. I'll be here during the entire visit, of course, for your safety and guidance."

Chapter Twenty-Eight

SULLY. I'LL SEE SULLY before nightfall. And Rasta, and Emmett. I've only been away one day, but it seems like forever. I haven't talked to Rasta alone since early Sunday. I really, really want to know what she thinks about her da signing off on the kickshaw drug.

Unless . . . a flaming arrow pierces my thoughts.

What if he didn't?

Your parents and guardians know of this drug, of this practice. Is that a carefully chosen truth?

I press the komodo's metal claws into the pad of my thumb as I pace. If I trust Machete, if I decide to go that route, it'll be so easy. But it's wrong, something is wrong, something is bigger than wrong, and the lizard knows it and I tried burying the lizard deep in the earth but it popped back up. Rasta knows that it's wrong, too, but she doesn't know any more about the what and why than I do. If only there were someone who could —

Nona.

I jerk the dragon out of my pocket and hold it close to my ear because I could swear it spoke. The komodo doesn't speak or squirm in my hand. I scratch my ear for the benefit of anyone watching me on cam, and put the komodo back in my pocket.

Nona. Back to pacing. Nonanonanona. I haven't thought about her one time through all of this. *You're the only one she actually likes.* That's what Rasta said. Why isn't she part of the delegation? Sully would never include her, that's why. Besides, she answers questions with questions, like Machete. Maybe she's a Machete spy. No. Not with the way her face pinches when she says "Ms. Mischetti." Not a spy, but something different. Something different from everyone else.

The evening slowly ticks away. The music stays off. The gong rings for dinner, then for Cleezies. Now it's Social, and everyone is on the Quint. The room gradually dims, and my stomach twists and writhes and chews on itself. I want Rasta. And Sully. And Emmett. I want to be with my comrades. If I cooperate with Machete, she'll let me out of here, and I'll tell Rasta everything, *every* everything, and we can decide things together, maybe convene with Nona.

Finally, footsteps on the stairs. Machete opens the door and switches on a dim overhead leddie.

"Get in the bed." No kickshaw voice now. "They're waiting upstairs."

"Why in the bed?"

"Because you and I have not yet resolved anything. Because this is my camp, and I can expul you — and I will, here tonight, if you don't cooperate with me on this completely. Don't make me do it, Kivali. I will."

I cross my arms and look into her eyes. I try to look past the dark brown and the black centers, into the depths. I smell no fear. She is solidly in charge. The darkening room casts deep shadows beneath her eyes. She looks old, older than Sheila.

"If I tell them that you're holding me here because I asked questions, then you'll expul me?"

"Immediately."

I get in the cot, still fully clothed. Tomorrow I'll be out, and Rasta and I will talk, and I can go forward from there. I pull the covers up, and shove the komodo down to the point of my pocket. Machete nods, steps into the hallway, and calls up the stairs.

"Come on down."

Rasta comes through the door first, breaking a huge grin at the sight of me. Sully is right behind her, and then Emmett.

"Lizard!" Sully's voice is the best thing I've ever heard. "So you've had it with the crops, have you? Couldn't hack the dirt under your fingernails anymore?"

"Not too much noise." Machete comes up behind Sully, finger to her lips. "We don't want to tire her."

Sully whirls, dips a shoulder, and crashes into Machete's stomach. Machete folds with an *oof* and slams into the wall. Sully jumps on Machete, and they both hit the floor.

"Go!" she yells.

I thrash my legs free of the blanket as Rasta and Emmett practically levitate me off the cot.

"No!" Machete yells from the floor. "Kivali, no!"

"Come on," Rasta rasps in my ear.

She yanks my arm with a strength that I wouldn't have guessed. I look over my shoulder and catch a glimpse of Sully-Machete tangle. Sully laughs out loud as she tries to contain Machete's thrashing limbs, and Rasta and Emmett hustle me out the door. Emmett closes it and turns the dead bolt, locking Sully in with Machete. I turn back, can't leave Sully in there, but Rasta pulls me along.

"Sully knows what she's doing; come on."

Up the stairs, the three of us. Down the hall and through the foyer we go, out into the gray-dusk. Cool raindrops pelt my face as we run across the gravel. Gravel jabs at the soles of my feet.

"She needs her frods," says Emmett.

"No time." Aaron steps out from the dense tangle of wet green at the edge of the gravel lot. "This way."

"This way where?" I ask.

"Hiding place in the woods." Rasta pulls me along. "Aaron knows the way."

Emmett nudges me from behind, and Rasta pulls my hand, and we follow Aaron's broad shoulders through the gray and the rain.

Blur, it's all a blur. The dripping trees, the cold damp, Aaron's back and Rasta's hand and Emmett close on my heels, from the enforced quiet of the Quarry to this wild wet ride on the wind. The cool dirt feels better on my feet than the gravel, but I still hit every sharp stick and root, stubbing and scraping.

A wet, leafy branch smacks me in the face. I stop to wipe my eyes, and right there, fear catches up with me and douses the fires of escape and excitement. We've gone too far. They'll Blight us all, every one of us, they'll throw us with the violents, the Sabis and Liams with their empty icy eyes and —

"Stop!" I yell.

Aaron and Rasta stop. Emmett runs into me from behind. We're at the top of a rise. The path ahead drops off sharply into denser brush and creeping darkness.

"Wait!" I'm breathing hard. "We have to go back. We can't leave Sully."

"No!" Rasta's hair plasters flat to her head, and her eyes are enormous. "There's no back."

I look over Rasta's head to Aaron.

"Why are you in this?" I ask.

"Sully." He wipes his face and shoves the dark curly hair back from his forehead. "Follow that switchback path." He points down the slope.

"You're not coming with us?" Emmett's voice cracks.

"No. I told her that I'd show you the way, and I've done that — keep going, and you'll find the grove. I'm out."

Rasta grabs his arm.

"Aaron, you can't be out," she says. "None of us can, don't you get it?"

Aaron turns to go back the way we came but Rasta is latched on, and Emmett steps up to block his way.

"We have to stay out of her control," says Rasta.

Aaron shakes her loose, flinging his arm up, and she loses her balance. She teeters for a long, slow-mo moment, grasping at air. Then Rasta falls. A tumbling shape, down and down, she crashes through the brush and the rain to the gathering gloom below.

Chapter Twenty-Nine

EMMETT AND I HURTLE down the rough slippery slope, pushing and holding, grabbing at bushes and trees to slow our descent, trying not to fall and not to stop and not to disintegrate in the darkness. We slide, splitting apart at a tree trunk and stopping on either side of the dark crumple on the ground next to a big rock.

"Rasta!"

Her posture is all wrong, the twist of her torso, the angle of her head. Emmett grabs my hand.

"Don't move her."

He takes off his warmer and drapes it over her.

"Go get someone."

"What happened to Aaron?"

I look up from where we came. Nothing but dark and steep and leaves. The night has swallowed it all. Just below us is a narrow path leading into the woods and I take it, hoping it will lead to Pieville. I squint and stumble, cursing Aaron and looking for known ground, any entry to the familiar. Wet grass licks my ankles, and the occasional vine or prickle darts out to snag my skin. I push forward through the deepening dark and steadily dripping rain.

The cold, heart-pounding *what if Rasta is dead, or paralyzed, or . . .* stumble goes on and on until the tangled woods open to something a gray-shade lighter. I run toward it, and the oak grove throws itself open as if it's been waiting for the touch of the bare soles of my feet. My grove. Aaron could never have led me here; it's mine. The grass is blessedly non-prickery, and I run into the center and scan for the main path to Pieville. The grove is surrounded by a tangled snarl of darkness, and I can't see the path or much of anything else.

Despite my channel-locked focus on hurry-up, I pause, because — what *is* that? Some sort of a current, a pulse — a magnetic something — embraces me in the center of the grove. It wants me to stay, but I can't leave Emmett and Rasta alone in the cold, going under, drowning in the dark. I shake myself loose from whatever it is and walk to the edge, hand held out in front of me until I touch wet leaves. From there I skirt the edge of the opening, trailing my left hand, feeling for the break in brush that means the opening to the main path and Pieville and people and help.

Finally, open space. I grope my way into it, away from the force in the center of the grove. I can tell that I'm on the path by the cold-packed mud beneath my feet, and I run sightless through now-solid black, hands out in front of me, one high and one low, so that I don't bash into a tree. I navigate by feel — tangle and thistle to the left; I veer to the right. Deeper dead leaves and underbrush on the right; I steer to the left. I cannot see at all, not a shadow, not a glimmer.

"Lacey!" I yell into the dripping dark. "Lacey, are you there?"

Nothing. Fikewise fiking fike.

"Anybody? Hey, help!"

Rain smatters leaves all around me.

"Help! Hey, help!"

A leddie shines through fabric ahead, and I run toward it.

"Who's out there?"

"It's me, Lizard."

A door zips open, and Risa pokes her head out. Somehow I got completely off the path and came up the back way on Pie Three.

"Rasta's hurt, back past Lacey's slice. Can you run up and get someone? I'm barefoot, no leddie."

"Get who?"

"I don't care, anybody! Someone who can do something."

Light glows in other slices. Pen leddies bob toward us.

"What's going on?"

"Rasta's hurt."

"What happened?"

"Lizard? I thought you were sick. Are you okay?"

"Where is she?"

Risa is ready to go, rain-warmer on and pen leddie in hand.

"There's an oak grove, a big clearing just right of the main path, way past Lacey's slice. If you bring them to the grove and yell, we'll hear you. Rasta's just beyond."

The thin beam of Risa's leddie bounces off toward the slope

up to the fields. Adrenaline-jacked and exhausted, I turn in the other direction, back to the grove, back to Rasta and Emmett. A hand grabs my shoulder.

"Come with me."

No mistaking Nona's voice, and I almost fall to the ground with relief. *Nona. Nonanonanona.*

"Come on," I say. "Rasta's this way."

"Let's get a blanket to keep her dry till they get there."

Sense in that. Nona pulls me past the gathering crowd to our pie. She zips open my slice, follows me in, turns on the leddie, points at the cot.

"Sit."

"No time! We gotta get back there. She'll be freezing and drowning and—"

"You can't even talk with your teeth chattering like that. At least dry your face."

She throws me a towel, and I sink my face into it, the rough warmth of it, the dry of it, just for a second. The ends of the towel move, rubbing my hair dry. Nona takes the entire towel from me and moves it across my head, the back of my neck. She rubs the towel over me and tousles me around until I land back in my soaking wet shivery body.

"Put on socks and boots; your feet are wrecked." She pulls the towel away from my face. "I'm getting blankets and my rain warmer. Hurry up."

Nona zips out. I yank socks and boots onto my battered feet. The beam of Nona's leddie pierces the fabric wall.

"Let's go," Nona calls.

Nona carries a blanket wrapped in a rain-warmer. Off we go, the leddie lighting a few steps in front of us. As we turn into the grove, I hitch to a stop. The pulsing. It's stronger now, and although it clearly comes from the center of the grove, it rebounds in my gut. I'm suddenly dizzy, a little bit nauseous. I stop, put my hands on my thighs, try to steady myself. Nona puts a hand on my back.

"Where's Rasta?" she asks.

"This way." I stand, shake my head, and move on. "Emmett's with her."

I reach out to touch the leaves, and the cool water on my fingertips lessens the dizzying pull of the — what *is* that? — in the center of the grove. A rough wet oak trunk helps me focus as I skirt the opening, searching for the narrow path on the opposite side. Nona shines the leddie beam from behind, and we find the break in the trees. The path is narrow but definitely discernible. Nona grabs me by the shoulder again, and I sidestep, almost losing my balance entirely.

"I'll find Rasta and Emmett," she says. "You have a different call to answer."

She flashes the leddie back toward the center of the grove, and it illuminates moving shadows and shapes. As I turn and squint to see what they are, Nona pushes me between the shoulder blades so hard that I stumble forward and fall on my face in the wet grass.

Chapter Thirty

I RAISE MY FACE from the dank earth to an open darkness that rolls with texture and movement. The magnetic pulse surrounds me and is me. It is the amplified essence of Lizard Radio, and it saturates all sensation, inner and outer.

I nose the crumple in front of me, recognize it, and roll into my lizard skin. I stand, rising horizontally off the ground on four short, powerful legs. The beat sways me from snout to the tip of my heavy tail. I take a step, and my claws drag across the grass. I pause, raise my head and chest, and flick at the night air with my tongue, tasting the sounds and scents of mystery and wonder.

Scores of geckos emerge from the earth, and agamids drop from the oaks. Chameleons and skinks and whiptails skitter through the underbrush and spring into the clearing. A cluster of water monitors and a Gila monster stomp to the rhythm, and six-lined race runners ripple circles through the grass. Sungazers and anoles loop and pitch, and tiny teiids gambol and stutter-skip. Tokays dash across my broad back, croakity-chirping as they launch in every direction.

I plant my feet on the rock of the planet and flick out my tongue to draw sweet water from the grass. I inhale the furious wind, igniting a sizzle of mad joy and crystal-dark clarity. I flow into the elements like hot lava. Each step, each motion feeds my komodo heart and fires a fierce love for the world, for the sky and the dark and the night and the rain. I roar from the core of my soul, my boy-girl human-lizard bender-comrade soul.

A reply comes from the dark treetops overhead, a tiny raw *caw*, a wing-flutter in the breath between dragon beats that catches my throat for a quick second. But then the saurian song rises and flames through my heart, lighting up the grove.

I dance with the lizards. I bellow the beauty of the night, surrounded by others like me, others who see me and know me for exactly what I am. I sway and ripple and stomp in a rush of ecstasy that extends backward and forward in time, never-ending and never a start, on and on and —

A human hand materializes from above. It seizes my left front leg at the joint and flips me on my back. I snap and thrash, but it pins and holds me.

"Easy, Kivali. Easy."

Another hand lands gently on my cheek. I jerk away and scrabble backward. A blanket of pressure and restriction envelops me and pins my arms to my sides.

"Kivali, shh, come here. You're cold as ice."

Machete wraps a blanket around me in the dripping dark, smothering me in a full-body hold. I jerk to one side and the other, pushing her away, and waver up to my own two feet.

"Where's Rasta?"

My human voice is so small in the night.

"I'm taking you back to the Quarry." Again Machete pins me, the blanket trapping my arms. "We'll talk there."

I thrash loose from the blanket and her grip again, and step back.

"Tell me now."

The rain has stopped. Machete flicks on a leddie. She bends over, picks up the blanket, and hands it to me.

"Come on. Walk with me." Her voice is no longer soft. "You need to get inside. You're chilled."

"Tell me." I push the blanket away and cross my arms over my chest. "I'm not moving until you tell me."

We stand in silence. The pitch-black chill of the grove dampens everything. The silence stretches longer and thinner until finally, Machete breaks it.

"Kivali. I'm so sorry. Rasta is dead."

The komodo roars from my core, but the sound that emerges is something between a whimper and a moan. I fall to the ground and cover my head. Cold. I shake so hard, it hurts my teeth and rattles my ribs.

"Ms. Mischetti?"

Footsteps approach in the dark.

"I've found her, Lacey."

A light bobs through the bushes. Lacey's leddie flashes across Machete and then into my eyes. I turn away from the light.

Machete drops the wet blanket on me. My teeth begin to chatter, and I wrap into the blanket.

"Lacey, please get dry clothes from Kivali's slice, and another blanket, and put them in the Quarry. Then go tell the other guides that we'll meet before CounCircle — at first gong. Guides, counselors, teachers. Then get some sleep. I'll need you tomorrow."

The light turns and disappears, leaving the two of us. The chattering of my teeth rattles my skull.

"Let's go, Kivali. We need to get you somewhere warm."

I let her pull me to my feet and steer me to the path. I am frozen numb and cannot manage anything beyond one step and the next. We continue through Pieville, up the slope, across the fields, and into the main building. As we cross the wooden porch, I pull the blanket around my head like a hood, shielding me from the light.

I descend the stairs and enter the Quarry without turning or removing the blanket. Machete comes behind me, flipping on the overhead leddie. Lacey got here ahead of us; clean coveralls lie folded on the end of the cot, along with an extra blanket.

"Get a hot shower," she says. "I'll check back on you in fifteen ticks."

The door closes. I stand beneath the hood of wet blanket, wavering on two narrow, clawless feet. My belly is up off the ground and exposed. Shivers rack my body with each inhalation. My teeth clack and grip and rattle. I stick out my tongue to taste the air, and it gives me nothing. Like being blindfolded.

I step over to the curtained corner and turn the handle to hot. Water smatters around the circular drain. Steam rises from the concrete floor. I drop the blanket, unlace my boots, unbutton and drop my coveralls, and peel off my cold, clammy T-shirt and boxers. My human skin is smooth. No leathery beads, no protection, no defense. Just cold chicken flesh. I step beneath the hot water. This shower has a lot more pressure than the ones in Pieville.

The water pours on my head, over my face, across my body. I cross my arms over my chest and turn so the water pounds hot on the back of my neck. I squinch my eyes tight. On the backs of my lids, Rasta's form tumbles again into the rain and the dark. I snap my eyes open and try to step back, away from that image, but it follows me. My head spins dizzy and my stomach turns, threatening to climb up my throat.

I want the komodo. I do. I want it. I step out of the shower still dripping and shove my hand in the clammy wet pocket. Nothing. I check the other one. Nothing and nothing. It's not there — it's got to be. Again, I even check the back pockets. I rush over to the dry coveralls and check them just in case. Nothing.

I towel off in silence. The towel is harsh. It hurts my skin. I pull on the dry coveralls. I wish that Lacey had brought dry socks and boxers and a T-shirt, too.

The doorknob turns, and the door opens.

"You're dressed?" Machete's eyebrows furrow with displeasure. "You should be in bed."

No. If I get in the bed, then I'll sleep. And if I sleep, I'll wake up and it will be tomorrow, and the lizards in the grove will be the dream, and Rasta gone will be the reality.

"Did you lose this?" She holds up the dragon. My komodo dragon is in Machete's hand. "I found it on the ground near you. It's an interesting piece of work. I was sure that you wouldn't want to lose it."

"Give it to me."

"Kivali." She shakes her head with such sadness. "You've had one horrible shock after another. You must sleep. It'll help."

"Give it to me!"

Yelling is a mistake.

"I'll return it to you tomorrow. I'd like to examine it more closely. It's so beautifully crafted. For now, you need to settle down." She holds out a kickshaw. "We'll talk all of this through in the morning. I'm here for you. You're not alone."

The sight of kickshaw draws a warm run of water in my mouth. I can see no way to get the dragon so I palm the kickshaw, clenching my fingers tightly around it.

"I know that you care deeply about this community, about your comrades. You made some foolish, tragic decisions. We need to set this right, all of us together. Your comrades will need you tomorrow, and so will I."

"Where's Sully?"

"She's asleep."

"Will she be expulled?"

"We'll work everything out in the morning. For now, I think we all could use a little sleep."

I hold the kickshaw up in front of my face. Sweet little kickshaw. It is the way to CropCamp and humanity, to alla the One, to being an *us* in the *them*. It's my conduit to a safe and protected life with strong guidance and guardianship.

Looking directly into Machete's eyes, I tear the kickshaw in half, then in half again. I shred it like Rasta did in the field, walk over to the privo, and flush it. Only then do I face her.

"You're upset." She nods. "I understand."

She places another kickshaw on the little table by the cot.

"Sometimes," she says, "we get a second chance."

She crosses to the door and looks back at me with all of that sympathy. She pulls the door shut behind her with the familiar click of dead bolt. The kickshaw sits quietly on the table and waits for me.

It would be so easy. It would taste so good. I haven't eaten since breakfast, hours and a lifetime ago. I'm so hungry, and I'm so tired, and it would not hurt one thing in the world for me to take it. Nobody would know. I can't do anything useful for the next several hours, anyway. I'm locked in. I have no choice.

Kickshaws are not good.

I rip up the second kickshaw and flush it before I can change my mind.

Chapter Thirty-One

I PACE THE QUARRY. I want out. I tried to be a comrade with the humans, but now I've danced with the dragons, and I will not be tamed. I pace the other way, around and around. As long as I stay awake and pacing, I know what I am.

The dead bolt clicks. The doorknob turns, and I back against the wall. Machete has come to toss kickshaws into my cage. They'll pile high until I finally break down and eat one, and then I'll go on a feeding frenzy. I'll glut myself with kickshaws, strings of kickshaw saliva hanging from my serrated teeth until I collapse in a kickshaw coma and —

It's not Machete. It's Nona.

Nonanonanona.

"Come on," she whispers.

I grab my socks and boots and follow her on the tippiest of toes. It's hard to contain myself in quiet. I want to roar up the stairs and burst into the night air. Instead, we slink up and slide through the cracked-open door at the top into the entry hall, all lights off and doors closed. We creep out, nestling the screen door carefully into its frame.

The rain has stopped. The moon is big and bright, and it backlights a bank of clouds. We skulk around the edge of the Quint and stop in the bushes on the far side, away from the yard lights. I sit to put on my boots, and wet grass soaks my bum. Nona kneels beside me.

"Where are the others?" I ask.

"Emmett's back in Pieville. Sully is locked in a Quarry room like yours."

"Aaron?"

"Probably hiding back in his slice. Emmett told me what Aaron did. Not a surprise."

"Why are you out?"

"I was never in. I did nothing wrong — I just helped in a time of great need. Ms. Mischetti commended me on my commitment to community." She drops beside me on the wet grass. "I am committed. Just not the way she thinks."

"What way then?"

"Your way. Donovan's way."

My pulse begins thudding to the beat of Lizard Radio. Nona is a saurian.

"I didn't mean to push you so hard," Nona says. "Did I hurt you?"

"Do you listen to Lizard Radio?"

"What?"

"Did the lizards tell you to push me into the grove?"

"No lizards." She shakes her head. "No radio."

The lizard beat skips and fades.

"It was a knowing," she says.

"What's a knowing?"

Nona heaves a huge sigh, as if I've just asked her to recite all of the SayFree tenets. A cloud slides over the moon, casting a layer of chill and I rub my palms together, trying to up some body heat.

"Sometimes I hear things." She is hesitant in a way that I've never heard Nona be. I nod, and she goes on. "Not with my ears but sort of inside. Like coming to CropCamp." I nod again, and she starts to sound more like herself. "I hadn't seen Donovan for years but I got the knowing, and I asked to come to this camp. I saw him when we pulled into the driveway, walking behind Saxem."

Nona's eyes fill and shine in the moonlight.

"We talked before orientation that first night." A tear slides down her cheek, but her voice stays flat-footed. "He was still all Donovan."

"He didn't take the kickshaw." I remember so clearly the way he dropped it and covered it with his foot. "He ditched it."

"Nobody can ever make Donovan not be Donovan. He just is."

Her mouth moves in a sideways tug, and another tear spills, and I know. She feels about him the way that I do about Sully.

"So he still is?" I ask. "Even though he vaped?"

"Of course he is."

"You talk to him?"

A spark of Sheila-hope flickers, but Nona shakes her head.

"Not exactly. It's more like . . ." She scrunches her eyes closed, looking at something deep inside. "Everything is a particle and a wave at the same time. You know that, right?"

"No."

"Well, it is." She opens her eyes, and they are no longer leaking. "It's physics. I think vaping means becoming all wave."

"And the wave can talk?"

"No, no. It's not like that. Not like we sit down and have chats. It's a knowing, like I've always had, only it's from him. I think it is, anyway. Feels like it. I want it to be."

Knowings and waves. Beneath the drippy dark of the moon cloud, huddling on cold wet grass after a Quarry breakout, they seem as possible as Lizard Radio.

"So is dying like that, too? Is Rasta a wave now?"

"I don't think so," she says. "I think that vaping is vaping, and dying is dead."

I hug my knees in close, drop my head, and rock back and forth. Vaping is vaping, and dying is dead. Sheila's a wave. Rasta is gone. Nona loves Donovan. Lizards in the grove.

"Lizard. We don't have much time. Rasta's da is coming at seven, and Ms. Mischetti will—"

"Rasta's da?" That yanks my head up. "How do you know?"

"I listened under her window when she was reporting to the gov. She lied about everything. She said that Rasta and Sully and Emmett were on an innocent lark. Didn't mention your name. Not once."

"But why is he coming here?"

214

She looks out across the Quint. The moon has escaped the clouds again, and Nona's features are bright as day. Sharp-hook nose and stubborn chin.

"Docs," she says. "There are docs to sign before he can take — you know."

Even with the moon, the night is so thick, so hushed.

"Does everyone know what happened?" I ask.

"Just me and Emmett. And Lacey. Ms. Mischetti said that she'd tell the camp in the morning. Set up grief counseling and all."

"Not even Sully?"

"I don't know. I didn't see Sully. She was already locked in."

"Can you get her out?" I ask. "Like you did me?"

Nona looks at me sideways.

"We have no time for the likes of Sully," she says.

"We do," I say. "Emmett, too. And Aaron, I suppose. They're in it as much as we are."

Her eyebrows lift. I wish that she didn't know so much.

"Aaron?"

"Safer to have him with us than not. Do you know which pies he and Emmett are in?"

"Emmett's in the third. You're not going down to Boyville, are you?"

"I am. You get Sully, and I'll get them, and we'll meet in the grove."

Nona shifts, turns to face me directly.

"What was in that grove?" she asks.

215

"Go get Sully," I say.

The lizards felt realer than real and more powerful than a thousand Machetes. I don't know where they went, but they'll come back. They have to. No one else can free us from this endless tangle of night.

"I'll get Emmett and Aaron," I say. "We'll meet in the grove and figure out the next part together. We have to hurry, before it gets light."

I stand and pull the wet coveralls away from my bum. Nona looks up at me.

"It's so risky," she says. "Getting the boys all the way over there. Can't we meet somewhere in the middle?"

"The grove," I say.

Still Nona sits there, looking up at me.

"I know that Sully doesn't like me, but don't cut me out, okay?"

"I won't cut you out."

"Don't. I can't stay here. It's wrong."

I shiver deep on that. Nona and her knowings.

"Promise that you won't leave me here," she says.

"I won't. I'm getting Aaron, aren't I? You think I'd include Aaron and leave you?"

"But promise."

"Okay." It seems like an easy enough promise to make. "I promise."

Nona gets up and heads back to the office building. I make a run for the boys' Pieville.

Chapter Thirty-Two

THE BOYS' PIEVILLE IS set up very similarly to our side, and even in the shifting moony darkness it's easy to find the third pie. The problem is that I don't know how to wake Emmett without waking anyone else. I walk around the pie, trying to guess which slice might be his. One slice has an open window, and I step up close, framing my hands around my eyes so I can see in.

I am nose to another nose, and I leap back with an out-loud squeak. Emmett steps out and wraps himself around me, startling me again so badly, we almost both go down. We bobble and recover and then he's right in my face, hollow-eyed and quivering.

"I tried," he whispers.

I put a finger to my lips and fast-foot it away from the pies with Emmett right behind me. Once we get clear, I turn to him.

"I tried," he says again. "I did. I tried so hard to find a pulse, kept telling myself that it was because of the rain and the dark and the shivering, and if I tried harder, I'd find it, or make it happen, or —"

I put a hand on his shoulder. I've never reached out to touch someone else. Never, not once in my life. He leans into my hand so hard, I almost lose my balance again on the steepness of the slope, so I pull him toward me a bit, and he collapses against me.

No quiet tear-trail on the cheek for Emmett. He's crying for real, sobbing even, and I don't know what to do with my hands. I pat his back a couple of times like I've seen people do, and then I take his shoulders and gently set him away from me because his crying is jiggling something loose in my own chest and I'm not ready for that.

"Where's Aaron's slice?" I ask.

Emmett shakes his head, and I nod.

"No," he says. "Aaron says to leave him out of anything we do or he'll go to Machete. Says he's not going to Blight for Sully or anyone else."

"Come on, then," I whisper. "We've got to hurry."

I don't want to be relieved, but I am. The dream-memory of Aaron's bloody smile looms a little too vivid in the dark. Besides, I don't want him in my grove again. I'd like to be above that, but I'm not.

Emmett and I pop up near the Pavilion, and I scan the grounds. The moon is winning its hide-and-chase game with the clouds. I'm not cold anymore — with all the nerves and running around, I've broken a sweat.

"You're not kickshawed?" I ask.

Emmett pulls a kickshaw out of his pocket. I take it from him and rip it up and grind it into the dirt with my boot.

"I knew I shouldn't take it," whispers Emmett.

I nod, still watching the Quint and the fields. I hope Nona got Sully out okay. You'd think those Quarry rooms would be more secure. But then, how secure does anything need to be? The bio-sensor corral gives Machete all the security that she needs.

We skirt behind the Pavilion and the far side of the fields, around the toolshed to the potato field, and then slip-n-slide down the path into the girls' Pieville. I keep expecting Lacey to leap out at any second, but Pieville is dark and quiet. When we approach Lacey's slice I put an arm out to slow Emmett.

He takes my hand, and I pull him past, quiet and easy. The woods help us sneak along. Nothing rattles or cracks on the wet ground, and the wind stirs the treetops and smatters leftover rain on the leaves and the ground, covering the sound of our movement and breath.

Bringing Emmett to the girls' side is clear folly by human standards, but tonight is a new world. When we get to the grove, the saurians will be there. Not just dancing geckos, but actual adult physical saurians. Not waves but particles. They'll push my hair off my sweaty forehead and warm the uncertain chill in my spine and tell me that I'm a good lizard, a fine lizard, and that I am enough. They will take charge. They will take care of me, and of Emmett and Nona and Sully.

All the way to the grove I repeat this to myself, make it loud and true in my brain because it has to be true. I need it to be true. I stop just before the turn into the grove to listen for the lizard pulse. Something rustles on the path, and I spin and Emmett latches onto me. Sully stops smack, and Nona runs into her from behind. I step away from Emmett, putting space between our bodies.

"We don't have much time." Nona cuts the freeze-n-hush as she steps between me and Sully, breaking our eye-lock. "Come on."

She walks into the grove, just like it's the Quint or the potato field or anywhere else. I follow her with a hammer-fast heart.

The grove is perfectly still. No saurians. No rescue mission. No dancing lizards, no singing geckos. Just wet grass and wind and a dapple of leaf-patterned moonlight. I turn away from the others and fold my arms over my suddenly sickish stomach.

Why aren't they here? Korm's gone. Sheila's gone. Rasta's gone. The saurians are all I have left.

"So what's the plan?" Nona asks.

I turn and bump Emmett, who's right on my heels. Nona comes closer. I try to catch Sully's eyes, but she's looking somewhere over my right shoulder.

"The plan," I say.

After a very long, empty pause, Sully meets my eyes. No warm glow, no flashing lights.

"Yes, Lizard." Her out-loud words cut sharp, harsh. "You know, the plan. Nona said that you had one."

"Why did you say that?" I turn on Nona.

"Because you're the one to save us." She nods. She's sure. Emmett nods, too. "Donovan said."

"Who the fike is Donovan?" Sully crosses her arms. "And when does the saving start?"

That is the question of the night. The saurians aren't here, and neither is Donovan Freer. My dragon is under Machete's control. There are no otherworldly saviors. Nothing but disintegrating options for the four of us. I can only see one way out.

"The plan is this," I say. "Nona and Emmett, you go back to your slices. Emmett, you are super-sorry tomorrow. You got led astray. Sully, I'm taking you back to the Quarry. You're super-sorry tomorrow, too, and you beg for another chance. You tell Machete that I was a terrible influence, that I'm full of delusions, that I told you to break me out, and now you realize what a bad choice you made. Emmett, you tell her that I've been plotting to overthrow camp from the start. Both of you tell her that. She'll believe it."

"And you?" asks Nona. "What will you do?"

"I'm going out to meet Rasta's da."

"She won't let you leave." Sully is still looking at me like I'm someone she's never seen. "She just about lost her bowel train when you got away last night. She said that if anything happened to you, I'd never make it to Blight because she would personally kill me dead where I stand and sign the docs."

"Kill you dead? She said that?"

"I want to know what happened to Rasta." Sully's voice is harsh and flat, Nona-style. "Machete said that she couldn't see the path and she fell. Aaron was supposed to be with you. What happened?"

"He didn't push her," Emmett says. "It was an accident."

"Then why isn't he here?"

"He said he's out of this, no matter what you say."

"Exactly what will Rasta's da do?" Now Sully turns on me again. "Help you overthrow the gov? Bomb the camp? Are you Sabi now?"

"He must know about the implants," says Emmett. "He signed off on them."

That knocks Sully and me both loose. All three of us stare at Emmett.

"What are you talking about?" asks Sully.

"Kickshaw implants. That's why the camps work. They keep us from jazz, and they keep us from violence. My cousin told me. It's kickshaw implant, or it's Blight."

We stand in the sinking moonlight and register that.

"What do we do, Lizard?" asks Nona. "We'll do whatever you say."

But do you like it or fear it?

"Just go back to your slices, okay? Please? And do like I said?"

Nona and Emmett stutter around, fluttering their hands and trying to make words. Sully stands apart with her arms crossed. She's not flashing any lights. She's just watching me.

"I mean it." I point back toward Pieville. "Go. If you trust me a titch, you'll go now, and you'll hurry, and you won't get caught."

"Remember your promise?" Nona asks.

"Yes, I remember."

Emmett throws himself around me again, wraps one leg around one of mine, and kisses me on the cheek. Then he takes off at a trot. I watch them both leave, brushing past Sully. She does not move until their rustlings are out of earshot. Then she speaks.

"So are Emmett and Nona dropped from the saurians, too?" Each word is a blow dart. "I don't like that Emmett kid. That holy-halo thing he does with his dimples. When did you get so close to them?"

Her voice breaks on the last word, and she turns away. Suddenly and again, I love her more than anything. She's so — so — so Sully. So completely human, powerful and vulnerable and untouchable, all at the same time. She sucks air, then turns to face me with her jaw set hard.

"What the fike happened out there in the rain? Was it really an accident?"

"It was. Aaron said that he was going back, and Rasta tried to stop him, and she lost her balance and fell. Then Aaron took off."

"If he pushed her, I'll kill him dead myself. I might anyway."

"He was scared. We all were."

Sully steps closer.

"So you're not jealous of him anymore? Is that because you've got Emmett following you around, thinking you're some kind of grand wizard-lizard?"

"No." I shake my head. "It's because I don't want jazz from you."

She blinks as if I smacked a cold palm across her face.

"I can't handle it." My voice comes out shaking with truth that I didn't know was there. "Rasta's gone, and I can't stand it if

I lose you, too. Sully, whatever happens next, even if I never see you again when I walk out of here, I want it to be okay between us. Like you said out by the fields. Friends."

Her eyes move over me, reading me like a booktron, and I open my covers and my eyes and my chest and my insides and I let her. I show her my delicate human skin and let her feel the pulse of the grove and the way it rocks deep in my veins.

She takes another step closer. I stand my ground. She reaches out, pulls me in, and hugs me hard. She actually pulls my weight off my feet, up onto my toes. All that heat, all that electricity I've felt at her every touch for the past three weeks, it comes through heart to heart in a way that pounds with power.

Not komodo power. Human power. Sully's power. Lights and jazz and the layers of deep and different below, the secret places she hides even from herself. I feel liquid-heart love for this person in a way that I have never felt before. Still and again and more than ever.

She sets me back on my feet, pushes me away, takes a deep breath, and draws herself taller. The moon has dipped into the western treetops.

"So what happens now?"

"I take you back and lock you in and pray that Machete buys your story."

"Are you fully lunar? I laid hands on her. She didn't like me to start with."

"I'm going to meet Rasta's da. He'll help us."

"I'll come with you."

Oh, I want that. I want it more than a mountain of kickshaw.

"No." My full weight settles onto my human feet. "I want it to look like I'm acting alone. Machete will believe that. Make her believe it, Sully. You can. You can make anyone believe anything."

"Anything?"

She flicks just enough grin to give my heart a skip.

"Almost. Now come on, it'll be daylight soon, and none of this will work if Machete catches us out roaming around."

We trot through the woods, across the Quint, and quiet-quiet back to her Quarry room. We have one more hug that pounds power to my heart. Then I lock her in. I sneak up the stairs, across the lot to the gate. Before I cross the sensor, I look back at CropCamp.

This gecko can hold eight times its body weight with a single toe.

Me, Emmett, Nona, and Sully. That's not eight. It's only four. And just for another hour or two. Then I will find Rasta's da on the road, and he'll take over.

Chapter Thirty-Three

I CRAWL UNDER THE FRONT GATE. Simple as that. I suppose it would have been smarter to sneak out some back way, but I cannot let Rasta's da get by me. So I crawl under the iron bars and slink around the left-side hulk of granite boulders.

There's a niche about shoulder-high. I climb into it, pulling myself up and scrabbling the toes of my boots against the bottom rock. I settle in there, curling myself into a tiny rockish ball. The moon casts long shadows from the west. Trees toss secret whispers back and forth overhead.

I don't have to wait long. The screen door bangs, and feet crunch across the gravel. They stop between the boulders. I hold my breath.

"Kivali."

Machete isn't fooled. She knows that I'm here.

"Kivali, I'm sorry. I should have stayed with you until you fell asleep. And now you've bolted."

The dragon-beat thumps in the back of my heart. Does she know how I got out of the Quarry? Will she send a search?

"Come back. We'll figure it all out together. We both want the same thing. Together, we can do this. Comrades."

Comrades don't lock comrades in.

"I'll give you ten ticks to come back, and then I'll have to alert GovCentral that I have a runaway."

Comrades don't threaten each other, either.

"This is your last chance to walk back in. Do it now, and everything will be fine. More than fine. Kivali, you need guidance. Let me help you. I can be the mother you've never had."

Mother? Machete wants to be my *mother?* Lizard flesh rises bumpy across my arms, the back of my neck.

"If you're caught outside, I can't control what happens to you."

I don't move. Not even an eyelash.

"It'll be out of my hands. No chance for me to foster you. No chance for you to cert here, or probably anywhere else, either. You'll end up in Blight. And what a loss that will be."

She sounds sad. She sounds really, genuinely sad. Like Sully, she can make anyone believe anything. Almost. The trees rattle and swish. Machete and I wait. She knows that I'm here. She does. I can feel it.

Finally, she turns. Her footsteps crunch back across the gravel. I let my breath out slowly. The screen door hits the frame. I don't think she will report me right away. Maybe she'll give me enough time to meet Rasta's da. That's all I need.

I crawl down from the rocks, cut across the tall grass to the road, and start walking. I let the wind blow me through the early gray toward the north-south highway. Rasta's da will come from the south. He will be a fierce adult crow with all the safe fluffy arrow-true strength of Rasta. He'll look like her, only more. He'll take charge. Me and Sully and Nona and Emmett — he'll take care of things for us.

The puffs of cloud ahead are dark gray-blue against the east sky, which gradually mellows to bluish gray and then pink and then yellow. The raggedy dark tree line slowly sharpens and takes form. The sunlight behind me tips the undersides of the clouds, lightening them to white, and the sky gradually deepens to a true blue. My shadow is long and lean and walking, still walking.

At last, a lone dot of motion appears on the road ahead. It's a single skizzer, traveling at a good clip. We draw steadily closer to each other. The solo person in the driver's seat is small. Barely bigger than I am. Soft. Balding. And pale, so pale. He brakes, stopping a few paces from my kneecaps. Grief scalds his mild features.

"Who are you?" he asks.

"I am Rasta's strong alliance."

His face crumples as if my words sucked all the air out of him. He pulls over to the side of the road and gets out of the skizzer, propping himself against it. When I approach, he reaches for me, and I expect a protective wraparound of adult crow feathers.

Instead, I am enclosed in a larger version of Emmett. He leans on me. He is heavy. I feel smothered, like I'm sinking into the dirt on the side of the road. I pat his back until he steps away and I can breathe.

"Tell me." His voice is nothing like Rasta's. It's weak, airless, fractured. "Tell me what really happened to my baby."

Shame washes over me. Imagine having Rasta in your nest for sixteen years, and then gone forever. I've only known her a few weeks.

"She was trying to help me," I say. "She —"

He doesn't give me a chance to confess.

"I told her to be careful, told her over and over before she left, told her in every inflow. Told her to keep her head down, to just get through camp and come home to us."

"I'm sorry." I don't sound like a dragon or even a comrade. "It's my fault. I —"

"No." Rasta's da shakes his head. "Don't tell me your name or anything about you. Whoever you are, and whatever you're doing, if you are Rasta's strong alliance then you're mine, too. But the less I know about you, the better, because they'll ask and I'm not a good liar. Just tell me this — was she scared? They said that she hit her head and died quickly. Is that true? Or did they hurt her?"

"No!" I say. "Nobody hurt her. She fell."

"You were on a lark? Outside in the rain?"

"No. That's a lie. Rasta was trying to rescue me, to get me away from Ms. Mischetti."

He nods. He's looking at me but he's very far away. I'm a distant planet that he's peering at through a telescope.

"And you?" he asks. "You're all right?"

His ask has no force behind it. I don't think he wants to know, not really.

"Did you know?" A desperation for a complete truth seizes me by the throat. "About what they do here? The implants?"

His shoulders curve and cave. Weighed down. Defeated. He knows.

"What are they?"

"You've already been on the oral dose." He won't look at me. "Same stuff; they plant it near the spinal cord. High-emotive frequency triggers a biorelease."

"But why?" I whisper.

"Suppresses aggression, violence. Eases anxiety. Adults my age take it orally, but the implants are better, if they get them in before the brain fully matures. Fewer side effects." Now he sounds like an infodoc. Or someone trying desperately to convince himself. "No addiction, no black market, no guessing at titrations before blood tests."

"But — do you think it's good? The drug? Is it good?"

"It works." He still won't look at me. "If you take it, things are easier. And Blight? I couldn't want that for my Rasta." Her name comes out on a sob, and his shoulders shake as he turns away. "What was the last thing she said? Were you there? Do you know?"

I close my eyes, seeing Aaron's back and Rasta turning to me in the gray twilight rain. I see her plastered wet hair again, her huge eyes, and I see the tumble on the backs of my lids.

"'We have to stay out of her control.'" I repeat Rasta's last words and open my eyes to find Rasta's da really looking at me for the first time. "She said that right before she fell. She meant Ms. Mischetti."

"And that's what you're doing now," he says. "Getting out of her control."

"I came to find you. To ask you what we should do."

He turns away quickly, as if I've hit him. He wraps his arms around himself like a child.

"I gave my Rasta." His voice shakes so hard, I think it might crawl out of his throat and rattle off on its own down the road. "This camp business is all wrong, but it's too big to fight. I can't help you."

He gets into his skizzer and pulls onto the road. I stand in front so that he can't move without running me over.

"You can't help me?" I whisper.

No, no, he shakes his head no. He stares at his hands on the steering wheel, tears sliding down his cheeks and dropping onto the sleeves of his light blue jacket. "I have to go sign their docs." His hands clench tight, so tight that the end of one thumb is red; the knuckle of the other one, white. "They won't let her come home till I sign their fikewise papers. I have to sign their . . ."

Shaking his head, tears falling, hands clenching. I step back. How dare I ask him for anything? It's inhuman and unlizard. I get out of his way. I can't bear to watch him anymore. I've barely gone ten paces before he calls.

"Wait."

I stop, but I don't turn back. I don't want him to see my tears.

"Here. Take these." Footsteps approach along the road behind me, and then stop abruptly. He drops something at my feet. It's his jacket. "You can't go walking down the road in camp coveralls."

His shirt joins the jacket. I unlace my boots and kick them off, start to unbutton my coveralls. Glance over my shoulder. Facing the other direction, he steps out of his pants, tosses them back toward me, and stands white-bodied in sky-blue boxers and black socks in the middle of the road.

I quickly put on the shirt, drop my coveralls, and push them behind me. I pick up his pants and put them on. Buttons, zipper, belt.

"Rasta would want me to help you," he says.

I close my eyes and take a deep breath. It's not what I'd hoped, but it's something. His clothes fit me well enough. Plenty roomy but not ridiculous. I turn to thank him but he holds his hand up, stopping my words. Both of our faces are wet. He finishes buttoning the coveralls and walks back to the skizzer.

He picks up a bag from the passenger seat, looks at me for one brief glance with Rasta's eyes, and hands it over. Then he gets in and skizzes off, wearing my beige CropCamp coveralls. I watch until he fades to a tiny dot on the horizon and disappears.

Chapter Thirty-Four

MY LAST KNOWN OPTION leaves with Rasta's da. On my right is a stretch of crop fields. On my left a scraggle of brush is backed by a line of woods. I have to get off the road. I step into the shallow ditch on my left. Climbing out the other side feels like scaling a mountain, even though it's only a few steps. I trudge through the brush into the protective shadows of the trees and collapse against a big oak trunk. An enormous branch stretches above me, and the canopy blocks most of the overhead blue.

I look in the bag. It's food. And water. I immediately drain the half-empty water bottle. I unlace my boots and yank them off. Between last night's battering and this morning's long walk, my feet are killing me. I peel away my damp socks to take a look. My left heel is scaggy with a popped blister and some dried blood. The hot spot that's been smoking on my right heel is only red — no fluid. I stretch my toes apart, airing the sore spots in between.

Then I rip into the cold baked potato, almost choking myself as I gulp down huge bites. It tastes like CropCamp, like hands planting and weeding and mounding and digging, and like sunshine and rain and soil. I wish that Rasta's and my hands were in that potato-field dirt right now.

I'd talk. I'd talk and talk and talk. I'd tell her about Sheila, and Korm, and the komodo. I'd show it to her. I'd let her pet it. I'd tell her all about the saurians and the Radio and the komodo's mysterious movements. I'd tell her about me and Sully, and about how it felt to step out of my lizard skin, and ask her if she saw me roll back into it with all the lizards looking on. I'd tell her about that creepy dream where Aaron ate the bird. I'd ask her if Nona is right, if vaping is vaping, and dying is dead.

By now the CounCircle gong has rung and the CropCamp day is in motion — but what does that motion look like? Which carefully chosen truth is Machete telling everyone about the rain and the dark and the fall and the night?

I devour the apple, core and all. It's sweet and wet and soothing. When I've licked the last of the juice off my fingers, I lean back against the trunk and close my eyes. I have never been more alone in my life. Lizard and human — they're both so very far away. The problem with living in two realities is that neither one gets to be entirely real.

If I could stomp with lizard music into eternity, I wouldn't need anything else. In that deep night dance I was a dragon, aura to core. But Machete flipped me to human and stole my komodo, turned me into a freezing, drenched little comrade who lay dreaming in the rain instead of rescuing my friends. Pathetic. Now I'm a weak, foot-blistered thirsty runaway. I am a throwaway whose mother wanted it not. Raised by a vaping foster.

When Donovan Freer vaped, he raised his arms and begged to go. Did Sheila do that? Did she leave me on purpose?

Maybe the dragon left on purpose, too. Because I chose CropCamp and Sully. But how could I not? For all her faults, Sully is real, a flesh-and-blood conglomeration of particles that I can smell and touch. Lizard Radio is a bunch of waves at best. At worst, it's nothing but random chemical and electrical impulses in my head, planted by two delusional adults who never figured out how to live in the world. Sully can shatter my ribs and splat my heart on pavement. Lizard Radio can't hurt me like that, and it can't touch me the way Sully does.

It can't touch me the way Rasta did, either. Water begins to leak from my eyes. It's nothing like the wild grief ride in my slice after kickshaw. Tears trickle salty to the corners of my mouth as I remember Rasta's elf-face and serious eyes, her magical baby-crow voice and her fingertips on mine. A steady current of loss flows down my cheeks, dripping from my chin. Rivers and streams of sad that I think will be pouring out of me forever.

There is nothing left for me. I'm neither human nor dragon, not Sheila's, not Machete's, not Korm's, and not Rasta's da's. I belong nowhere. Certainly not here in this foreign wood, with nowhere to go and nowhere to be. The only thing that I am is nothing.

Before you can be what you are, you must be all things.

The whisper comes from the inside, like *gotothefields* my first night at CropCamp. I wave the words away. I don't want to be all things. I don't want to be anything. It's too hard.

"Please."

My voice is so shaky. I force myself to my feet, straighten, and stretch my hands to the sky.

"Please."

Donovan dropped his clothes. I pull off Rasta's da's shirt, unfasten the belt, and shed the pants. I stretch again for the sky, bare-chested.

"Please."

Nothing happens.

"Please?"

I try to make my voice sound like Donovan's, but I can't get the right tone of plea into my *please*. The slanting sun and the breeze lightly touch my skin, and the trees whisper around me. Everything is so sharply defined; the colors so bright, they hurt. I drop my arms and look around.

It's no good. They won't take me. I'm surrounded by particles of color and light and shape. Temperature and texture. My breath rises and falls, and pulse beats blood through my body. A couple of cheery birds whistle back and forth. Why do birds get to be so happy? Surely they've seen other birds fall and crash and disappear. Birds die all the time.

I draw a deep shudder-breath and blow it out. I pull the clothes on, lie back against the tree, and close my eyes. The grove still beats somewhere near the base of my spine. Here, alone in the woods, I can have my delusions and hold them close. I look for the lizards on the backs of my eyelids. Breathe in, two, three, like Sheila taught me all those years ago. Like Korm taught me. Empty your mind, two, three. Listen, listen sideways.

After a long, long time, I'm able to sidle off the straight-forward center of things. There's a shift in balance, a whirling of form. Faint footsteps approach from beyond sideways, and I keep breathing so they won't stop. Korm strides across the insides of my eyelids and turns to face me. Keep it steady; don't drop the signal. In and out, two, three.

Like me, Korm is dressed in pants, a shirt, and a jacket. The smell of her basement room holds me in familiar comfort. The windows expand, and the walls separate into trunks and stretch up to oak leaves. Korm's outline wavers but her eyes burn with intensity. *Kivali.* She steps toward me. Her voice is deep, and it's suddenly difficult to see Korm as her and not him.

Where is the dragon?

"She took it," I say.

Korm's outline shimmers and wavers and disappears completely, leaving only green leaves and ferns. Even so, someone or something circles me. I slowly spin, trying to see all sides at once. I'm unsteady and unprotected, fully exposed.

"Korm, it's you, right?"

I reach out, wanting solid touch. Korm laughs and material-izes, wavers and melts and re-forms. Just as she is man/woman, he is particle/wave. I can't settle on one perception or the other. I see both, and I see neither.

And you? Are you human or lizard?

"I'm neither."

Wrong answer. Lizard or human? Choose.

This isn't Korm. Korm wouldn't make me choose.

CHOOSE! WHAT ARE YOU?

Korm's roar crashes inside my head, and I hit the ground with a *whoomp*. I snap and thrash and roll upright, using my muscular tail to launch a jaw-snapping lunge at the screaming air. There is nothing to bite, nothing to take down, nothing to conquer. I tongue-flick, searching for scent and movement and finding nothing at all. I open my dragon jaw and speak with my human voice.

"Neither and both."

Somewhere in the ethereal cross-section of particles and waves, Korm smiles. And when Korm smiles, the leaves dance, and the breeze floats soft and warm around me, and I relax.

That's where your power lies.

I spin away and bury my face in my arms. Korm is wrong, and Korm is right, just like Sheila, and just like Machete.

Kivali.

Machete's hand drops on my shoulder and rolls me over. It's not Machete, though. I am alone, below a single oak. A disembodied whisper breathes in my ear.

Give Darlene my love.

The birds are gone, and the sun is higher. The leaves and bushes whirr and buzz with daytime insects. I rub my face. Everything is unreal. My feet, my hands, the birds, the fat bee buzzing past—none of it is real. Maybe I'm not even real. Have I ever been real?

I stand and brush myself off. My body is my body. It's mine. I look down at myself. I've never worn men's clothes. No boys' clothes since that winter boy-boots day in the school yard. They feel good on me, and right. I widen my shoulders and broaden my chest, and run my fingers through my hair. I look like a boy now, for sure. I'm not, though. Man and woman: they're both familiar and foreign. Like beautiful pasture planets I travel in my dreams, speaking each language with a heavy accent.

My dragon is caught in Machete's trap. It's bait, I know. But I have to go get it.

The sun hangs high as I trudge along the road. I tie Rasta's da's jacket around my waist. My feet hurt, but it's a relief to move toward something. The road goes on and on. It doesn't move under me as fast as it did when I was walking to Rasta's da. I wonder what Machete did when he turned up in CropCamp coveralls.

The occasional skizzer passes, and a couple of gov trucks. No one slows down. No one seems to notice me at all. Maybe I'm not really here. Maybe I'm already gone, and I just don't know it. Maybe everyone I know has vaped. Maybe I have.

Maybe Sully will still be there. I hope that Sully is still there.

The hot spot on my right heel gets hotter as the road slants upward. Just keep going, a hundred more steps. And a hundred more. What will I do when I get there? I'll make Machete give me my dragon. I'll take it to the center of the grove. We'll beseech the skies and the moon. This time it will work, and the dragon and I will vape to the land of Lizard Radio. Korm will be waiting for me, and Sheila, too. Donovan Freer too, I suppose.

It's a long hill, and my blisters really don't like it. Where is the CropCamp turnoff? I must be close. A hundred more steps. Thirty-seven, thirty-eight. A skizzer passes and slows, then pulls over to the side of the road. The person driving the skizzer wears a yellow head-scarf. She gets out and looks back at me.

I should duck into the woods but the little dip in and out of that ditch seems like more than I can do. I'm so hot and thirsty and hungry and tired and footsore. That person puts her hands on her hips just the way Sheila does.

I stop walking. That person shades her eyes with her hand.

I think that person is Sheila.

We are about fifty paces apart. I must be mistaken.

"Sheila?"

That person breaks into a run. I'm too tired to run but somehow I do, and we slam into each other and her arms are around me and she's holding me in a tight, tight hug.

Sheila is not a hugger. Sheila is hugging me.

She pushes me away, looks at my face, and pulls me back in again. I collapse Emmett-style. She is not only holding me; she's holding me up. She's holding me up like she has since the baby days, with the moon, with the rinkety-dink, with the komodo, my whole life.

When I'm finally able to draw a breath and stand on my feet, she looks me over.

"I didn't recognize you," she says, "with your hair like that, and those clothes. What happened?"

"Are you vaped?" I ask. "She said that you vaped."

Sheila's eyebrows drop, and her mouth narrows to a thin line. I know this look. This looks means that Machete is in trouble.

"Kivali. I did not vape. I'm right here."

"She said that you vaped."

"Darlene is a liar," says Sheila.

I catch my breath. *Give Darlene my love.*

"You know her." It's not a question. "You've known her for years."

"Yes." Sheila nods.

"Korm knows her, too," I say.

Sheila's wide-eyed jaw-drop would make me laugh if I wasn't so tired.

"Darlene told you that?"

"No. Korm did."

Chapter Thirty-Five

LESS THAN A THOUSAND paces from the CropCamp
entrance, I lie flat on my back and stare up at the world. My damp
socks hang from a low, dead branch. The breeze licks my sore
feet. The birdies chirtle and warble back and forth. I am amazed
at how the appearance of one human face changes everything.

Once we establish that Korm is not actually, physically here,
and that both of us are, Sheila leaves to get food and water from
the skizzer, and to hide it off the road while we figure out what
to do. I'm well hidden in underbrush down the hill and into the
woods. Shards of sunlight slice through the pine tops. The soft
earth pulls me in, cradles me, sings in the voice of the cooling
breeze, and I roll over and close my eyes. No shadows move, and
dragons do not dance. It's just dark, just easy, just—

Loud. Running, crashing footsteps. Sheila slides in as I yank
my eyes open and lurch up. She rams my head down, and my
nose hits the dirt with a sharp jolt. Sheila pants through her nose,
trying to quiet herself. My heart ponies up like it's trying to keep
pace with hers.

"What happened?" I whisper.

Sheila shakes her head. The birds are gone. No sound at all beyond the thrum of blood racing through my body. The silence stretches, and high red fades from Sheila's cheeks. A cicada buzz begins and builds. It rises to a pitch and falls. A chippie hops up on a stump, looks us over, and scrabbles away in the brush.

"They found the skizzer," whispers Sheila. "I don't think they saw me — I belly-crawled back into the woods while they were searching it."

"Who?"

"Gov uniforms. They can't ID me from the skizzer, but they'll be looking. We need to move."

I put my socks and boots back on, and we creep deeper into the woods, watching our feet so we don't trip or crack sticks. I try to map CropCamp in my head and figure where we are in relation to Pieville, the Quint, the grove.

Sheila holds up a hand, and we both stop. We stand in silence, listening, listening. Only woodsy sounds. Leaves murmuring in the breeze, a rustle here and a tweedle there. Sheila unwinds the rinkety-dink scarf and releases her sweaty curls. She hands it to me, and I wipe the sweat from my face.

"Why are you out here?" she whispers. "Does Darlene know where you are?"

I shake my head no and hand back the scarf. Sheila drapes it around her neck, takes one more scan of the woods around us, and eases to the ground.

"How could you leave me with her?" I ask.

"I gambled on the Darlene I used to know." Sheila speaks so soft and low, I have to crouch in to hear. "It was a bad bet."

She pats the ground next to her, and I drop to one knee but I won't sit next to her. Not until she gives me some answers.

"So it's true?" I ask. "You were friends?"

Sheila nods.

"I hadn't heard from her in almost twenty years, but she Deega'd me the same day I got the gov order for early camp. Told me that if I sent you to her camp she'd watch out for you, get you on track and off the gov watch list."

"Why didn't you tell me?"

"Korm went on a fire-spitting rage when I told her." I'm annoyed that Sheila doesn't answer my question, but I want to know about Korm, so I don't interrupt. "Wanted you to underground right away. We fought. That's the last I've heard from her. Word is that she vaped."

"So you bet on Machete over Korm."

"Machete?" Sheila hints a smile. "That's what you call her?"

"Not to her face."

Leaves rustle behind, and Sheila grabs my hand. Someone is coming. Step, step. They've found us. Step, pause. Creeping, crafty.

The birds tweedle and the cicadas buzz. My mouth is too dry to swallow. Another step, and then another. Sounds like just one person. Maybe we can overpower them, throw a tackle, escape if we can take them by surprise. There — there, the leaves move. Another step — a flash of brown — a face.

It's a deer. Big ears pricked. It steps forward, nods. The black nose twitches. *What are you; will you hurt me?* Another head bob, a step closer, and then it jerks back with a quick stomp and a whistle-snort, and crash, crash, crash, and away.

Sweet free air rushes into my lungs, and Sheila and I gasp and laugh together.

"That definitely means that no one is close."

Sheila speaks right out loud. My heart continues to pound, not with fear now but with wonder. A real, live deer. In the woods. With us. Those eyes, that dip-bobbing hesitant walk, those delicate legs, that glorious bounding flight into the woods.

"So what exactly did Korm say about Darlene?"

I let the deer go and turn back to Sheila.

"'Give Darlene my love.'"

"How?" Sheila asks. "Mean like a weapon?"

"Soft," I say. "Sad."

"Sad, huh? About time Korm got sad."

"About what?"

"Whatever happened between her and Darlene. All of our plans to change the world, take it by storm — they all fell apart at once. Korm went underground; Darlene applied to SayFree. I thought that we were close, all of us, and suddenly I was left solo."

"So how could you leave me with her? Why would you do that?"

Sheila lies back and puts the rinkety scarf over her face. I think that she's not going to answer me, but then she starts talking again in a very low voice.

"Two things. One was hope — that she was sorry, trying to make up for things. The other was fear. Darlene made it clear that she wanted you in her camp and was going to make it happen." The thin yellow flowers shift as Sheila speaks. "I know Darlene. If you'd disappeared, she'd rip up the entire sector looking for you."

"So it was better to hand me over so she could jam up my head with some implanted drug thing?"

"Darlene said no implants on potential decision-makers, and you'd be a candidate if you'd cooperate. She said that the whole deal was off if you knew about our connection, though."

I wish she'd quit talking through that stupid scarf.

"Darlene knew that I'd bite on a chance to keep you safe. She knows what matters to me, same as I know what matters to her."

"What matters to her?"

"Vapes. Her older brother vaped when she was seven and broke her heart. Stopping vapes — that's all she's ever cared about. I guess that's why she went with the gov. Figured she could stop them that way."

Oh. The image of Machete rocking under the moonlight, hands over her head — I can almost see her as a child. Almost.

"And apparently, you matter," says Sheila. "She Deega'd last week and said that she wanted to take over fostering you. Said you asked her to."

I yank the scarf off Sheila's face.

"She said *what*?"

Sheila nods.

"And you believed that?"

My voice squeaks at the end. Sheila closes her eyes.

"You were so angry when I left you. And then the updates were all about how well you were doing, how you had friends, how you were larking around with the popular kids. She said that you were happy, well adjusted."

The skin below Sheila's eyes is so dark, almost like bruises. How did I not notice that before?

"I doubted myself." Finally, she looks at me. Water rises in her eyes. "All the choices I've made for you."

I'm tempted to put the scarf back over her face.

"Some of it must have been true. Did you really have friends?"

"Yes," I say. "I had friends."

"Can you tell me about them?"

No. Watered eyes or no, I cannot tell Sheila about Sully or Rasta. Not yet. I don't answer, and I still don't, and at last she sits up, rubs her face, and ties the scarf back over her hair.

"Time for that later, I suppose. Korm's underground connections heisted a skizzer for me today, and they won't be happy about losing it, but they'll still get us out of the sector if we can get back to the city."

"Korm's connections are helping you?"

"I went to them last week. Asked them for help. They know about you—Korm told them. They want me to try to get you away from Darlene."

"How? Just skizz in and pick me up and Machete will say, 'Okay, fine, see you later'?"

It feels good to be childish and petty. Sheila doesn't even flinch.

"I came on impulse and hope — and here you are, so it worked. Who knows, maybe your radio set it up for us. As soon as night falls we'll get on our way."

Sheila's in charge now. As if CropCamp never happened to me. But it did. She left me there, and CropCamp happened.

"I'm going back in." Same as in Machete's office, words fall out of my mouth before I can catch up with them. "She has my komodo. I need it."

"Don't be absurd. If Darlene gets her hands on you again, she'll never let you go."

"Then I'll vape."

"It's not that easy. Korm tried to vape for years. Decades. Studied, practiced, researched. You don't just decide and do it."

"I know some things that Korm doesn't."

Sheila looks me over, up and down. She'll see my bluff. She'll see how scared I am to go back in there. She will stop me.

"That may be," she says, "but there's something that you don't know, and you need to know it before you set foot back in that camp."

"About vaping?"

"No. About you. Where you came from."

"The saurians?"

"Aren't you curious about why Darlene took such an interest in you? Why she cares so much?"

I shake my head no.

248

"I first saw it when you were three, or maybe four. The way your eyebrows dip when you're mad."

My eyebrows dip. A small black-headed bird lands in a tree to my left with a know-it-all *bee-bee-bee.* I raise my eyebrows as high as they'll go. No eyebrow dipping. No.

"I think Darlene knew exactly how old you were."

My face fires hot, and hotter. So I dip my eyebrows sometimes. So what?

"A baby would have ruined her gov career. She knew that I'd take care of you."

"You never said that." My voice quivers. "You said the lizards dropped me. I believed it."

"No matter who birthed you or which stories we tell, my gecko, you're still you. I've never understood your radio, and now I understand it even less, but it's something real and so are you."

I'm not her gecko anymore. Not since I stepped out of my lizard skin.

"Listen, Kivali. Stories and theories aside, they don't let asolos foster babies, Blight or otherwise. It made no sense for them to let me keep you. Someone had to pull some strings."

"I think you are wrong," I say.

"I didn't want to tell you unless I was one hundred percent sure. When I saw the two of you together, I upped it to eighty. When she pulled the foster maneuver, I passed ninety. And now—why are you running around free? Don't you think that's odd?"

The black-headed bird flits off. The wind gives another puff, a stronger one.

"I'm going back in now."

Sheila will not let me go back in there.

"Of course." She nods. "I'll be here waiting. Do what you need to, and then come back to me."

"What if I don't come back?"

Sheila lies back down and closes her eyes.

"Just for the record, my little whiptail"— she speaks so softly, I can barely hear—"I never stopped thinking that you might save the world."

"Save it from what?" I cannot believe that she would let me go again. "And for what?"

"We don't know, do we?"

Chapter Thirty-Six

TEN PACES SHY OF the yellow boundary sign, my anger and bravado join hands and walk off, leaving me alone in the woods. Keeping clear of the boundary, I pace back and forth trying to figure out where I am in relation to Pieville or the grove. I don't want to come crashing out right next to Lacey's slice.

I turn my back on the boundary and look for the last rinkety-scarf scrap. That was Sheila's idea, to mark my trail so that I could find my way back easily. I rolled my eyes when she tore the yellow scarf into strips, but I'm not rolling them now. The scraps are just the sort of thing that Sheila thinks ahead about and I don't.

Here I stand on the yawning maw of CropCamp grounds, still with no plan and no clue. What do I do — walk in and ask Machete for the komodo? And she'll hand it over, pack a lunch for me and Sully and Nona and Emmett, and wish us a nice journey?

No. I might not be Sheila's gecko but I'm not a Machete-slaying dragon, either. The best I'll find inside that boundary is caged, sedated lizard-dom. I can't go back, and I can't go forward. Everywhere I look is both and neither.

That's where your power lies.

Well, that's a stupid place for power to lie. I'm not an adult yet. Sheila will take care of me. All I have to do is let her. But I haven't gone ten steps back toward her before my teeth start chattering. I stop and look, forward and back. CropCamp and Sheila.

If I leave now, I won't be both or neither. I'll be the weak, shivering human that Machete rolled in the grove for the rest of my life. Her foot will be on my tail forever.

I sink to the ground and wrap my arms around my legs, forehead on my knees. My stomach chews itself from the inside out. I can't puke it out of me because it *is* me. I curl in on myself, smaller and smaller.

What *am* I?

Liam's icy eyes rise again, and I shiver like I'm back in that winter day, knocked to the ground by those eyes and held there by a boot on my scarf. The lizards saved me that day. Where are they now?

You must find yourself. That's what Korm would say, but Korm isn't here. It's just me, Kivali Sauria Kerwin.

Before you can be what you are, you must be all things.

I don't know how to do that. But maybe I can try, just try the way Korm taught me. Just for a second, here and now in the limbo-land of both and neither. It can't hurt. I close my eyes and inhale all that I can: the green grass beneath my feet, the air and the trees and the heat and the day.

Be a rock.

I find the rock. I find mountain, and then earth. I breathe

the wind. The wind finds a spark and blows into a fire that blazes until the rain begins, and then I become water, drowning the fire, flowing and roaring and dripping and swirling, cleaning my insides, washing my outsides, splashing and crashing inside and out, running over the rock.

I open my eyes and suck in the afternoon air. I still have no plan, but the direction is clear. Ahead, forward, and in. I'd best move quickly, or I won't move at all.

Twenty or so paces in, I spot a pie-top and head directly for it. I stride into Pieville bold as daylight. No one is here. Not a moving, living soul, unless they're spying secret from behind the trees. The spigot water is the sweetest thing I've ever tasted. I drink and drink, and run it over my head and neck. I flip my hair back, combing my fingers through and soaking the collar of Rasta's da's shirt.

Since the privo is right there I use that, too, and then drink some more. Where is Machete? She must know that I'm here. She's waiting for me somewhere. Maybe in my slice.

I head over to my pie and zip in. My slice is just as I left it, with Nona's towel in a heap on the floor. I take off my boots. Footsteps approach as I peel away my dirty, damp socks.

"Lizard."

It's Lacey.

"I know you're in there. You need to come with me to Ms. Mischetti's office."

I am still afraid but my stomach is no longer eating itself. I pull on clean, dry socks, lace my boots, and step out to face Lacey.

She clearly wants to handcuff or corral or lasso me, but I walk past her before she can make a move. My feet still hurt, but the dry socks are a wonder of comfort. Lacey follows me through Pieville and up the slope. At the top, the fields stretch out and glisten emerald-green. Not a comrade to be seen.

"Where is everyone?"

"At dinner. Ms. Mischetti is waiting for you in her office."

"I'm not going there. I'll wait for her in the Pavilion."

I half-expect Lacey to tackle me from behind, but she doesn't. She leaves me at the Pavilion. The screen door squeaks as I open it. I guide it gently closed and enter the hush. I've never been in here alone. A faint scent of wood smoke lingers in the solemn silence.

The rocks rattle as I walk to the back row where Sully and I slipped in the very first night. I sit on the low, rough wooden bench, breathing hard. There — across there — that's where Donovan Freer met my eyes and held them. And there, that's where Machete stood.

I stretch out my hand, palm up. What if someone laid a kickshaw on it right now? Would I take it? I close my eyes and let the kickshaw shine spread through my body. Here in this Pavilion is where I found some kind of One, such warmth and ease and sweet feeling — friends and fun and camaraderie and a sense of belonging that I'd never known before CropCamp.

I step up on the bench nearest the door and watch Machete stride across the grass. Darlene. My bioparent. I once lived inside of that body. Did she love me even a tiny bit? Or did she hate having me in there and think only about how to get rid of me?

I want my komodo, but I want more than that. I want to know a few things about Darlene Mischetti. I can't see any other way to get her foot off my tail.

Chapter Thirty-Seven

"GOOD AFTERNOON, KIVALI," SHE SAYS. "I was pleased when the biosensor alerted me that you were on the grounds."

She steps onto the bench on the other side and walks the outer circle, away from me. I hop a row in, walking the inner circle. She doesn't know what I know. I want her to tell me. I want her to want to tell me.

"Congratulations on your dealings with Mr. Shorlen. That man is so deep in grief, I have no idea how you got him to comprehend anything, much less act. But the docs are signed, and I'll keep my agreement with him. No expuls for anyone involved in last night's incident."

No expuls? Sully is still here? I almost miss my footing on the gap between two benches. Machete continues a slow prowl around the outer ring.

"I have to admit, when I saw him in your coveralls, I had a moment of thinking that you might not come back — I put out alerts to all the sector borders, just in case."

I jump to the outer ring and walk quickly so that instead of her being behind me, I'm behind her. She keeps walking, too. The rocks below gnash their teeth. First one to fall loses.

"I wonder where you've been since this morning. What you've been doing."

"Shall I give you a carefully chosen truth?"

Machete turns and walks toward me. I jump in a row and keep walking.

"People don't want the whole truth, Kivali. They want to feel safe, and they want someone to tell them what to do."

"Which truth did you tell Rasta's da?"

"There was a terrible accident on a rainy night — the sort of tragedy that sometimes happens when young comrades play loose with the regs, even with good intention."

We both circle, and my mind scrabbles busy like a chippie with things I want to say and things I want to ask. Machete takes big strides. I jump another row in, steady my stance, cross my arms, and face her.

"I have answers to your questions," I say. "My independence isn't an asset or a liability. It just is. And leader or follower? Both."

Machete continues to walk, and I turn in place so she won't be behind me.

"Both," she says. "The problem with both is that it ends up being neither."

"I don't see that as a problem," I say.

She shakes her head sadly at my foolishness. My eyebrows dip.

"I've learned some things about vaping," I say.

Machete stops walking. She looks at me, cocks her head.

"What do you know?"

Not a test or a challenge. She's actually seeking information.

"It's nothing to fear."

"Not true, Kivali. Anything that rips us away from our comrades and from the One cannot possibly be good."

"Maybe there's more than one One. Maybe some of us choose the both-and-neither one."

Machete turns away, walking again. I stand in place and watch.

"Are you saying that people vape by choice?" I'm surprised by the bitter edge of her voice. "They just up and leave everyone and everything, forever? Did your Sheila take off because she'd had enough of you?"

I watch this woman who is my bioparent, who abandoned me, who lied to get me here, who is still lying. *Her older brother vaped when she was seven and broke her heart.* I step off the bench and cross the still-snarling rocks. They allow me to pass.

"That's why you were sad when Donovan Freer vaped. Because it looked like he wanted to."

Machete looks down on me. Color flushes high in her cheeks. Her eyebrows dip and then rise. This is the time for me to be like Rasta, who knew when not to speak.

"Yes. That any young person would choose that — that he —"

She's not lying now. Her broken heart bleeds through her eyes. She swallows, collects herself, steadies her voice.

"And yes, you saw my doubts, and yes, that was unnerving for me. My entire life, my whole career, has been based on saving young people from vaping. I don't think that's been wrong. But maybe it hasn't been entirely right."

Truth and emotion from Machete are wonderful things. They sweep through my system like kickshaw juice and explode a new vision, a world where the truths aren't carefully chosen and young people have no need to escape-vape. What if we can actually work together, me and Darlene?

"Then let's change it," I say. "Let's make it different."

"Make what different?"

"This." I wave my hand across the Pavilion. "All of it. GovCentral trusts you. If our crop production is good and nobody complains — the teachers and counselors and guides, they trust you too, right? You have all the power here."

I wish that I could open up my bony skull and let her see the beautiful world inside, with the best of CropCamp mixed with the best of Korm's ways and Sheila's color, with no need for Blight or carefully chosen anything. If I can only make Machete believe in it, then maybe together she and I can . . .

"So you want to work with me to create the best world we can, starting here at CropCamp? And you'll commit to me, to your comrades, to the community?"

For the first time since Machete entered, I look outside. Lacey and Saxem hover on the Quint, facing the Pavilion. They are guarding Machete, I suppose. I step back up on the benches and begin to walk the outer ring. Could it happen? Could we do it?

"You are an amazing young person, Kivali Kerwin." Machete and I are on the same route again, walking in the same direction. "You have it all — power and compassion, vision and ability. Together, we can do some very good things."

Machete and I working together is a ridiculous idea. But is it any more ridiculous than Sully's kiss or Nona's knowings or Rasta's fall? If Machete will just be honest with me, truly and completely honest, we can do it.

"First," she says, "I have something difficult to tell you."

Yes. The truth is ready to pour.

"If you know the truth, then no one can use it against you."

The beautiful world of the future, one where I fully belong, surges before me.

"Sheila planned her vape."

I stop at the end of a bench and teeter. The rocks below snap and gnash.

"She begged me to take you in this camp session, and asked me to keep you safe, which has turned out to be harder than I expected. But I could not refuse Sheila Kerwin."

I turn to face Machete on the opposite side of the Pavilion. No redness in her cheeks now. Just the cool color of lies.

"You see, I've known Sheila for years. In the earliest days of SayFree, we resisted together. Youthful visionaries we were, like you are now." Machete's laugh sounds like a growl. "But we made different choices. I've put my vision to work in a useful way. Sheila refused to work with others, and she didn't want you to know that we were connected. She wanted you to think that you were finding your own way here, on your own power. Which you are, of course. I'm just giving you some extra help. Because of my old bond with Sheila."

I stand tall with the rocks at my feet and the air in my lungs, the fire and the water in my heart and soul, and I look into Machete's eyes so that I won't miss a single glimmer of reaction.

"Darlene," I say. "I know who you are."

Machete's knees waver visibly as if a strong wind blows from behind, but she recovers quickly.

"Then you also know who you are?"

I nod. Her quick inhalation is visible. She settles, nods, and forges on.

"Then you know how important it is that you're here, and that we move forward together. You and me. Together at last."

I plant both feet solidly on the bench, my weight balanced, my head high.

"Korm sends her love."

Machete steps off the bench and sits down. She tries to collect herself, and fails, and tries again. She is afraid, but she's not a coward. She could call Lacey and Saxem. They could Quarry me in a second, and I could rot down there with no expul. Sheila couldn't rescue me, and neither could Rasta's da. Nobody could.

"Where is Korm?" she asks.

"She vaped."

Water shines in Machete's eyes.

"Recently?"

"Very."

Machete closes her eyes as she inhales, and when she opens them, the shine is gone. Her eyebrows dip and stay down. She's made her decision.

"That leaves you with me." She stands. "And this is still my camp."

She walks across the CropCamp rocks. They don't bite. They don't even growl. They belong to her.

"Come with me." She reaches a hand up to me. "You must be exhausted. You need some rest."

"I don't want rest, and I don't want kickshaw. Not by morsel nor needle."

Her eyes soften, and she drops her hand.

"But Kivali, the implants were never meant for you. You're not like the others."

"What if I am? What if I'm exactly like the others?"

"Mmmm, of course." She nods, and her eyes are so understanding. "Of course, you're worried about your friends, your comrades. This is what will make you such a fine leader. You see, none of the guides get implants. We'll make Sully and Emmett guides. I can work with Sully's rebellious streak."

I almost ask about Nona, and then I remember — Machete knows nothing of Nona's involvement. Another thing I know that she doesn't.

"Trust me, Kivali. I've been doing this for many years."

I came in here seeking information. I have all that I need.

"I'd like my metal lizard back," I say. "Please give it to me."

"You're upset. And so exhausted. Kivali, it's been an awful

few days for you. This is not the time to make any decisions. Rest first, and eat. I bet you didn't sleep at all last night."

I back away from her hand.

"Do you have it? The lizard?"

Damn the quiver in my voice!

"Of course," she says. "It's obviously important to you, so I've put it in a safe place. Come with me. I'll get you some dinner, and we can talk more, work things out."

"No. I'm not staying here."

"Where do you think you can go? I'm your only option now, Kivali."

She is so sure of herself. If I stay, I'll feed on kickshaws and carefully chosen truths for the rest of my life.

"Remember what you said in our very first meeting? About how some young comrades have an internal intuitive guide? You were right." As I speak, the dragon — not the toy one — fires my words. "That's what happens when you leave your child. Your child becomes something that you know not, with a power you know not."

Her eyes flick outside. She's going to call them. She's going to Quarry me. She lies when it suits her, and when lies don't work, she has all the power of the gov behind her.

"You're the one with choices to make now." Lizard Radio sings in my ears, and the dragon speaks from my heart. "They'll have consequences. You need to let Emmett and Sully rejoin their comrades with no sanctions and no culpas. I will walk out of here without interference."

"And if I interfere?"

"Then you'll have more vapes to explain, plus some disruption from my connections on the outside. Don't doubt that I have them."

"If I do as you say? Then what?"

"I will quietly disappear into the woods." Carefully choosing my truths, keeping my options open. I am the offspring of Darlene Mischetti. "Maybe I vaped, or maybe your biosensors malfunctioned. Report whatever you want — whatever makes you look best. I don't want to be your enemy."

Again, her eyes flick outside.

"Kivali." Her voice is so soft. So kickshaw. "It doesn't have to be like this."

I turn and walk toward the door.

"Please."

Machete said please. I hesitate.

"Tell me one thing." I keep my back to her. "What did the lizard mean?"

"What lizard?"

"The one on the shirt. The one you left me in."

"I don't know what you're talking about."

I turn and study her eyebrows, her cheeks, the color of her skin. She's not lying. She really has no idea. I shake my head and turn for the door. Rocks rattle, and before I can escape, her hand falls on my shoulder.

I spin, springing at Machete with a full-throated roar. She stumbles back and catches her balance on the nearby bench, looking up to meet my flat-eyed lizard gaze. I do not take my eyes off hers.

"What are you?" she whispers.

For the first time in my life, I have a complete answer.

"I am me."

Chapter Thirty-Eight

POWER. WHEN YOU FIND it in your hands you'd best act quickly, because nobody holds it forever. Machete makes one last grab as I cross the threshold of the Pavilion.

"What about your toy lizard?"

I turn and meet her eyeball-for-eyeball.

"Keep it to remember me by."

I stride past the fields and down into Pieville. My back itches with the expectation of a hand, a fist, a lasso, a laser, but nothing lands. At the bottom of the slope, I finally look back. Lacey stands at the brink of Pieville looking down with her arms crossed. Surveillance, not interference. So far, anyway.

I am clearer than I've ever been in my life, and ideas come fast and sharp. I jog past the privo, round my own pie, and drop to my knees in front of my slice, hurrying while I'm out of view. I scrape away the pine needles and dig, sifting the dirt through my hands. I gather a clump of dirty hair and yellow shreds in my fist and zip inside.

Taking my secateurs from the shelf, I crawl under my cot and use the point to punch through the fabric wall that separates my slice from Nona's. Then I snip along the seam until I have a hole big enough to put my fist through. I ease my arm through the hole up past my elbow, and with a sideways flick I toss the ribbon and hair into the center of Nona's floor.

Nona and her knowings. She'll know that I've been here. I scramble back out from under the cot and look at the center pole. There's no way to put something in Sully's slice without Lacey seeing. Nona will have to tell her. She'll have to believe Nona. It could happen.

I pull my own clothes from a pouch and toss them on the cot. Quite the young lizard I was, last time I wore these clothes. At first I think I'll take them, and the secateurs, but then I remember that I'm supposed to be vaping. I take my kaggi anyway. Sheila will be thirsty.

When I poke my head out of my slice, Lacey is posted between my slice and hers, leaning on a tree, watching. I guess her job is to be sure that I really leave, without contaminating anyone on my way. I head over to the spigot, fill my kaggi, and drink it dry twice. I fill it again. Because you have to be hydrated to vape, right? What do they know?

I hit the privo, wash up, wave to Lacey the sentinel, and head out of Pieville the way I came in, directly into the woods, trying to strike the same angle. When I'm well out of view I stop, ease to the ground behind a thicket, and wait.

Eventually I hear footsteps, crunch-crunch. Lacey stops

maybe thirty paces shy, and although I can't see her, I can feel her look, watch, search. I barely breathe. Footsteps rustle, turn. Stop and listen again. Recede. Stop. Recede farther.

I count slowly. At six hundred and forty-seven I hear footsteps approach off to my right. They advance, then stop, and recede. I start the count again, slower. When I hit one thousand, I cautiously rise and stretch. The sun is on its way west, and the woods slowly rise to life along with me — a tweedle here, a chippie scurry there.

I force myself to move slowly, picking my way quietly through the brush. Finally, I spot the splash of yellow boundary sign and let out the breath that I didn't know I'd been holding. Before I can figure out how to get to Sheila without yelling, she steps from behind a tree. Right there, waiting. I should've known the scarf scraps weren't just for me. Of course she'd follow me to the boundary.

I slam my finger against my lips, look back so she knows that I might have been followed, then turn forward and toss the kaggi underhand. It lands on the other side of the border. Sheila looks down at it and then back up, eyebrows drawn.

I point from one sign to the next, tracing the boundary with my finger. Sheila picks up the kaggi, drinks, nods. Drinks some more. When she caps the kaggi, I begin to walk in the direction of the grove, signaling her to follow me on her side of the boundary. I carefully spot the next yellow sign and stay clear of the boundary line. Sheila walks with me on the other side.

Every fifty paces I stop, listen, wait. I keep watch to my right for the path that leads to the grove. On the fourth stop, I cup my hands around my mouth to keep the sound from going behind me, and speak out loud, soft and low.

"I'm waiting for my friends to come meet me. We'll cross together."

"Did you see Darlene?"

I nod. I want to say more but not here, not now. Sheila nods. We understand each other well enough.

We walk on. It's not easy, staying close to the boundary but not going over, tramping over fallen logs and through pricker thickets. We each struggle along on our own side. I thought the grove path was much closer, but it's hard to tell how far we've actually gone. Finally, I spot the path to the right and stop.

"After dark," I whisper. "They'll come in the night."

I settle against a fallen tree, hidden from the path but visible to Sheila. Sheila settles as well, taking another drink.

My heart slows, and I breathe deeply. My komodo stays with Machete. I mean what I said — I really *do* want her to keep it to remember me by. What might that mean to her? Anything? Will the komodo walk in her dreams the way it does in mine?

I hope that I'm right about my friends coming. It's hard to see how it can happen, and it's not safe to try, but if they come, I'll be here. Maybe *safe* isn't even the point. I've always been so afraid of Blight, but if it's full of people like Korm and Sheila and Nona and Sully, how bad can it be?

I am fully out from under Machete, even if she catches me. She can cage me or expul me or Blight me but I'll never put my tail beneath her boot again. When night falls, I will set my feet on grove ground one more time, and I want to touch the place where I last saw Rasta. Once I cross the border, I can't do those things.

Dark takes its own sweet time strolling into the woods. I wait while the sun dips lower and lower still, eases itself to the purpling horizon, and finally gives up the day. I wait while the birdsong droops from sleepy to silent and the cicadas hush. I wait until the moon is on the rise, cresting the treetops.

Then I stand, and Sheila mirrors me.

"I'm going in." I pitch my voice even lower than before. Noise carries at night. "I'll be out before sunrise."

Sheila nods. She drinks from the kaggi again, and holds it up to me. I shake my head no. I watered up plenty at the spigot. Besides, who knows how late it'll be before I come back, and how long it'll be after that before we have access to water?

I set my feet on the path to the grove. It's easy to follow in the moonlight, and much easier to be quiet when I'm not crashing through brush. The closer I get, the slower I walk. Maybe Machete has sensors or cams all over the land. Maybe she knows exactly where I am. She might even be there waiting for me, ready for her next strategic move in the like-it-or-fear-it game. I make myself stop every ten steps and listen.

Finally, I'm only a few paces from the grove. The path opens ahead, and the oak leaves glint silver in the moonlight. I don't think Machete is here. I don't think anyone is. No magnetic pulse, no dragon beat. Only the night air on my skin, the musky deep smell of the oaks, and a shiver of nerves from the inside out.

The grove is silent. I skirt the edge. I haven't heard a gong since I came onto the CropCamp grounds, but it must be past curfew. I trail the bushes until I find that faint opening out the back side.

I retrace the narrow path, finding it with my feet in the glow of the moonlight. When the ground begins sloping up and the path takes a sharp left turn, I stop and look around. There. The rock. It's not quite as big as the ones outside the CropCamp gate. Only waist-high, I approach, touch the cool granite.

Yes, this is it. The ferns and bushes are well-tromped, and the slope stretches sharp and steep. And this tree, right here — yes. This is it. I swallow hard and wrap my arms around myself. It's all so real and so unreal, and somehow Rasta and death seem like the realest real of all, and that hurts. It hurts like a knife so sharp that you don't know right away when it cuts you. But then you see the damage.

I fall to my knees and feel the earth. I curl my body next to the rock, as close to Rasta as I can get. I close my eyes and see how she looked in the double kickshaw haze. Shimmery purple, spread out on the grass. Nobody else shimmered.

She was the one who knew her power not. Her feathers are stitched into my dragon heart. Rasta didn't know one thing about Sheila or Korm or Darlene or any of it. She just knew me, and somehow that made me more me. Or maybe more her. I'd give anything to have her come walking into the grove. We'd find a way to get to her MaDa. We would. Imagine how happy her da would be. Maybe he really was all-powerful when Rasta was still here. Maybe she made him that way.

I push myself to my knees, close my eyes, and imagine wrapping that shimmer of purple around me like a warmer. I open my fingers in a curled spread and touch the tips to the earth. Just for a second, I swear, the dark earth meets me with a breath of human baby-crow touch.

How I wish that dying wasn't dead. I stand, bow my head, and touch the rock. The rock meant no harm. No more than the trees or the rain or the mud underfoot. Or me.

Chapter Thirty-Nine

AS I WALK BACK to the grove, Rasta's purple shimmer puts a quiet on my nerves. This might be Machete's camp, but it's my grove — and tonight, she is not welcome here. The moon hangs high, draping the woods with a light that fills and swells my entire chest. My heart pumps its own steady pulse, strong as the dragon beat and light as lizard feet.

When I step onto the grass, the surrounding oaks hold me in a hush. If ever there is a place and a time to believe in other worlds, this is it. Not faraway worlds but worlds right here, dancing just on the other side of the moonbeams. Worlds after worlds after worlds, particles and waves, lizards and lightning, neither and both. Radios and knowings and trance-missions of freedom. Sheila and Donovan, Korm and Rasta, maybe even a very young Darlene.

I bathe in that silver moonlight of possibility. I breathe in deep. I don't need to tune in to Lizard Radio because it is broadcasting live, here and now. It surrounds me, and I only have to reach out my fingertips to touch it, strong-alliance style. This is an all and a one that I can live with, even if I never see another kickshaw for the rest of my days.

I move into the middle and turn in place, using the moon-shimmer for a spot. The oak tops whirl around me as I spin like the child I was before anyone starting asking what I was. When I stop moving, the treetops spin on. The ground tips softly to greet my knees and my hands. I crawl across the grove, lifting one heavy dragon foot at a time, claws dragging the dew-wet grass.

I roll over on my back and look up at the stars. They are so close and so far. Like everything. Like every single everything. I lie there for a long time, immune to night chill or fear shivers or worries about anything, as the moon passes slowly across the clearing. It is on the downside of its peak when I hear movement from the direction of Pieville.

Footsteps plod along. Not hurrying. Not sneaking. Just walking. A shadow approaches the opening and pauses at the entry. A shadow with a poof of hair. My friend Nona. She steps into the clearing. I wonder what she feels. Pulse? Chill? Peace? Can she see the worlds and worlds?

"Lizard?" she whispers.

I rise from the shadowed ground.

"I knew it!" She lurches and hops. An awkward skip-dance that only Nona could do. "I knew that you'd be here."

Nona and her knowings.

"Emmett?" I ask. And barely daring to hope, "Sully?"

"I whispered to Sully in the privo. I couldn't get to Emmett.

Katrina is on watch outside our pie. Probably someone on Emmett's, too."

"How'd you get out?"

It's the first time I've seen Nona smile with teeth.

"Found your split on the seam. Made it bigger. Crawled through to your slice and out. I thought for sure that Katrina would hear, but I made it clear away."

I smile, but the no-Sully disappointment drags on my heart. Emmett, too.

"So you think there's no chance on the others?"

"Can't think of any way to get to Emmett. And Katrina is planted right in front of Sully's slice."

So that's that. I close my eyes, and on the backs of my lids, I see Sully with her lights behind the lights, her own breed of both and neither. And Emmett's endless gentle warmth. I can't see any way to save them. Like I did with the komodo, I'll have to leave them to their own powers.

I open my eyes to the moonlight and nod at Nona. We head out of the grove. Once we are well along the path but before the boundary, I stop and whisper a short summary of Rasta's da and Sheila and my face-off with Machete.

"She thinks I've vaped," I say. "But when we cross the boundary, she'll know. Sheila's waiting there to underground us. We'll probably get caught. It's not too late for you to go back—"

But Nona is already shaking her head no, bigger and harder as I continue to talk.

"I'm a Blight baby. My fosters are just as happy to be shed

of me. Donovan Freer is the closest thing I have to family, and you're the closest thing I have to him, and worst case I go to Blight where my real parents are."

She shows me her leddie and full kaggi and extra socks, and for the first time I notice that she's wearing precamp clothes. She brought her secateurs. Nona came prepped. Nona is a good person to have along. I nod, and we walk on. I take the leddie and flash it ahead, searching for the yellow splash of border sign. I don't want to cross by mistake.

"Sheila's just on the other side of the boundary," I whisper.

Ten paces later, I flash the leddie again and catch a glimpse of yellow, maybe two hundred paces away. I flash the leddie on my face, then on Nona's, so Sheila will see that it's us. Then I turn it off, but before I can take a single step, Nona grabs my arm.

"Sully," she says.

"Sully what?"

"Sully is moving — she's out of her slice."

Nona's voice is as flat as ever but my pulse skyrockets.

"How do you know?"

"I know. Go back and get her. I'll wait here." Nona hands me her leddie and sits on the ground. "Be careful."

I'm halfway back to the grove before the chitter-bang of excitement in my chest eases off and an uneasy wondering creeps in. Maybe it's a trap.

No, this is *Nona*! NonaNona. I've lived right next to her for the past —

Right. Not even a month. I don't know her at all. And now

she knows where Sheila is, and she knows where I am, and . . . I stop dead on the path, between this and that. Of course Machete knows that I'm still on the grounds, and that I'm trying to get Sully out. Of course she wouldn't just let me go.

I stand still for a long time. The moon has started to drop west. A single bird begins its first sleepy morning song, and still I stand in indecision. The east is completely dark but it won't be for long. I can't walk away. Not from those first days of being Sully-chosen, that rush-n-wash of excitement, the splitting open of my lizard skin, the pound of our hearts together on that last hug.

I continue on the path. Step, step, step, pause. Listen, listen, listen. The entry to the grove is just ahead. I step off the path behind a tree trunk, and I wait. Those are not footsteps I hear.

Are they?

Yes, they are. And that's a moving shadow. My heart pounds so hard that it rocks me back and forth, and blood roars in my ears, and surely the whole camp can hear it. The shadow hurries closer, looking for me, coming to find me, to get me, and—

It's Sully. I step out and startle her, and her startle startles me so we leap away from each other. I recover, step closer. Still cautious. Sully's hands are in her pockets. She is in CropCamp coveralls.

"Okay, so fiking Nona fiking knows more than I do."

"Yup." I nod. "Nona knows stuff."

"I coughed a few times for cover when she was sneaking out your slice so Katrina wouldn't hear. Where is she?"

"Up ahead."

"Why are you still here?"

"Didn't want to leave without you. Come with us?"

Sully's expression blurs, an uncertainty I've never seen on her. She shakes her head.

"I can't." Her voice quavers. Not like Sully's voice at all. "I thought you were gone, and for once in my life I made a decision, and now here you are."

I reach out to her but she pulls away.

"No, you don't understand. Machete — she's letting me off this whole thing without even a culpa. She says that she'll work with me. She'll make sure that I cert."

"She lies," I say. "She lies whenever she can get away with it."

"Maybe so, but Lizard, I'm not a kid. It's grown-up decision time." She doesn't sound very grown up. "This is my chance. You're the one who said I could do it, make her believe in me. She says that she'll make me a guide."

"Is that what you want?"

Even as my heart is crashing down into my feet, down underground, I am seeing how smart Darlene is, and I am remembering that guides don't get implants, and that Sully might stay Sully. She's not shining any lights in my eyes. I love her more than I ever have but she's far, far away from me. Getting farther every second.

"I don't know. I'm not good at choosing."

"Don't choose." Again I reach out to her, and this time she doesn't step away. I touch her cheek. "Just be Sully."

She's already chosen. I can see it. But still, she came to see if I was here. A choice within a choice.

"Will I ever see you again?" she asks.

"You will." I can't see how, but I'm sure that it's true. "If you're a guide, you won't get the implants. Machete's first name is Darlene. Remember that she lies."

"You could stay," says Sully. "She'd let you back in. We could be guides together. We could shut up and do what we're told until we've certed and gotten some cred, and then we can change things from the inside. You and me, together."

"Shh."

I put a finger on Sully's lips and shake my head, and then I hug her. It's different now. Warmth but no fire, no electric jazz. Our hearts beat close but not together, and the staggered rhythm strikes me so sad. I remind myself of the worlds and worlds, and impossible possibles.

We step apart. Sully reaches across the space between us and catches a tear as it falls from my eye. She holds her finger up in the moonlight.

"Lizard tear," she says. "It'll keep me safe."

I nod, but it's not true. Nothing is safe. Some things are free.

"Mind the regs," I say. "And do me a favor — watch out for Emmett?"

Sully looks me full in the eyes and there she is — all the contradictions, all the wrongs and rights, jazz and loyalty and fear and good fun and everything in between.

"Friends?" she asks.

"Friends."

This time I say it and mean it with all I can feel and all that I know, which isn't much, but it's more than it used to be.

In the last of the lingering moonlight, I leave the oak grove and Sully and CropCamp behind. I take with me my skin and my heart and my tears and my light. I believe that there are gaps in the boundary. I'll find them. I will.

Acknowledgments

This book, more than anything I've written, absolutely required community to bring it forth. I'm grateful to the people who helped me in so many ways — to envision, to draft, to keep writing drafts, and to search and search again for the book's dragon heart.

Mary Ann Rafferty gave me the beautiful sketchbook where the Lizard first appeared. Mat DeFiler, Jane Resh Thomas, Annetta Wright, Laura Greene, Sara Aikin, Susa Silvamarie, Jane St. Anthony, Mary Lynn Morales, and Catherine Friend plowed through early drafts and ideas with me.

Background music and inspiration came from John Coltrane and Ferron. In particular, Ferron's song "It Won't Take Long" from the 1984 *Shadows on a Dime* LP has kept me thinking for years about freedom, strength, and dreamers in the making, and with this book I finally had a place to put some of those thoughts.

My former agent Andrea Cascardi helped me to believe that *Lizard Radio* could grow up to be a book. Fiona Kenshole and David Bennett at TLA stepped in with more suggestions, and David launched the Lizard to the next stage with a shiny brilliant idea and professional guidance at the right time.

Many friends, family members, and colleagues helped with the feeding and care of the komodo over months and years: Maryasha, Ponch, Nora, Lisa, Merry, Ruth, Terry, Kim, Amelie, Emily, Eddie, Jeremy, Jane, Denise, Yerp, Kate, B.E., Barbara, my

Minneapolis book club, the Writing in the Woods group, and others.

Jane Resh Thomas, who taught me about the power of endowed objects, gave me a toy Komodo and a gang of metal lizards to help me tune in. Becky Stanborough, Alice Deighan, and Mitzi Mize took me to smell the breath of a real-life Komodo dragon. Mitzi's magical artist-eye gave me my screen saver, and Becky Stanborough waded through chapter by chapter and came back with incredibly smart and careful suggestions. Thanks to Babs and Meg for bringing the nonfictional Sully into my world, and to Babs for the eagle-proofing eye. Special thanks to Maryasha Katz for asking me to try that last paragraph again.

What a relief it was to turn the Lizard over to Joan Powers at Candlewick Press! Joan had the Lizard's back (and mine) at every turn. She has a very clear, focused way of asking for clarity and specificity without shutting anything down. I absolutely trust her gentle editorial hand.

Working with the Candlewick team on a book is the best. I can easily appreciate the tangibles, like Meghan Blosser's meticulous copy edits and Pam Consolazio's otherworldly cover design, but there's so much more above and below the surface. Each Candlewick person I've met seems like part of something magical, working for the forces of good in the world. I can't believe I get to be part of it.

Above all, I'm grateful to the Lizards that came before, those who've walked with me, and those to follow. Let's hope we keep finding the gaps in the boundaries.